Anna Babiashkina was born in 1979 in Yaroslavl region, Central Russia. She graduated with honors from the Department of Journalism at Moscow University, and is currently editor of a women's magazine with a circulation of 180,000. She has a number of prize-winning novels to her name, including *Nothing There*, *The Time Difference*, *I Need You*.

In 2011 her novel *Before I Croak* won the Debut Prize; it also won the Bestseller Prize for best "urban novel".

Babiashkina cites Jonathan Safran Foer and Ian McEwan as her models in fiction.

"My novel is about children of the late Communist era, now around 30," says Babiashkina. "It's a glance into our not-so-distant future... All the characters and situations have been taken from life."

Muireann Maguire is a Fellow of Wadham College, Oxford, and teaches Russian language and literature at Oxford University. See her blogs: <u>Russian Dinosaur</u> and <u>Snail on the Slope</u>.

GLAS NEW RUSSIAN WRITING

contemporary Russian literature

in English translation

Volume 58

This is the eighth volume in
the Glas sub-series devoted
to young Russian authors,
winners and finalists of the
Debut Prize.
Glas acknowledges their
generous support in
publishing this book.

ANNA BABIASHKINA

BEFORE I CROAK

a novel

Translated by Muireann Maguire

GLAS PUBLISHERS
tel./fax: +7(495)441-9157
perova@glas.msk.su
www.glas.msk.su

DISTRIBUTION

In North America
Consortium Book Sales and Distribution
tel: 800-283-3572; fax: 800-351-5073
orderentry@perseusbooks.com
www.cbsd.com

In the UK
CENTRAL BOOKS
orders@centralbooks.com
www.centralbooks.com
Direct orders: INPRESS
Tel: 0191 229 9555
customerservices@inpressbooks.co.uk
www.inpressbooks.co.uk

Within Russia
Jupiter-Impex
www.jupiterbooks.ru

Editors: Natasha Perova & Joanne Turnbull
Cover design by Igor Satanovsky
Camera-ready copy: Tatiana Shaposhnikova

paper book ISBN 978-5-7172-0098-1
ebook ISBN 978-5-7172-0099-8

BEFORE I CROAK

Near Moscow, September 2039

Finally, at the ripe old age of sixty, I'm writing my first book. All my life I've dreamed of this and never managed to make it happen. And now, before I croak, I've finally found the time to turn my Lifelong Dream into reality – to commit to paper sixty thousand words of coherent text in my own voice. I can write about what I've always really wanted, not whatever the editor-in-chief or the advertisers want to read (the way I see it, they were the only ones who ever cared about the trash scribbled by me and other journalists, in all the media where I managed to work during the long, dull years I now grandiloquently call "the making of my career".)

So now, before I croak, I, as a woman in full command of her faculties, born in the year 1979, still able to recall what life was like before mobile phones, the Internet, Putin and electric cars, sit down at my computer and, with a glow of profound satisfaction, open a new Word file and tap out the title of the novel that will open a new chapter in my life: *Before I Croak*. The computer instantly underlines the word "croak" with a green squiggle, warning that this expression is inappropriate. It adds (in parentheses): only suitable for referring to animals. Since my theme is myself and my fellow inmates in this old folks' home, the word "croak" is perfectly appropriate.

Ours was the first generation of old folks whose children handed them over to residential homes on a mass scale and forgot them there forever. There is no point in searching for reasons why the shunting of ancestors into this proto-cemetery stopped being considered shameful or even immoral by our children. We'd given birth to them reluctantly, at the last moment before the menopause, muttering regrets like "now I'll have to find the rent for a two-bedroom apartment, instead of a studio" and "no more foreign holidays for me". Naturally, we loved them after they appeared. Our lack of love, our reluctance, lasted only until they were born; after that, we gave them only too much love and care: we hired nannies for them; bought wide-screen televisions to enhance their cartoons; occasionally we even allowed them to play on the parental iPad. Our children grew up healthy and strong, with the world at their feet. In our technological era it simply makes more sense to stow all the old folks in one place, cared for by those rare people who aren't too fussy to tolerate the whims of the elderly and the shuffling of their slippers. They would look after us, and we'd live in our mildly pared-down, geriatric version of a summer camp just the way we'd always wanted: we were spared worries, spared responsibilities, spared work, left to our own devices. Exactly as in that TV program from our youth – the reality show "Big Brother". Although, of course, all our lives we'd had other plans for our declining years.

But now, like children, we no longer need to concern ourselves with anything; not with wangling a pay raise, or buying an apartment in Moscow, or who looks after the kid when you're called into work on a weekend, or how to split the property after a divorce. Each of us can do whatever we'd spent our lives wishing we could do. Mostly, for the men this means playing computer games non-stop and watching the sports channel, while for the women, it's obsession with TV serials, reading, chasing men, and pathological concern for one's external appearance (we are the first generation of elderly women to wear G-strings, epilate our bikini lines and sauté ourselves in tanning salons).

I threw myself into the routine of the old folks' home with all the enthusiasm of a total beginner. The truth was I'd had my fill of being lonely over the last three years, while my son tried unsuccessfully to persuade me of the advantages (for me) of residential care, stressing how much he (and that girlfriend of his) needed my apartment. Their education certainly wasn't wasted; somehow they knew just how to find the best arguments and the right words.

Now I've been here almost four months. And, finally, I'm writing this long-anticipated book, which could never have come to pass if I hadn't found myself precisely here. The old women give me the richest possible living source material, although I doubt that any of them will exactly rejoice to see my words in print. One of them, I suspect, might even commit murder to stop me. In spite of such reasons to hold off, I'm still writing this book. I've turned down too many opportunities in life because I was scared. Quite often, as it turned out afterwards, my fears were entirely exaggerated. Hopefully, this time too I'm overestimating the extent of the risk hanging over me; I'm jumping at shadows, without any justification.

But I mustn't get ahead of myself. I'll begin with my first days in this residential home…

Near Moscow, May 2039

I wept all night long. Then I spent all morning combatting the aftermath of my nocturnal tears – swollen rings around my eyes – with the aid of teabags. For the first half of the day I tried to wipe the yellow circles of tannin off my skin and powder them over. But my wrinkles showed through the powder more clearly than ever, and I had to wipe it off and go out just as I was. That's how I came to be known as the Cobra. It took me a week to discover that the other pensioners had given me this handle from my very first day. "Well, let them!" I thought. "Surely, once in my life, looks shouldn't matter.

At least I've still got a nice bottom; and it still does what it's supposed to do." What's more, I still had a hedgehog-style hairdo, enhanced by dark chestnut hair-dye, as luxuriant as a fake Christmas tree. The scarves, which I always wear in public, lend me a piquant air and cunningly hide the scar from my thyroid operation. I never had much in the way of boobs, but I could always afford an uplift Wonderbra and shaping underwear. Moreover, even as a young woman I trained myself to hold my spine as if I had a resistance band stretched down my back from shoulders to bottom; I never allowed myself to scooch up pathetically and walk with a hunch. In a word, for my sixty years I looked as fresh as a Polo mint.

We drove up onto the asphalted court fronting the old folks' residence. My son and his girlfriend enthusiastically hauled my bags from the car into my room. Saying, "Good luck in your new home!" they handed me a remarkably mangy-looking stuffed toy cat ("so I wouldn't be homesick") and rolled off to Moscow. That same evening my apartment was to be viewed by potential tenants. The idea was that in this residential home in the country (this nice expression concealed the fact that it was almost 200 km from Moscow) I would spend no more than three summer months. "Mama, it'll do wonders for your health!" my son told me. And if I didn't like it, then in autumn I could go home to my Moscow apartment. Of course, everyone except me had an interest in making sure that didn't happen. Or so it seemed to me.

I had no intention of striking up close relationships with the other pensioners. I hadn't had any friends of my own for a long time, and I'd learned to live without them. I had the Internet, my anonymous on-line chat groups, my books and my films. Moreover, I planned to spend these three months in the country working on my First Book. Nightingales, meadows, poplars would, as I thought, finally lend me the inspiration which never visited me in Moscow. At home, I'd already started on a dozen books, but I wasn't able to write a single one to the end. Every time I'd have a more brilliant idea or more urgent business to deal with (my cyst, my thyroid, my cataract). Or I'd think I really wanted a break. "This is just the right time and place," I decided.

As it turned out, there weren't any meadows or poplars near the residence; all you could see from the windows was the pot-holed asphalt, long-unclipped acacias and flower-beds, lined with broken bricks, where a delicate-looking herb with crimson-veined leaves had broken through. From far-off came a sweetish smell of pine needles and manure. There was a cow-byre less than a mile away. And within a hundred yards of the home there was a charming little lake with low, swampy banks and a boardwalk.

I had another reason for not wanting to be too familiar with the other pensioners; this was the fact that the home belonged to the cheaper sort, and I didn't expect to meet my own kind of people here. After all, I was accustomed to mingling with imaginative, creative, eccentric types. It was not for nothing that I'd been a journalist for a major newspaper! To a shit-hole like this, for this kind of money, they packed off losers who had earned very little all their lives and couldn't even send their children to university. I considered myself an unlucky exception; the private pension fund into which I'd paid my premiums unfortunately went bankrupt. The insurance (really the best part of my pension), which had been accumulating almost all my life, was gone for good (although my son feels that it isn't all lost yet and is still suing somebody over my money). As a result I now get the same pittance I would if I'd never held down a job in my life. In fact, that unpleasant incident was one of the reasons why my son insisted on sending me to this residence (The Mounds) and renting out my apartment. The main reason was concern for my health, naturally.

However, as became clear afterwards, I was quite wrong to suspect that I would be the only bright spark among losers. Half the residence proved to be crammed with people about whom I had either read or heard from friends, that is, people from my circle, who had certainly never thought that they would live to old age and had carelessly blown all their cash in their youth, hoping that if they did last until they turned sixty, the banknotes would take care of themselves. Which is to say they hadn't saved anything for their old age either. I'd been in the establishment for a couple of days before I found this out; it boosted my self-esteem no end.

At dinnertime (timetabled for 7pm), I descended with a cold, collected air. I hoped everyone would ignore me just as sternly as I meant to ignore them. A girl in a frivolous white hospital coat was wheeling a cart loaded with plates. "I'd like to take my suppers in my room," I said, stopping her. "But you're still on your feet, aren't you?!" she exclaimed, measuring me with a glance. I wasn't about to reply to that kind of rude comment. Since I was undeniably still on my feet, I headed for the dining room.

I had vainly hoped that everyone would ignore me. However, some female, evidently part of the management, decided to introduce me to everyone present, just as if I were the new girl in school. She swiftly picked me out (although we'd never met), grabbed me rather painfully by the arm and yelled to the whole room: "Ladies and gentlemen! Pay attention! We have a new guest to welcome: Sofia Arkadyevna Bulgakova, born in 1979, a famous journalist, who is hoping, as her son mentioned to us, to write a novel!" A giggle ran around the hall, which I put down to this noisy woman's way of expressing herself. I'd always known that modern young people have no feeling for language, but I'd never before been exposed to such a complete lack of discretion.

"Maybe you'd like to share my medical records with the group as well?" I whispered, quietly but viciously.

"That reminds me, you still haven't handed in your medical records to our health officer!" this she-functionary replied. "Well, not to worry, hand them in tomorrow. Grab your supper, let's go, I'll take you to meet the gang."

Eating in this woman's company was the last thing I wanted, but I somehow found myself trailing after her with my tray.

"I'm going to put you right beside our celebrated Alla Maksimova!" she mumbled through a mouthful she'd already managed to grab. "She's our local literary superstar."

The literary superstar, bent over her plate like a cocktail twizzler, picked out three stringy pieces of asparagus and fixed a far from friendly stare on me.

"So, Sonya dear, you write too?" she asked, her ceramic dentures sparkling.

I immediately had to find a rebuff to that condescending "Sonya dear".

"Yes, my love!" I gave her a wide smile as I replied to show everyone that unlike some people I had managed to keep my own teeth. They might be yellow with nicotine, but they were still mine.

"Alla is our most widely printed writer in the home," the staff woman, whose precise function here was still obscure, added proudly. "Her stories are usually printed out by other members of the community. She writes so entertainingly that some of our guys decided to make her a website of her very own, so that other people can download her stories!" she continued assiduously digging the hole deeper for Maksimova. "And we give her lots of support. If you manage to write something as interesting, they'll probably make you a site too."

Here I lost my self-control and chuckled sarcastically.

"Actually I'm a professional journalist," I snorted, still chortling to myself. "And I hope to write something that will actually have major literary value, and not some geriatric drivel that only a pensioner would want to read."

In my fellow diners' expressions I read that I'd said something dangerous. How dangerous it was I only found out later. As would become clear, I'm not the only one here who can read and even write a little. Practically everyone (!!!) in that home was dreaming of writing their own Great Novel.

And many of them were even working on it. They even printed their own Literary Almanac in the residence. What the fuck! I'd expected anything from this God-forsaken place, anything you like, but not that.

"When my mother used to work in this home," the woman from the staff was prattling on again, "all the old grannies, the older they got, got more interested in the soil. You can hardly imagine the way they went on! Every old biddy, if she still had enough strength left to totter about, insisted on having her own plot of ground. And she'd dig it up compulsively, just like some instinct or mania. I heard that in the old days all the old women did it for a hobby. They say that even when it was cheaper to buy potatoes in the shops, the old ladies would still creep out to their little plots and plant potatoes until they dropped dead on their vegetable beds. When I was a kid everywhere around here was planted with something, and Mom didn't have a clue what to do with all the vegetables every year. And now they've got a new hobby. Everyone writes. Every single one of them! Although, what's so surprising about that? In the old days the old women spent their whole lives digging the soil, they worked with their hands and they couldn't stop when they got old, and today's old biddies… that is ladies of a certain age, have worked in offices all their lives, typing on keyboards. And they can't stop either. It's progress! But we'll help them develop. We'll support them with pleasure. Since working with information is very useful for withering brains…"

When she got to withering brains my attention just switched off.

When I woke up the next morning, I'd already lost the desire to write my Novel. I wanted to express random creative dissonance by conking out on a patch of garden, the way our ancestors had died, and not at my laptop, like the stupid modern-day old women. I hurried to announce this on my blog and my Facebook page. After that, I deleted from the computer all those ingenious ideas which I'd been storing up on it all my life in the hope that, some day, one of them would blossom into a masterpiece, the kind of thing for which a Nobel Prize would be too little, to quote the poet Anna Akhmatova.

Since my idealistic plans for a three-month writing binge had been abruptly destroyed by the interference of ugly reality, I no longer had any idea what to do with myself in this provincial dump, overrun by idiots who ran off at the mouth. I certainly couldn't imagine what more there was to do in life than sit in front of a magically flickering screen and press keys. Hell! Why had I turned into such a banality? I'd always thought of myself as an extraordinary, unique person, robbed by circumstances of the chance to become my true self. "Sonya, go and jump in the lake," every letter of the alphabet screeched at me.

I spent two days feeling like Stalin after he discovered the failure of the Revolution (the one in 1905). He'd been in prison then too. And after finding out that his (and not only his) revolutionary future was all over but the shooting, he fell into the bitterest depression: he spent a week lying on his side, face to the wall, quietly weeping. Stalin never rose from his bed. He couldn't eat or sleep, he didn't wash. He just lay there, stinking and oozing tears. His will to live was paralyzed. (I borrowed this interesting fact from Edward Radzinsky's biography of Stalin).

For two days I had the same paralysis of willpower. I even thought I might die of it. That's to say, I didn't want to live. I didn't want to wake up, because I had no reason to wake up. And I dreamed of quietly expiring in my sleep (secretly, I'd figured out an additional bonus in this sort of death: my unworthy son would then understand what he'd sentenced me to by sending me here! He'd bang his forehead against the wall and spend his whole life regretting what he'd done. At the very least, I could then be positive that he wouldn't just forget about me and that my little grave would be looked after. What a thing to happen: you shove your mother into an old folks' home, and she turns up her toes just three days later!)

I'd have to think of something right away, so as not to die from disappointment and sorrow. And salvation presented itself.

Either my grief wasn't so great after all, or I'd never really been obsessed by the idea of becoming a Great Russian Writer. In any case, two days later I got up and ate a hearty breakfast. What's more, during my two days of silent protest and suicidal fantasy nobody had troubled themselves about my fate or rushed around oohing and aahing: "What's this, Sofia Arkadyevna, won't you get up?"

So then and there I decided to become the local Zoilus. If these pathetic creatures could pollute the entire information field with their literary weeds, preventing me from planting the Rose of my Great Novel, then I would tear them up by the roots! I would poison them with the herbicide of literary criticism, and open up literary elbow room for myself. After I'd privately made this decision, I felt an unprecedented rush of energy. I even did some morning exercises, epilated (in fact I find that with age the hairs on my legs have practically stopped growing), painted my nails purple, put on my best thong and all the stylish clothes I had with me. In this triumphant get-up, I went down to breakfast.

My plan was to attack from ambush, and go straight for the kill. As a mass-media journalist I knew that to make a new brand attractive you had to hook it onto a label that had already been used, a bit like a conga line. As a critic, in order to pull in my audience straightaway, I had to hit the most vulnerable point hard: literary superstar Alla Maksimova. The harder I hit her, the likelier it was that my campaign of self-promotion would catch on. All I had to do was find her weak spot.

I'd borrowed the superstar's stories and as a treat for after breakfast I started reading them right there over my porridge.

"Ah! So you've also decided to relax with some light, improving reading?" Alla remarked, glancing at the stack of printed pages on my table and recognizing the familiar words.

I gave her a sort of smile in reply, silently pronouncing "just you wait…" and shrugged my shoulders.

"Incidentally, I have a jacuzzi in my room. If you like hydro-massage, come round!" winked Alla. "We'll have a natter!"

"Try to stop me!" I nodded enthusiastically, like a horse tossing off its harness.

I wasn't planning to make friends with her. I'd already selected as a friend the only inhabitant of the home not infected by the scribbling virus: Natasha Sokolova, or Nata. This sweet-natured woman lived in the room next to mine. At least I'd been lucky in my neighbours.

"No, I'm not writing at the moment. I've already written everything I wanted," Nata had sniggered when I asked her about it. "More precisely, I've got one story left to tell. I swore to myself that I would write one and only one story before I die. But it's still working itself out. It's not finished yet," and, with an enigmatic smile, Nata had handed me her print-out of Alla Maksimova's complete works, which I studied over breakfast.

Nata had been a screenwriter. She gave off a cosy cinnamon fragrance, and on that little table where all the other pensioners had their laptops, Nata had a pretty basket full of balls of wool. She herself might have been made of mohair, she was so soft, warm, cuddly. Even her red curls were cleverly bunched up in a knot on the crown of her head. She had such luxurious shoulders and bosoms that whenever I saw them I involuntarily longed to plunge my nose between them, hide in them from everything and wail pitifully while she'd pat me on the head and comfort me maternally. However, this was all mere fantasy, my real mother never did anything like that.

But behind Nata's fleecy softness one sensed firmness and strength. The accuracy and abruptness of her movements, her direct laser-like gaze, and her always crooked smile did not encourage one to lower one's guard too much in her company. "She's like a concrete building surfaced with velvet," I thought to myself. "No pushover, but not a battleaxe, either."

As might have been expected, Alla the super-scribbler turned out to be a nauseatingly dedicated writer. It actually took me a week to study her literary legacy. The most promising quotations I immediately copied and pasted in a separate file. Meanwhile, I used every available means to find out about Alla's life before she wound up in the old folks' home. After all, a compulsive scribbler becomes a writer not because of words arranged in sentences, but as a result of his or her biography. A writer without a biography, like an actress without a role, is just a pale shadow, not even a pawn on the literary chessboard. And if you want to destroy someone who writes, you have to strike their text, their face, and their back-story all at the same time.

Unfortunately, Alla Maksimova's website, which was being set up for her, wasn't ready yet, meaning that there was nowhere I could dig up her official biography. However, Alla was very chatty and most of the pensioners in the residence were more or less up to date with her past. "The Start of the Glorious Path" dragged out a heroic love story, featuring a string of miracles and triumphs of willpower. Straightaway it was obvious that this was a fake. A lie. A made-up tale. Our youth coincided with the times when grandfather Yeltsin was already "working with documents", and threatened with daily extinction. Until we grew feathers and tumbled out of the nest, other kids, who were just a little older, had already appropriated all the possible miracles and magical transformations, leaving us just a few shoddy magic tricks, which wouldn't even have impressed a snake-charmer. And, illustrating how she'd taught herself to haul out of her empty hat an endless supply of "white rabbits", Alla openly lied…

In fact, the latter part of her life story proved that there was a lot she hadn't revealed about the early part.

It turned out that Alla was actually an orphan, from Kazan, raised in a Kazan children's home, where she found herself after her mother's death. She trained as a hairdresser and escaped to Moscow. There her genius was recognized, and soon Alla was working as a stylist in one of the most fashionable beauty salons.

When she was almost thirty, she had a brilliant idea; she opened her own, very profitable business. She planned to build a chain of express-hairdressers all over Moscow, placed close to metro stations. She understood how women often need to get their hair done quickly, in just ten minutes, on the way to work, or from work on the way to a rendezvous. This fortunate period of Alla's life was crowned by a very auspicious marriage – she tied the knot with a successful cinema producer, Rafael Oganesian.

Here her good luck ended. Her husband unexpectedly deserted the rising businesswoman, and what's more, by some miracle her business now belonged to him. Everything that had been acquired by their joint hard work – the garage full of stylish cars, the vast apartment on the Garden Ring Road, the country house – he kept it all. After the divorce, all Alla got was a tiny one-room bedsit with a view of the car park in a Moscow suburb.

The most puzzling and insulting part of the whole affair was that Rafael didn't leave her for some young actress-model, or for a cute TV celebrity; he just left her. He never married again, although a few days ago he had celebrated his 75th birthday. And this comforted Alla, just a little. She gloried in being the only woman who had managed to drag the freedom-loving Rafael to the altar.

Alla unsuccessfully strove to start a new business; nothing worked out. And this former celebrity with the glamorous sheen, who used to give hundreds of interviews about how "a woman can succeed in business without neglecting her looks", ended her career as an administrator in a shabby suburban hairdressers'. And after she retired, she rented out her Moscow apartment and moved here, to this residence.

"At first Alla was terribly lonely here. She didn't even have visitors," Nata, the former screenwriter, told me during our evening stroll. Nata herself got visits from three handsome sons and a smiling daughter, graceful as a ballerina, with warm grey eyes. "I was really terribly sorry for her."

"Listen, how do you know that Rafael of hers didn't run off with some little actress?" I asked, snuggling into my coat and happily breathing in the slightly chilly May air, scented with bonfires.

"Well, I just know," Nata shook her head vaguely. "We're all part of the same group. Judge for yourself: if he'd wanted a bit on the side he could have had it without a divorce. Alla would have looked the other way as long as he kept his feet under her table, as they say. If he'd really fallen in love with someone why not marry her? Could he really have found someone who wouldn't marry him? Well? Remember him 25 years ago, a really handsome guy, with charisma, hordes of admirers, a sense of humour, a shiny Bentley. What more could you ask?"

"That's true," I nodded. "I remember I interviewed him once. He made quite an impression."

"So as for Alla's life in this home," Nata returned to her tale, "all of us here went to her for advice about make-up, we literally gave her no peace, simply to stop her from dying of misery. When a person starts helping others, she doesn't have enough time to feel sorry for herself and be miserable. And then she recovered, sat down to her laptop and started setting herself up as a writer. You can see for yourself what happened next…"

By now, Alla had made her mark in four genres. She could already proudly call herself the author of one short story, one long story, one novella, and even a novel.

I am an attentive reader. Very attentive, one of those people who scribble all over books with pencil and stick notes on the pages. This isn't because I'm a great admirer of other people's writing. It's because I myself have always wanted to write. In other people's books I mark those pages where, through the screen of a fictional plot, truly genuine, sincere, personally-experienced emotions burst out. There are few people who are capable of becoming demiurges in the full sense of this word and of creating, even on paper, full-blooded images of absolutely separate, different individuals. The majority pretty much write about themselves. They divide their personal schizophrenia into a multitude of characters and play with them, like little girls playing with dolls in kindergarten. Some little Masha sits in the sand pit with half-naked, sand-smeared dollies and puts on three different voices: "Oh, Princess, why don't you want to come to the ball with me?" "Viscount, I want to go with you. But my mother forbids me to go to the ball. She thinks I'm still too little." "Hey, you two! If you go to the ball, I'll tell the princess's mother everything and she'll make her stand in the corner!" "Princess, if I chop up your neighbour with an axe and no-one finds out, will you come with me to the ball?" "Oh, Viscount, can you really do that for me? Then I'll go right off and put on my best ball-gown. Shall I pass you the axe?"

And straightaway everything about little Masha is clear to us, as well as everything about her family and her neighbours.

Extracts from the work of Alla Maksimova
made by Sofia Bulgakova, 26 May 2039.

The Prince in the White Mercedes (a short novel)

We learn from fairy-tales not to marry anyone less than a prince on a white stallion. But today we must reconcile ourselves to the fact that there are no more princes on white stallions. Now only jockeys and septic tank-cleaners in the countryside ride horses; today's ideal match is a prince in a white Mercedes. It's no worse than a stallion, and in fact, a lot trendier. But even here it's not worth being too fussy – one can settle for a prince in a black, red, silver, or indeed any other kind of Mercedes. As long as he has some kind of mount: if not a stallion, to extend our analogy, at least a gelding. You won't notice the difference straightaway, but you should bear it in mind. A gelding is a castrated stallion, whose lack of balls makes him enthusiastic for work. A gelding has a slavish disposition, and unlike a stallion, it won't kick the bucket from overwork.

Every man has an animal alter ego. It's not for nothing that modern-day Prince Charmings ride geldings, not stallions. No kids! No family ties! All your Prince cares about is getting the highest-calorie oats and the newest horse-shoes. And his work, his work! Don't wait for him to get down on his knees to beg you to present him with an heir. He simply isn't able to do this. He doesn't have the equipment…

The only time Dimon ever brought up the topic of kids, he said: "Listen, what if, let's suppose, you happen to get pregnant? Now imagine you were expecting, what would you do?" Ksusha's husband asked her.

"Well…" Ksusha tried to guess which was the right answer to this provocative sally of her husband's. "I think we'd do whatever you wanted. If you wanted, we'd keep the kid…"

"And if not, then you'd get an abortion. Right?" Dimon checked, and not a single muscle moved in his face.

"Absolutely," Ksusha agreed.

Her husband nodded approvingly and turned back to his computer.

The Lacquer's Edge (A Novel)

"In a beautiful female, everything must be beautiful: soul, thoughts, deeds. Even her nail polish has to be perfect." One ragged nail can change the whole course of your life. Ruined lacquer can ruin your luck forever, if the man of your dreams notices dents on the shiny armour that screens your nail from the cruel world and hides the hangnails on your hand as it tries to creep into his wallet... If a pair of unlacquered pincers catches his eye, he'll never give you a second chance to get inside his most sacred spot: his wallet.

And you'll finish your days in a miserable two-room apartment on some outskirts in the company of boiling borsch and the nauseating shrieks of small, impoverished children, that is, your kids. "Look after your hands!" Dasha was thinking, sitting with her manicure girl and watching closely to make sure all the cuticle was stripped off each finger. She really needed some luck today. She'd even turned off her mobile phone, so that her wicked bank clerks wouldn't be able to remind her about her urgent three-month-old-debt for that loan for her Audi TT.

If Love Was for Real (a short story)

"If love was for real, I'd have fallen in love at least once in all these years," Alla figured, dreamily going through the elegant wedding dresses lined up in front of her like a row of soldiers. "But I've never been in love! Not once! In all my thirty three years... You might well ask why. Maybe I never met the right guy. No way that's the problem. I've met every kind of guy there is. I dated a banker, and an oil magnate, and an athlete, and a yachtsman, even an artist. They were like a selection box: rich guys, ripped guys, smart dressers, smooth talkers. If I couldn't fall for any of them, the pick of the crop, who else should I fall for? But, hand on heart, I couldn't fall in love with a single one of them. And if the best and worthiest guys couldn't make me feel butterflies in my stomach, it seems like nobody can. If not even one of them made me think: 'I could live on bread and water with him', love's got to be an invention.

As for them, did they love me? By the standards of all these dreadful, utterly false films about love, they weren't in love with me either. But if the sort of love which makes money for writers and film makers genuinely existed in this world, would they really have been able to resist me? Who else but me should they fall for? Objectively, absolutely everything about me deserves ecstasies of delight, worship, adoration. Intelligence, shapely figure, style, good looks, education, career – I had it all… Well, not all, not love.

If love was for real, then every single one of my exes would be dying of despair right now, hanging on to the hem of my wedding dress to stop me crossing the threshold of the registry office. However here I am, choosing my wedding outfit, and all they do is send me congratulatory text messages. And that's just the way it should be. I've stopped waiting for this stupid thing called love and am calmly getting married…"

Three Big Macs for Cinderella (a short story)

A lady writer once observed that there is nothing more beautiful or impressive than self-sacrificing love. Every good film that makes its viewers cry at the end is inevitably about self-sacrificing love. When one lover is prepared to give up everything for the other's sake, there's something about it. You can give up the most precious thing you have, even your life.

In the cinema, victims of love make a big impression on everyone. And everyone wants to be in Kate Winslet's place, the girl for whom Leo sacrifices his life. Or to be in Leo's place, dying for Kate's sake and remaining in her memory for life. Or in the place of Luka or Sabaha from Kusturica's "Life is a Miracle"… Billy Elliot and his father… Take any Oscar-winning film, and you'll see that they're all about one thing: self-sacrificing love.

However in real life things don't happen like they do in the movies. In reality, the people we love are not impressed by the sacrifices their lovers make. They take them for granted. Take me, for instance: every day I perform a Feat with a big 'F' for the sake of love: I don't stuff myself. I maintain my girlish slenderness, delicacy and grace. But where are the tears of tenderness I'm entitled to from the person for whom I make this sacrifice? When I turn down French fries and profiteroles, incidentally, my heart weeps no less than King Edward's did when he abdicated in order to marry the commoner he loved. But while half the world shed tears over Edward and his horrible American midget, my sacrifice is accepted with a casual yawn. My loved one doesn't act as if a small Feat has just been accomplished under his nose, but rather as if an ordinary suburban train had passed by. And sometimes I think to myself: "My dear, if I fall out of love with you sometime, the first thing I'll do will be to go out and gobble up three Big Macs. Straight up. In one go."

When I read other authors, I picture them to myself as little children like that imaginary Masha in her sand-box, playing with butt-naked dolls. And I try to guess which character, in which plot twist, speaks for the author, or instead of the author, or about the author. I underline the words which inspired the Masha-author to play with her dolls in the first place. This isn't so difficult to do. This was just why I decided from the start that I had to write my book in the first person. There's no need for the mincing coquetry of "Sofia Arkadyevna thought", or "Ivan Ivanich couldn't even imagine". Forget about Ivan Ivanich. Those readers who still remember written words, and for whose sake authors still bother to ruin their eyesight, aren't fools; they understand immediately what Sofia Arkadyevna thought, and when she manipulated Ivan Ivanich's words as if he were a doll, and where Sofia Arkadyevna expressed someone else's idea, like the thoughts of some Ivan Petrovich who made an impression on her.

Come to think of it, we shouldn't be surprised that although little girls traditionally like to play with dolls, the most prolific writers tend to be men. Girls simply fulfil their passion for playing with imaginary people in childhood. While still in kindergarten and junior high, they play their way through all the real-life scenarios they can dream up. But little boys grow up a little later. They're not mature enough at the age when you play with dolls. So, especially for them, a more serious kind of game was invented, including "mothers and daughters", "sisters", "neighbours", "rivals", "love", "husband and wife". It's called writing. Thus girls who didn't play with dolls enough or who simply never grew up also often apply to Masters' programs in creative writing. I'm one of them.

Some men, however, are aware of this infantile aspect of writing and prefer playing computer games. For them it's like playing "imaginary people" without leaving any traces behind: no page proofs, no papers, no files drifting through the Internet. After a computer game nobody can leap out, like a prosecutor from behind his stand, waving a sheet of paper: "Aha! I know everything about you. I've read your books! Come with me if you please, you latent paedophile, you shit-eater, homosexual, serial killer!" But every word you publish can bear witness against you and betray you for long years to come. The lives of our famous authors such as Limonov and Sorokin prove it. I think fear of exposure is one of the reasons why, after those two, there stopped being so many outspoken, crazy, talented writers in our country. They probably still exist, but they're afraid of ending up the same way. It's easier for women; they have an inborn passion for striptease, including the spiritual kind. Which means that even the wickedest of their insane fantasies are just kids' pranks by comparison with the slag you can dig from the dark depths of the male unconscious.

Throughout my long life as a reader, I learned to faultlessly filter out the author's real voice from the choir of his characters, and track down those words which were really written from the heart: those which come directly from the writer, describing himself. I know the problems of every hack writer today better than their own shrinks. This was how I could copy out from Alla's works the particular passages which revealed her voice recognizably and unmistakably. She opened herself up.

I turned over the last page of "Three Big Macs for Cinderella". It was pretty clear to me where Alla had obtained the start-up capital for her hair-washing salons and why she had lost them after the divorce. I could guess why they didn't have any children. There was just one thing I couldn't understand: why after just a few years of happy partnership Alla's "gelding" had galloped away from her. After all, to all appearances, she understood him perfectly and was an ideal companion-in-arms. What had overturned Alla's carefully constructed, de luxe existence and sent her on the road to ruin? Probably Rafael Oganesian could throw light on this, but I was hardly going to pester him with idiotic questions. It was certainly true he'd been quite a man twenty years ago. I remember how his large brown eyes had ogled me when I was interviewing him for some motor magazine or other about his automobile collection. And he'd even invited me for a spin in his Bentley. I think I might just have kept his phone number in my notebook. Might a man keep the same mobile number for so many years? And why shouldn't he?

I tossed Alla's manuscript onto the dresser. My glance slipped over the calendar-alarm clock. Damn! Today I certainly wasn't going anywhere and I'd hardly be able to talk to anyone. Today was the most troublesome and exhausting day of the week – Saturday, the children's day.

On Saturdays our children poured into the home to prove that they still gave a damn about us and that somewhere, on the edges of their consciousness, our images still flickered. Their presence was as noisy as it was awkwardly prolonged. For the most part the children had nothing to say to us. They lived just as pointlessly as we had – after all, from whom could they learn a different way of life? They busied themselves buying new furniture, scheming about their bosses, getting drunk with colleagues, winning two-dollar pay rises, and worrying about their health.

Here was my own half-grown offspring awkwardly shoving a shopping bag containing some sort of fruit into my hand and muttering that my apartment was let to really, really, extremely nice people. And for decent money. And that there was so much work that he wouldn't even manage to fly to Sochi for the weekend with the guys. And that he was being sent on a business trip to Yekaterinburg – the local branch had too small a piece of the local market. They had to take a look and see what the local agents weren't getting right. And what's more, they were starting a new project, and here – drumroll! – there was a chance that he might be made project leader. And that meant he'd be moved up to a directorship.

"About time, at thirty years old," I growled.

"Mama, I'll only be 29 in September," my son clarified.

"What's the difference?" I shrugged. "When I was your age I was head of my section at a major newspaper."

"Yes, there were two people in your section, including you," Peter pointed out mildly.

"Exactly! At your age I was already directing staff! And you're still just a senior manager. Your father and I, at your time of life, somehow or other bought our own studio apartment. It's as if you didn't belong to either of us. It's lucky your Dasha got her parents' apartment. How would you manage without that? Where would you raise your children?"

My son pretended that out of the many things I said he'd heard only the last phrase, and muttered something about how, fortunately, Dasha still wasn't pregnant. And what's more, she might soon come in for a major piece of luck: she'd met a fashionable music producer and given him her demo

always very softly. When we played poker in the evenings, she looked on from a corner, never picking up any cards, just watching the game. If Tatiana did open her mouth, she always pronounced all her words with an apologetic half-smile, as if asking forgiveness in advance for the foolishness she was about to commit. All the time she would mercilessly pluck at her bob, dyed with the blackest dye from L'Oréal. Simple-minded women usually think that only black dye can be trusted to colour grey hair. I think Tatiana never played poker so as not to betray her dim-wittedness to her neighbours. Yet here was her perfectly nice daughter in floods of tears in Nata's room. What could be the reason for this?

Nata put a finger to her lips. I nodded understandingly and quietly pulled the door to. I automatically took an apple out of the bag my son had brought, bit into it and headed down the corridor. The time for collective TV news-watching was almost upon us.

Although each of the pensioners had a TV set in their room, everybody preferred to watch the news and the eight o'clock soap together. This way we gained general topics for conversation and even forged a sort of sense of unity.

"How's your daughter?" I asked Tatiana. "Is everything OK with her?"

Tatiana actually shuddered, she was so startled that I spoke to her.

"Yes, she's great, she left not long ago," Tatiana answered with a mousy smile.

"Hmmm… You sure about that?" I didn't want to give her any information. If her daughter was sitting and secretly crying in another woman's room, there was probably a good reason behind it.

I watched the soap and the news to the end. There was nothing of importance on the news – at least the Third World War hadn't broken out yet. We could peacefully put ourselves to bed.

On the way to my room I thought of looking in on Nata, but I decided against it. She came to see me herself. Sitting in one of the standard-issue chairs, she started on the bag of fruit my son had brought. She chose a red apple. For some reason I resented her taking that apple, but I kept quiet.

"Did you want something, when you came by to see me today?" Nata inquired.

"Yes, well, I did want something," I nodded, searching under the mattress for the Scotch I concealed from the staff. "I wanted to weep on your bosom; I really like your bosom. Ever since the first day I saw it, I thought to myself straight away: if I ever want a bosom to weep on yours is the one…"

"So what happened?" Nata asked in a tone which suggested that she wasn't the least surprised by my admission, as if her bosom was just a general place for sad ladies to weep on.

"I saw my son off and somehow felt really miserable," I said, pouring myself some Scotch and offering Nata some. She nodded. I got a second glass.

"Do you love him? You miss him?"

"Ye-es," I waved my hand undecidedly, as if brandishing an imaginary fan. "I have mixed feelings. It's not like I smother him with love, but I want for him to love me. And I'm not sure he does. He talks to me as if I were a stranger. And he's grown up so awkward. I think that if I croaked tomorrow he wouldn't even be able to come to an arrangement with the gravediggers. And I'd end up being buried somewhere by the side of the road. And dogs would run by and piss on my tombstone. And he'd forget to come visit my grave. Put more precisely, he wouldn't even remember me. And after all, I don't have anybody else left. My husband died, my mama too… I don't have anyone."

I wanted to cry again, so I downed my whisky. Nata also tossed back her glass. The whisky put heart in us.

"Did you want to have Peter?"

"We planned him," I said after a brief, awkward pause.

"Plenty are planned and few are wanted," Nata nodded meaningfully. "That explains a lot."

"Why was Tatiana's daughter weeping all over you today?" I changed the subject.

"Oh, she's having a thing with my son Oleg, and he's hurt her feelings. She came to complain."

"Really?" I was genuinely astonished. "But what a coincidence! Your son Oleg is having a fling with Tatiana's Katya, and you and Tatiana wound up in the same home!"

"What's so surprising about that? They met here. Oleg came to visit me, Katya came to visit Tatiana," Nata looked at me as if I were an idiot.

"Well, okay," I thought about it. "And how long have they been seeing each other? Have you and Tatiana thought about being relatives?"

"I think they're going to break up," said Nata decidedly. "They're too alike. People who stick together have to be different. Today I tried to prepare her for things turning out that way."

We drank a bit more and ran out of conversation. I lay down and never even noticed when I fell asleep.

Thanks to my hangover, I almost slept through breakfast. Although today even a corpse would have stirred for our morning porridge as the residence echoed to someone's deafening howls. I leaped out of bed with my face all wrinkled and raced down to the breakfast room to try and find out who was wailing.

In a chair, wringing her hands, sat Alla Maksimova, lamenting picturesquely.

"What, did someone finally tell her that her novels are total shit?" I asked Nina, the grey-haired lesbian for whom all the inmates had mixed feelings. Neither the men nor the women wanted to accept her into their group, so she kept to herself. It didn't seem to bother her much. She had long ago retreated into herself and showed no sign of returning.

"No," Nina answered, doodling curlicues on a sheet of paper, "Rafael Oganesian died."

"Hardly a surprise," I felt relieved. "The old guy must have been well past seventy."

"But he was her only husband," Nina replied, glancing over at Lena. Her glance seemed to suggest that Lena was Nina's only wife and also at death's door.

Everyone had long ago noticed that our lesbian colleague was a little too interested in Lena, a former medic, such a demonstratively strait-laced individual that some people suspected her of a riotous youth and exotic sins. Nina's unusual interest drew attention and even Lena herself suffered many uncomfortable moments because of it. Everyone was waiting with unhealthy curiosity to see whether Nina would manage to corrupt the oh-so-proper Lena into an unnatural intimacy.

Meanwhile, no-one wanted to get too close to Nina; she was an object of gossip, confusing everyone. Everywhere she went she carried a pile of paper, cut up into palm-sized squares on which she was constantly scribbling. She took clean squares out of the left pocket of her jeans and shoved the scribbled-on ones into the right pocket. In the mornings her left buttock bulged, in the evenings, her right buttock. No-one had a clear idea what she did before she wound up in the old folks' home. There were rumours that she'd been a copywriter in some advertising agency, inventing slogans. They said this was why she still had the habit of scribbling short notes. Our men were constantly plotting to get into Nina's room, steal a folder of her papers and finally reveal the dreadful secret – what was she endlessly writing on her scraps?

The news of Rafael's death created quite a sensation. On television, old folk as ancient as Oganesian himself talked about his invaluable contribution to Russian television and cinema. Amongst us, in the home, everyone was discussing the imponderable size of the dead man's legacy. And we looked enviously at Alla.

The cinema and television stars of Moscow also awaited with interest news from Oganesian's executors. Naturally, they weren't concerned with his apartments or his cars, but with the dead man's shares in the film studio and production company he had founded. He had been building this business all his life, cunningly attracting capital from all sides, never relinquishing his role as co-owner. As the company grew, Rafael's stake in it shrank, but nonetheless remained significant.

That morning when an antediluvian, petrol-stinking taxi rumbled up to the residence, its painfully familiar smell of exhaust fumes overpowering even the fragrance of flowering cherries, so unfamiliar to a Muscovite, everyone knew that Alla was heading to Moscow for the reading of the will. Apart from her, only very close relatives had been invited to this legal proceeding: Rafael's elder sister, who had successfully survived to senility, and a couple of his nephews, just approaching pensionable age. Nata had begged to accompany Alla on this nerve-racking occasion. As Alla's closest friend in the home, her muse and her comforter-in-chief, she was permitted. And thus both of them, dressed in black, stifling outfits despite the late May heat, ceremoniously walked to the car between pensioners stretched out on their sun-loungers. As they went, they loudly drenched the Kleenexes they held under their noses, elegantly lifting their sunglasses which lent them an especially funereal air. The taxi doors slammed loudly. To be precise, Nata slammed both doors. She punctiliously seated Alla, who was as grief-stricken as she could contrive, on the rear seat and closed the door after her. She herself sat beside the driver, tucking up her floor-length black skirt with a businesslike gesture before shutting her own door. Just before arranging her dress, she brushed yellowish-red dandelion fluff off the hem; at this time of year the pollen was carried all over the home like curry powder.

Nata always remembers details and never loses her head, even in the most stressful situations. Hard to believe that this same Nata committed, in her lifetime, four hideously senseless deeds: she bore four children, alone, without any sort of husband in the picture… It was probably only in old age that she became so observant and cautious.

I saw Nata's four children on the second Saturday after my arrival in the home. Honestly, I would never have thought that all four had the same mother: that's how different they looked. I would sooner have believed that Nata, influenced in her youth by Angelina Jolie, had followed the actress's example and joined in the craze for adoption. Nonetheless, as Nata assured me, the three young men and one daughter were her own kids. But… from different fathers. Nata refused point-blank to talk about her children's fathers, and answered my questions only by saying, "Trust me, all of them were amazing guys. All but one."

"Why did none of these amazing guys marry you, then?" I asked nastily.

"I didn't need marriage. If I had got married every time I got pregnant, then I would only have borne one man's kids. Then I wouldn't have accumulated this wonderful collection of children."

Nata's approach to motherhood was anything but traditional. She took pride in each of her children as if they were trophies, like an Oscar or a lottery million, or as an artist might be proud of some perfect aesthetic creation. She exulted in them as if she had succeeded, with unusual cunning, in appropriating originals of, say, the *Mona Lisa*, the *Last Supper*, Picasso's *Girl on a Ball*, Malevich's *Black Square*, and Aivazovsky's *The Ninth Wave* all at the same time.

This quirk developed after the birth of her first child. "I knew instantly that a miracle had happened – I had given birth to a completely new, unique person, who had never existed on earth before. I felt almost divine. I felt such euphoria that I wanted to give birth again. And again. Everywhere I went, I looked greedily for the father for my second child. Who would be outstanding enough? As an artist mixes paints, imagining in advance how to capture some sort of amazing, never-seen-before tint, I could think of nothing but whose essence I could mingle with my own to create a result that would astonish even me. And that was when I understood that I did not want to have children by the same man twice. To constantly give birth by one man would be the same thing as for an artist, having once created a masterpiece, to spend the rest of his life making copies and variations from it. There would be no drive for innovation and no creativity."

However much Nata created an atmosphere of total secrecy around the fathers of her children, that evening she could no longer hide the identity of one of them.

Alla and Nata returned from town almost simultaneously, but in different cars. All traces of mourning had vanished from their faces like yesterday's make-up. Nata had a mien of troubled innocence while Alla could not hide her disappointed rage. Both swept into their rooms and locked themselves in. They didn't manage to maintain the mystery for long. Since that morning, even the canteen cockroaches had known that all of Oganesian's vast legacy had been left, not to Alla Maksimova, the only woman who had ever managed to haul him to a registry office, but to his only son whose existence no-one had suspected – Nata's boy Vagan.

Even among Nata's children, 29-year-old Vagan looked completely out of place. Dark, curly-haired, with short, bowed legs and an extremely broad back, he filled her room like an art-deco armchair; at one and the same time imposing and over-exuberant. His baroque cheerfulness and fondness for effects made him a constant sensation in our none-too-exciting residential existence. Every time Vagan visited, the old ladies waited impatiently for his next "prank", which they'd gossip over later. For example, once he brought along a whole case full of extraordinarily horrible-looking garden gnomes, each the size of a cat, and arranged them in a threatening phalanx under Nata's window. Another time he dragged along a diminutive priest, who barricaded himself in Nata's room, while Vagan tempted and teased the female OAPs into coming to make confession. He brought over diviners and astrologists, psychologists and celebrity cooks; he sent Nata "live postcards" – mini-troupes of actors who expressed his filial love for her in songs and dances and assured her that he was doing fine. He shamelessly used a familiar tone within five minutes of meeting a new acquaintance. Even I failed to notice at what point I became Sonya to him and not Sofia Arkadyevna, as all the other old people's offspring called me. No-one could avoid giving in to his ebullience. Nor, as events showed, was he wrong to get so much fun out of life and constantly expect happy surprises and miracles.

Today he was a sensation not just for the pensioners, but for everyone inside the Moscow Garden Ring Road. He was, I must say, well prepared to deal with this: a man who made advertising clips for the biggest companies naturally knows how to project himself in the most promising light.

Privately, I applauded Rafael Oganesian's choice: it was truly difficult to think of a more suitable heir for his empire. Vagan was clearly much better equipped to be a studio boss than a frozen old haddock like Alla. None of the others felt very sorry for her either. But not because they were happy for Vagan; rather, because Alla had been transformed from the local superstar into a loser. Her defeat outside the borders of our residence appeared greater in scale than the victories she had achieved within it; they were completely overshadowed. Unlike our parents' generation, we didn't feel pity for losers. It was our mamas and papas who loved to sigh over unlucky people, although without offering any help, merely repeating:

"If only someone would help, protect, save, take care of, help out, have pity on so-and-so!" We preferred, with cynical honesty, to stab the loser when he or she was down, to deal a mercy blow so that they wouldn't even hope that someone would rush to their aid. Respect and esteem for winners was inculcated in us, without success, all our conscious lives, but instead of learning how to admire winners, we've learned to viciously mock losers. This is as close as we got to the cult of success.

We couldn't learn to appreciate the successful, because most of us, despite the trophies of social success we had scraped by our fingernails, nonetheless considered ourselves part of the losers' generation. After all, none of us children of the late Communist era became as rich as Roman Abramovich, ran for election, bought a TV channel or invented a new kind of fuel, built our own film studio or won an Oscar. We'd lost even before we entered the game; the prizes for which we were invited to fight were like so many glass beads with no real value. What had we got to be proud of? A foreign-made four-by-four, soon to become a rusty heap of broken metal? Paying off a twenty-year mortgage on a two-room hovel in the arsehole of the world? Or the fact that we once had the use of a company car with a driver, or that some of us got to the top ten in the Yandex rating of online bloggers? Genuine winners from the previous generation conquered real lands, factories, TV channels, whereas we simply played around, sharing out the same virtual sand-box. Each of us, proudly bearing on his or her breast the badge "Russia's Top Blogger", knew deep down, of course, that this victory was, in real terms, a defeat. The bravado of our winners hid the grief of suicidal losers. So when verbally scourging someone who'd been busted as an even bigger loser, our winners gained all the more satisfaction, comparable with the bliss of a medieval monk flogging himself.

In a word, Vagan's success with the legacy worsened the positions of both Alla and Nata in the eyes of the OAP community.

"Well, my dear, our zoo has turned into a rats' cage as far as you are concerned," I summed up the situation for Nata, when I popped in to see her the following day. Nata deftly worked her knitting needles, creating a densely stitched scarf the colour of absinthe.

"Well I don't give a damn about any of them," Nata snapped agitatedly, pulling a stitch. "The only person I feel genuinely awkward with is Alla. And this has absolutely nothing to do with any of the others."

"Why should you be nervous around Alla? You didn't write the will," I snorted. "After all, you shouldn't be such a naïve idiot to wait for some guy who couldn't stand you for thirty years to suddenly leave you his goods, not even a broken toilet bowl. To live until your cleavage has wrinkles and still believe in that kind of Hollywood bullshit. Is she a complete idiot? Then it's twice as good for her to learn something about real life."

"I get all that, but it's still awkward," Nata sighed. "She really believed in this. She was twitching with anticipation and already making plans about how she'd let me run the main screenwriting section and so on. She and I really got on well here. And now it seems that I've spoiled her luck a second time."

"Come on, stop feeling sorry for Alla. Look, her hurt feelings might finally turn her into a decent storyteller. Nervous breakdowns are great for inspiration. If you ask me, you shouldn't be thinking about her right now, but planning an anti-crisis PR campaign. Every day they're getting less fond of you here. And the longer you try to sit it out, winding wool, the worse it'll get."

"Knitting helps me think," Nata answered seriously. "Trust me, the old dears in this place are not my biggest problem; I can sort them out in a day or two."

"You mean there's a worse pain in the ass?"
"You bet!"

Nata's problems turned out to be genuinely grown-up. Although it was in fact her children who had driven her to the brink of hysterics.

Not one of Nata's offspring, she admitted, had known before the reading of the will who their fathers were. But each of them had always desperately wanted to know. And now that, against Nata's will, Vagan had learned how powerful and brilliant his father had been, the others were also keenly demanding the truth. Besides their legally justified curiosity, the children were influenced by pecuniary expectations and petty vanity. Finally, each of them believed that he or she was the offspring of someone extraordinary, as their mother had assured them since the day they were born and which they had barely believed. Until Rafael's death. Now they had bought piles of glossy magazines and business journals and were searching with magnifying-glasses through all the major and minor celebrities, seeking a family resemblance.

"They've got me by the throat, they're suffocating me with all their questions," Nata hissed. But it wasn't yet time to tell them the truth. This mother of many children had a hundred and one reasons to continue playing her game: "They are my children, no-one else's. They are my collection of children and I'm not sharing them."

In the first place, as she explained, not all the fathers were as glamorous as Oganesian. And Nata didn't want to sow the seeds of envy and dislike between her children because of this. Secondly, if some of the fathers were eager, like Rafael, to play a role in their children's lives and enthusiastically kept in touch with their offspring, bestowing gifts and helping them choose the right path in life, others, on the other hand, resenting the whole business, had tried to insist that Nata have an abortion.

"You see, right now they're all equal, each of them

thinks he or she has inherited good genes and hidden talents and that somewhere in the world they have a loving father. Imagine if they find out that they weren't wanted at all by their fathers or had fathers less talented than I've always said," Nata explained. "That's why I forbade Rafael to have a father-son relationship with Vagan. I made him swear not to. You can imagine what the older boys – Oleg and Sasha – would have thought. They don't have fathers, and look at the father Vagan's got. I don't think they'd have got on. And of course Rafael wouldn't have had enough paternal energy for all three of them. Nor was he willing to take on other men's children as his own. Moreover, I doubt that if the children had found out their fathers' names they'd have been able to keep them quiet as I've done. They'd have tried immediately to get to know them, started writing letters, scouting out facts, chattering to friends. A lot of people who might be hurt by the truth are still alive. Oganesian was the only one who was so impressed by a woman who wanted nothing from him but a child that he wouldn't leave me alone for five years. Others have families, other children. Why cause so much trouble for people by creating instant relatives? And most of all, why can't I be enough for them? Why do they need someone else as well? It's pure egoism and I don't intend to indulge them. I've decided to tell them the truth only if I outlive everyone whom it might hurt. So the way I see it, I've got to live a long time. Only in the case of Alla and Vagan, the truth escaped. But I really never wanted Rafael to leave Alla. I even tried to persuade him to stay with her. But it was no use."

After reading Alla's book, I understood why Oganesian couldn't stay with her after he met Nata. But hearing this story first-hand was incredibly interesting.

Nata Sokolova had worked in Rafael's company almost since it was founded. She had been lucky enough to be included in the first call for screenwriters, when the newly founded production company had urgently needed a horde of cheap, undemanding writers, uninhibited by notions about great literature, in order to churn out a stream of soap operas. For the first few years she found herself on such a low level in the hierarchy of creative personnel that she had no opportunities to encounter the studio's Great Founder personally. And she was just about to reach a level where one might actually bump into the Great and Terrible One in person, when she got pregnant and stayed just where she was: writing plots and dialogue. In order to meet Rafael face to face, you had to be working on the storyline at the very least – these were the people who went to meetings in the top boss's office, reported the ideas brainstormed by the scriptwriters' group and carried Valuable Points and Mega-Ideas higher up the chain.

By the time she was 28, in spite of all the problems she had brought on herself with her pregnancies, Nata had managed nonetheless to become one of the main writers; she was entrusted with rewriting original TV series, working directly under the supervision of the scriptwriters' group. In spite of the fact that series were supposed to be completely "ours", the studio was by then already co-owned by Americans, and no productions went forward without their approval. The Yanks were unnaturally keen to know everything that was going on: being informed about the general concept wasn't enough; they wanted every dialogue to be just right. Because of this, every script had to be translated from Russian to English and, after corrections, back again. They eagerly picked the brains of the Russian scriptwriters, mercilessly making demands on their time and self-respect.

Conferences were generally held at night, while the sun was rising over California and the cheerful Hollywood residents, after filling up on their low-calorie oatmeal, washed down with freshly squeezed juice, were feeling a surge of good spirits, energy and loquaciousness. By then the Moscow scriptwriters had been on their feet for 16 hours and could barely use their brains or tongues. In a word, their strengths weren't matched. But that was the time invariably fixed for conference-calls with the Americans.

At the table in the Moscow office there would gather Rafael himself, the main author, two storyline writers, the chief series editor, the executive producer and the creative producer. Over a crackly line, choosing the English words with difficulty, "our" guys would try to defend their material, while "their" guys would try to show that everything they'd received by email the previous day was pure shit. The atmosphere became quite tense at times and some of the creative writers fell into a sort of apathetic trance. They would switch off, as if they'd blown a mental fuse, to protect their nervous systems from overload. People would doze off right at their desks. The only man who never dropped off was Rafael. He was able to make his pitch coherently and confidently in a foreign tongue, the language of Shakespeare, without retreating into Russian or his native Armenian or simply collapsing, until four or five in the morning. He retained his energy with the help of a flask of coffee, prepared earlier, and a bottle of cognac, which he mixed in varying proportions in a pint glass. As every hour went by, the proportion of cognac increased. By morning his cocktail was cognac with coffee rather than coffee with cognac.

The other person who held it together to the end was Nata. The others had already spent more than a year of all-nighters in the office, but for her it was her first independent and therefore genuinely stimulating project.

One October night, when in decent Moscow homes, well-brought-up girls snuggled up in feather duvets and dreamed pleasant dreams about new mink coats, and planned outings in the snow, Nata Sokolova, mother of two, was nervously chewing her wrist in a meeting room flooded with raw yellow electric light. The people around her were slowly but surely freezing on their chairs into unnatural poses and beginning to snore. Nata was infuriated by their casual attitude and, as if accidentally, she would kick her colleagues under the table with the soft toe of her fur-lined boots. Rafael was mixing his eccentric cocktails. Nata, despairingly, would try to defend her baby, quacking at the receiver, "But, but, but! Listen! Listen!" And, feverishly hunting for appropriate English swear words, she would rush to the dictionary, turning imploring eyes on her boss: "How would you say this in English?" Every so often she pushed under his nose ripostes to the Americans' objections she'd scribbled earlier. Perhaps she wasn't very good at being convincing in a phone conversation with America, but figuring out in advance the problems that might arise was entirely within her powers. Nata didn't even notice how, half-asleep, she had automatically grabbed Rafael's glass and, without grimacing, had drunk down the entire swill of coffee and cognac. Then she poured herself a top-up of pure cognac. By way of reply, he silently reached into the middle of the meeting table, took a clean glass, splashed cognac into it, passed it to Nata and reached for his own mug.

"I'll go and rinse it!" Nata trembled, full of remorse. Rafael just shook his head. He grunted and raised his eyebrows invitingly. Nata understood without further words: she took the drink. They clinked glasses.

Naturally, long before this episode Nata had evaluated Oganesian as a promising father for her future child. His thirst for life, energy, willingness to take risks, undeniable talent and enthusiastic goodwill had long ago shaped a simple statement in her brain: "I want a guy like this for myself. Forever." But for a long time she hadn't known how to get near Rafael. Moreover, she knew his wife Alla who sometimes turned up at the studio, when they needed to develop a particular look for the actors in a series. Alla Maksimova would chase all the actors into the conference room, look at them, talk to them, and then send them to her salon, from which they'd emerge as a genuine team, each with his or her unique image, so that the viewer wouldn't be confused by identical blue-eyed blondes on screen, trying to figure out whether this was a new character or the same girl who'd appeared in the previous scene. Alla was undoubtedly attractive: she had the tidy, slender figure of a childless woman. Cunningly injected Botox had somewhat frozen her forehead (into lines of surprise), and her upper lip (into laugh lines), lending her face a masklike charm. She had taught herself to convey a whole range of emotions with a single glance; she'd probably have made a good actress. She always smelled good, as if she'd just left a beauty salon. (But of course, she always came straight from her salon to the studio.) Unlike Nata, who rushed between office, clinic, and kindergarten, and sometimes, like today, the toyshop. Nata already felt slightly depressed, worrying she had been in too much of a rush to create her collection of children. It was clear that, with two children, she was no longer as attractive to men as she'd been. She looked slightly older than women of the same age. She didn't have time for all the important things: manicure, tanning salons, pedicure, permanent tattoos, massage, dermabrasion, saunas, cleaning, and anti-ageing procedures. But perhaps having a third little one would sort her out. Was this really the way it would all end, that she'd make herself just too unattractive, prematurely becoming an old hag?

She didn't know yet that her children would help her to believe in herself again and show her that she was doing the right thing. That she was very sensibly investing her present in her future: so much more sensible than wasting time lying on the salon table, being squeezed by a masseur, or peeled and daubed by a make-up artist, or pinched by a manicurist.

At seven in the morning, through the just-waking city (not yet log-jammed with traffic), Nata was driven home in Rafael's famous Bentley, which had been profiled in more than one photo-article. Nata found herself in its leather-seated interior for the first time. Rafael, although neither absolutely sober nor fully awake, managed to drive the car with bravado, but not dangerously enough to make Nata want to dive out of the moving vehicle. Oganesian drove his own car; he didn't see the point of buying the car of your dreams and then entrusting it to some driver. Why hand your happiness over to the chauffeur? No, he wanted to enjoy his own ride.

They had no energy left for talk. Besides, Oganesian was clearly so absorbed in watching the road that any chatter would just irritate him. Probably in order to discourage any attempts at "lively conversation", he was playing Black Sabbath at full volume. And Nata kept quiet, listening to the words of the songs.

Only when she was saying goodbye, and undoing the strap of her safety belt, did she sigh: "That was... stimulating!"

Rafael winked in response: "Wasn't it just!"

Nata lifted out the bag of children's toys she'd hastily bought the previous day. Her elder son, Oleg, had a birthday coming up. But that didn't mean Sasha, the younger, could go without a present. If he did, the big day would degenerate into a bloody, drawn-out struggle between the brothers, with howls and sobs. The bag was soaked by the October slush: it burst, spilling out two identical model cars, still in their boxes.

"Why did you get two the same?" Rafael asked with interest, helping Nata to pull one of the boxes out from under the seat. "Not a bad little car, by the way!"

"I've got two boys. And if I give them different cars, they'll fight over which one is cooler. No different from big boys!" Nata smiled.

"Good kids?"

"The best!"

"It'd be cool to buy my sons the toys I couldn't even dream of when I was a child."

"Yeah, and you'd play with them yourself – that's what all fathers do. They buy their kids train sets and spend hours playing with them themselves."

"What, really?"

"I don't know," Nata shrugged lightly. "My girlfriends tell me that's what their husbands do. We don't have any daddies, so the kids get to play with their own toys."

"And what models have they got already?" Rafael seemed to have woken up.

Nata stiffened, glanced towards her front door – two little boys aged six and three were springing out of it, their grandmother close behind. It was their regular morning expedition, taking them from the apartment to kindergarten via every puddle along the way. The boys ran right over to Nata.

"Now they'll tell you themselves!" Nata spread her hands.

Rafael, and especially his wheels, immediately won the kids' respect. The eldest, little Oleg, even showed off his grasp of the topic: "You know how much this costs?" He pulled his younger brother's hood back emphatically.

"How much?" the younger gaped.

"You couldn't even count high enough!" the older boy remarked scornfully and, breaking off, looked at Oganesian, evidently fearing the disclosure of some fact that might weaken his authority.

Naturally, the boys immediately begged Rafael to drive them to kindergarten, making him swear that he would give them a spin again another time; they even promised to show him all their toy cars. Along the way, they asked him whether he happened to have a gun, just to be seriously with-it. (They weren't put off by his negative reply, which didn't seriously damage Rafael's cool. "So just buy one," the kids advised, "in a car like this you need to drive with a pistol or else someone might shoot you in the head! Criminals are like that!") The elder boasted that he knew what gays were; he offered to explain to Uncle, in case the latter hadn't heard. And just in case, he wanted to know if Uncle was gay. (As it happened, just the day before both boys had insistently demanded to be told the meaning of this word, which they'd heard in kindergarten, and they were still enchanted by their new knowledge, seeking opportunities to use it.)

"Hear that, Mom?" Oleg suddenly turned to face the front seat. "Uncle isn't gay, you've got a chance with him!"

Nata also knew that she had a chance. Interesting children, even other people's, act like a stimulant on certain men, awakening their inner alpha male and arousing a desire to create "kids just like those". Life is generally ordered around bizarrely generous principles: work is offered to those who are swamped with it; girls hang around guys who've already got a harem; LiveJournal bloggers "friend" people who have a thousand followers already; money follows money; children follow children. Everything took its natural course, although not straightaway.

Over the next few days Nata was trying to sell Oganesian on "the latest fashionable thing" – streetracing. This trend was just catching on then. Raf heard her out with interest. (Yes, Raf, and not Rafael; he had suddenly asked his employees to stop addressing him by name and patronymic and to call him simply, American-style, Raf.) "Night racing, cool wheels, and all these vroom-vroom machines. Going for a spin with these guys once was enough to almost drive me nuts. They've got adrenalin coming out of their ears!" Nata stared at him with glowing eyes. Oganesian had no objection to taking a lungful of the air breathed by the "Generation Next". He and Nata very easily found a businesslike explanation for heading out together at night to join the street racers. Rafael was planning to expand his business: as well as producing TV series, he wanted to start making real full-length films. And cinemas, as everyone knows, generally attract audiences under the age of 35. If a company wants to appeal to that audience, the production chief clearly needs to be up to date. The fact that there were plenty of young people right in the company's office, who could be studied just as well, Raf and Nata very reasonably never noticed.

In a word, they started doing "the night shift". His excuse was to try out his new cars and "get a feel for things"; she went in order to record the boss's wise thoughts and to note down interesting types. Raf, who was 44 and in his second youth, was flattered that the young racers looked up to him as an authority and a guru; he really could speed like a lunatic. For propriety, sometimes they brought along someone else from the studio on these night excursions. But this "live weight" was very quickly put in someone else's car to "observe from within". The night, the speed, the risk, the sense of pushing limits greatly facilitated closeness and sexual desire. After a sharp turn or a sudden brake one's first thought was "Wow! I could have died just then! Aaaaggghhh! I'm alive! I'm ALIVE!" And that was followed by an urge for some life-affirming and life-creating action. Like making love in the back seat.

The youthful street racers' cars careened past swiftly and unpredictably; production of the blockbuster about night streetracing went forward slowly and anxiously; only the belly of a pregnant woman grew at its unchanging millennia-old pace. And ripened just when it should – nine months later.

At the end of July, Nata left the maternity ward with a little boy wrapped up like a parcel in her arms. She allowed Raf to give her son whatever name he wanted, as a sign of gratitude for his services. Raf called him Vagan. He decided not to visit the maternity ward – after all, he was married to Alla, and Nata herself didn't want to see him there. Later, the newly-found 45-year-old father admitted that at the last moment he'd been seized by an impulse to rush to the mother of his child, but he was so drunk he couldn't even insert the key in the ignition. Waiting for his first child to be born, Oganesian had boozed hard, shutting himself up in his dacha, chasing out both his wife and the maid; he'd never had a chauffeur to banish. After getting very drunk he anxiously called up Nata and asked, "Is he out yet?" After hearing "Not yet", he immediately hung up and abstractedly slugged whiskey from the bottle. So that when Nata was ready to let him know that He was out, he was already so exhausted by anticipation that he was sleeping an anxious, drunken sleep and didn't hear her call.

Nata told the story of Raf and of Vagan's arrival so smoothly that it was clear she had rehearsed it, if only in her mind, in order to tell her son everything one day. I was fascinated. Suddenly Nata interrupted her own story with a question:

"Do you remember how in Alla's 'The Prince in the White Mercedes' there's a scene where the heroine discusses children with her husband?"

"Is that where he asks what she'll do if they suddenly need to fly somewhere and she answers 'whatever you say, lord and master'?"

I suddenly understood exactly which scene Nata had in mind. Oh, how glad I was that I'd copied that extract into my "revelatory" file! I'd just known that it was based on reality.

"Yeah, that's the very dialogue I have in mind," Nata stared at me. Evidently, my response had put her slightly on guard, giving away too much interest in our topic. But she'd already trusted me with so much, she couldn't resist telling me the rest.

"She didn't think up that scene. It was a real conversation between Alla and Raf," Nata confirmed my expectations. "Only she completely misunderstood what was going on."

"It was a test for her, an experiment?" I didn't even try to play dumb.

"Yes, something like that," Nata nodded. "I was already very pregnant by then and Raf was pretty troubled in his mind. It wasn't that he'd instantly wanted to leave his wife and marry me. On the contrary, from the start he'd hinted that I shouldn't get any notions and start counting on that. And, of course, it wasn't my plan at all. I didn't need marriage. But he was bothered by something all the same. That's when he asked Alla, what would happen if you got pregnant? And she told him, 'I'll do whatever you want. If you want an abortion, I'll get one.' He obviously wanted to hear something different from her. He decided that since she wasn't the same kind of woman as me, since kids were not her heart's desire, she didn't really love him. Then he started thinking, 'Just imagine, she was ready to kill my baby! And she tells me she loves me! A woman like that could turn off my life support.' It was already too late to change his mind, although I won't say that I tried very hard. They broke up soon after that. Alla, as far as I can tell, never understood why it happened. Raf was that sort of guy: once he'd made a decision, he wiped that person out of his life, without seeing the point in wasting time explaining the 'politics of his decision'. It's entirely possible that if I hadn't come between them, sooner or later they would have gotten to the stage where they could have a child together. But here Raf had already gone off his head a little, he was convinced that all the girls in the world were dreaming of having his babies. And Alla, it seemed, was also so delighted with herself that, like him, she expected someone to beg her on bended knee to produce an heir. Do you remember that passage in one of her books, where she regrets that men no longer beg women on their knees to bear them children? Both Alla and Raf were superstars. Neither was prepared to talk the other round."

While our superannuated ladies were divvying up the late Oganesian's romantic attachments and reckoning his legacy, I regretfully realized that I had pretty much wasted my time studying Alla Maksimova's works. As things now stood, when everyone whose face wasn't actually paralyzed was laughing at her, it would simply be bad taste to snipe at her literary style. Her faith in her literary talents was basically the last thing she had left. If she took a pounding in the literary ring as well as elsewhere, she might hang herself from sheer despair. I'm caustic but not cruel, and I didn't want her death on my conscience. So I urgently needed to find a new target for my venom.

Once again I took stock of the literary landscape of our residence. Studying the in-house magazine, I joyfully seized on the gloomy mystical-moral fables published under the pen name of T. Losthope. They were written badly, lifelessly, as if the authoress had dictated them from beyond the grave. I read a couple of tales about the irresistible power of fate, the inevitable payout for every careless action, and a satirical pamphlet about Comrade Losthope began spontaneously forming in my head. Lines kept popping into my mind, in which I rhymed "Losthope" with "lost dope" and "nope".

For some reason I couldn't quite lose myself in laughing at this lady (I never doubted for an instant that these panicky homilies could have been written by anyone but a woman). The tone of fierce seriousness, the absence of the slightest attempt at black humour, put me on guard. In one of these esoteric pieces a boy drowned a kitten, out of childish cruelty. Then, when he grew up and became a father, some children, acting on the same murderous impulse, grabbed his son by the legs when he was swimming and accidentally drowned him. Naturally, the father immediately saw that this punishment had been visited on him in revenge for the kitten he'd drowned in his childhood. He decided to devote the rest of his life to atoning for his sin, spending his days near the Animal Market and rescuing the kittens abandoned under the stalls at the end of the trading day.

In another work by T. Losthope, an evil fate punished a careless young girl who had forgotten to water the plant bequeathed to her by her dead mother. She dehydrated the plant so severely that it dissolved into dust when she touched it. The red dust covering the windowsill reminded the girl of her cremated mother's ashes, and she immediately sensed that she had committed a terrible crime, for which she could never be forgiven. And that's how it turned out: when the girl became old, her children forgot about her just as she had forgotten about her mother's geranium. They didn't bring money or groceries home and didn't even bother calling her on the phone. The old lady suffered greatly, but she didn't simply call her children and ask, "Don't you need anyone to sit with the grandkids, or bring your clothes to the laundry?" No, she didn't do anything so silly: instead she tried to solve the problem through what she considered the only reliable method – mysticism. She tried to grow a new geranium on the memorial slab in the columbarium containing her mother's ashes. But no matter how many geraniums the old woman planted, not a single one took root. Each of them died or crumbled into dust, just like that original, fateful flower.

In a word, an even moderately discerning reader will have no difficulty guessing how the rest of the stories by this author ended. For example, what happened to the mailman who once accidentally lost a letter from his mailbag? Or what was the fate of the man who refused, in his youth, to be a witness in a court case, because he grudged the time? Or what happened to the carpenter who built swings for children so badly that one of them fell down and crushed a child? Or to the baker, who carelessly sprinkled nuts in the filling of a cheesecake and sold it to a man who came out in enormous hives if he tasted even a fragment of nut?

Clearly, all these individuals ended badly: their fates were simply dreadful. If I had even the slightest touch of paranoia and a slightly less irreverent attitude to the author of the texts, I would probably, after reading these stories, have locked myself in my room and not dared to move a finger, in case something horrible happened to me next.

After sitting down to write a thunderous critical assault on the mysterious T, I suddenly felt sorry for her. It sounded as if she lived in a permanent state of panic. I should try to find out first who's hiding behind this pseudonym and discover whether this author is psychologically sound, and whether all this gloomy rubbish is just a kind of joke, I decided. Although it wouldn't surprise me if she really believes all this stuff. In which case the devil knows what she'll come to.

Tatiana, the same woman who walked around as if she had a bag over her head, turned out to be the author of that esoteric-mystical rubbish. That very same woman who dyed her hair pitch black, who spoke to people as if instruments of torture were constantly dangling in front of her. The same woman who seemed to tremble in front of everyone even before she'd been criticized, the mother of that Katya who was seeing Nata's son Oleg. Tatiana, evidently, wasn't having fun with her stories; she was expressing her true view of the world. It was interesting to speculate what might happen in a person's life to make them believe that every act, even the tiniest, carries a punishment a hundred times more serious. At supper, I found myself watching Tatiana with interest for the first time.

I knew that she was a widow and that she had a daughter called Katya, Oleg's girlfriend. And that according to Nata, Katya and Oleg were about to break up. And that this upset Katya greatly, while Nata was rather pleased that her son would find a more suitable partner. That was understandable – I certainly wouldn't want Tatiana as an in-law. I decided that if anyone knew everything about Tatiana, it must be Nata. She would certainly have studied her under a microscope. But Nata unexpectedly admitted her ignorance:

"No, I've no idea why she was suddenly overcome by a wave of fear," Nata evidently wanted to dismiss the topic. "To tell the truth, I think it's so unlikely that Katya and Oleg will stay together that I haven't taken a close look at Tatiana. She's a typical housewife, she's spent her life between the dishwasher, the washing machine, and the oven. What could possibly be interesting about her?"

"Well you seem to know that she was a housewife all her life, that's something. And what did her husband do that allowed his wife to stay home?"

"He was some sort of doctor, I think," Nata shrugged. "But I don't know. If you're interested, ask her yourself."

Overcoming my repugnance for the woman that's just what I did. I set off to gather background information directly from the source.

Tatiana stiffened sharply when I sat down beside her on a bench on the lawn. She put aside her book, *Prophetic Dreams*, and arched her brows.

"You're on your own all the time, don't you get bored?" I asked.

"Do I really look bored?" Tatiana asked quietly and fell silent, evidently waiting for me to get up and leave. Well, she had the wrong idea there!

"I want us to get to know each other better. I'd like to learn more about you."

Tatiana fiddled with a lock of her hair in a habitual gesture, but she didn't say a word.

"I heard that you were a full-time housewife. I've always been a little envious of women who don't need to rush to and from the office every day. Tell me, what was your favourite time of day? When everyone had left and the apartment was quiet, or when everybody crowded round for supper in the evening?" I felt as if I were digging an oyster out of its shell with a pair of pincers.

"We had a house, not an apartment. And it was never completely silent. I had a helper, and a nanny, and a gardener, or I ran errands for my husband, collecting stuff, delivering things."

The poor woman obviously resented my insistence, but she didn't have the gumption to get up and walk away. That happens to people who haven't passed through the school of life in big gangs; they don't know how to deal with aggression, they've never learned how to say "No". They try to be polite with everybody, confusing correct behaviour with lack of character. Housewives like this are generally shy about telling the maid in so many words what they want done or how the cook or cleaner should behave, and therefore they have to fire their staff regularly. At the beginning they all wait for dear Galya to figure out that washing the floor while simultaneously spending hours on the house phone with Ukraine is in bad taste. Then they start hiding the telephone, but the cleaner still finds it and gets her dirty hands on it. And then, after torturing themselves a little longer, they fire dear Galya all the same, without explaining why, or by babbling something along the lines of "I've decided to do the work myself, we don't need any more help." Then dear Nadia arrives to replace Galya, and – surprise, surprise! – she starts greedily begging clothes from the housewife: "Oh, you haven't worn this for six months can't you let me have it? Oh, pleeeeaase!" For three months the housewife replenishes dear Nadia's wardrobe and then once again mutters something about how she doesn't think she can afford a cleaner any longer.

Although I'm not from Ukraine, I can get my claws into someone no worse than that dear Nadia. My interrogation was going very well. But it remained an undeniable interrogation; not even I, a professional journalist, could relax Tatiana and lull her wariness.

By the end of our chat I had obtained a little more personal information. Tatiana had spent her adult life living with her husband, a psychotherapist. She herself had graduated from the St Petersburg Institute of Culture, majoring in library science, and had worked briefly – for a year – in her field. Working for an established Moscow bookshop, she had assembled home libraries for important wealthy clients. Through her work, she met her future husband, Zhenya. He was looking for books to garnish his new oak bookcases and make the right impression on guests. He was considerably older than her, but that didn't bother her. They were happily married for twelve years, and then became even happier with the birth of their daughter, when Tatiana was 34. She didn't work before or after Katya's birth, looking after her husband and daughter to keep them comfortable and well-fed. For more than thirty years she lived in Zhenya's shadow, until it all ended abruptly. Three years ago, her husband died of cancer. He'd practiced medicine almost to his dying day. Immediately after his death the family's financial position collapsed, money stopped coming into her purse, and Tatiana moved to the old folks' home, letting the house where she had spent half her life at a high rent. When she arrived she'd been the home's youngest resident, at just 54.

All in all, it was a portrait of peaceful middle-class existence, which went no farther towards explaining Tatiana's terror of life.

"Tatiana, in all your stories the heroes are overtaken by punishment for sins they've committed in the past. You know, this made a very strong impression on me. I suddenly remembered all sorts of horrible things about myself, and shivers went down my spine." I took aim at my target and, in order to soften her up, I flattered her a little. "Do you really think that's how life works?"

"Yes, that's what I think." Tatiana stiffened even more than before.

"Tell me, has something similar happened to you?"

"Yes."

"Can you tell me about it?"

"No, I can't."

"Listen, there's no way I'm going to believe that you've done something so awful that even at sixty years of age you can't tell anyone about it. Surely by now you can let it go! I'd really like to know."

My insistence finally went too far for my interviewee. But even now, Tatiana couldn't say plainly, "No, I don't want to talk about it and I'm not going to. Get lost!" She simply jumped up, pressed her book to her bosom and sighed, "I'm sorry, I really have to go to the toilet."

And she scurried right off down the path.

Damn! People are so strange. At first they dig all their complexes out of their brains and let them run around in full view in cheap literary magazines, and then they bend over backwards to give the impression that this nonsense has nothing to do with them. And if they get so upset they have to let it all spill out, they don't want to be heard, like that peasant from the fairy-tale who whispered into a hollow in an oak-tree: "The tsar has horns!" without giving the storytellers a chance to create rumours or awake the unhealthy interest of the public.

I was so angry at Tatiana for her secretiveness that I decided to suppress my humane empathy with her and distribute the very next day my pamphlet about her "literary efforts". I burst into my room, opened the file and re-read it with pleasure, imagining Tatiana tearing her hair in despair. I don't like people who don't trust me. I'm the sort of person who would never poke a hedgehog in its soft belly, but who would firmly squash a snorting hedgehog that had rolled up in a ball! There's a price to be paid for stupidity. Besides, sometime I had to start the work I had in mind to uproot all the text-weeds in our literary garden.

Which all goes to say that I swiftly appeased my conscience. I printed off 50 copies of my critique and, as I drifted off to sleep, gazed admiringly at the pile of white sheets.

Sometimes I regret that all of this really happened, that I didn't just invent it all. If I had thought up this story then, of course, I'd have constructed a more elegant plot. If I'd written an imaginary tale rather than a documentary account, all of Nata's little secrets would have been revealed in the appropriate sequence for a bestseller. Every secret would have brought with it a substantial hook, to hold your attention, dear reader, and prevent you getting bored. But things happened as they did. Life, unfortunately, doesn't always follow the rules of art. Simpler, uglier, and more painful – that's life for you!

And the secret which, if I'd thought up this story, I would have kept back until the end, was exposed unexpectedly fast. My one-page critique of the talentless writer Losthope, which I'd distributed around the residence early in the morning, hurt me more than anyone else. And it hurt me so cruelly that I was lucky to stay alive rather than drowning myself in our shallow lake with its old-fashioned wooden boardwalk. All the same, it was a good thing that I'd dreamed all my life of writing a novel and considered myself a writer first and foremost, and only then a woman and a wife. If I had defined myself in terms of my family I wouldn't have been able to bear the whole truth which was revealed to me. But thanks to the fact that I never yielded my whole heart and soul, now, as my eyes filled with burning tears, I could say to myself: "This will be good material for the book." At last, my literary emergency runway had proved its worth.

As it happened, I sprang out of bed first thing in the morning, glanced happily at the pile of shitty reviews of the even shittier writer T. Losthope, fished a little box of pins out of my writing table, and set off to pin them up all over the house. Honest to God, my opponent seemed so weak and defenceless that there was no point in exulting over her. I acted rather from my consciousness of the need for literary weeding than personal dislike.

Of course, my little prank immediately created a sensation in our community. Somehow or other, everyone soon found out that I was the author of the vicious lampoon. From all sides, pressure was put on this independent critic.

For a start, the director attempted to summon me. She sent a messenger, apparently taking me for a little first-grader who would stand trembling in front of her, knees shaking, at her first request.

"You're wanted, come along," said a young woman, beckoning commandingly, curling her fingers into open fists, as if getting her blood pressure taken.

"If your director is desperate to speak with me, then I'm ready to see her in my room after lunch today," I shrugged and slammed the door in her face.

It wasn't as if I had grand plans for the day, I simply wanted to make it quite clear that I set the rules in this engagement. This meant I should immediately display my state of spiritual calm and relaxation. I decided that if I sat on the edge of the lake with a fishing rod, I would look both imposing and unconcerned. Therefore I went to the men's wing to look for hooks and lines. I was planning to extract them from Dimon, a guy who could spend days on end coaxing fish out of our pond, evidently hoping to find a golden one.

"Why you pick on Tatiana?" he gaped at me, mouth wide open, placing his tongue against the farthest-off part of his denture with a chomping, sucking sound.

"Why 'picked on'?" I defended myself. "I simply expressed an independent, critical opinion. Every writer needs an unbiased and objective evaluation of his or her work; he or she needs someone who will point out strong and weak aspects of the text, helping to avoid mistakes in the future. After all, that's why they founded the Institute of Literary Criticism." I could have gone on perjuring myself, but Dimon was not in a mood to listen.

"Look, Sonya, just don't get on the girls' tits! What do you think, that people here escaped from Moscow just to get stressed all over again? You've got to live and let live."

"OK, I get the message – you're not going to give me a rod!" I turned and went into the boat-room, where the leisure equipment was kept: balls, rackets, bicycles and fishing rods.

"If you bother Tatiana again, you'll get yourself in trouble," the old man threatened behind me.

"Yeah, right! I'm so scared," I snarled.

"It'd be better for you if you really were scared."

I could hear him hawking phlegm in my wake. What a disgusting old bastard! If I'd been in Tatiana's place, I'd have been ashamed to have people like that on my side.

Just as a precaution, I walked around the house and discovered that my literary critique had been torn down everywhere. I put up new ones in their place, adding a few more vicious sentences and including my signature – after all, everyone already knew it was me. I took from the blond boy who ran the boat-room a fishing rod and a sandwich roll, and set off for the lake.

It was a hot day: a whole swarm of horseflies and other bugs was buzzing around me. The fish weren't biting. My

Nike baseball cap didn't protect my head from the sun; in fact, somehow it seemed to intensify it. My head felt like a microwave oven on the grill setting. And if I took it off, my eyes started weeping from the blinding sunshine. My best course was to return to the courtyard in front of the home, sit under the century-old poplars, bury myself in a volume of Chekhov and sprinkle myself from time to time with mineral water. But going back to the courtyard would mean declaring open war. I didn't feel like hand-to-hand combat.

I lasted three hours in the sun-oven. I didn't catch so much as a lousy minnow. I was already thoroughly annoyed at myself, at Tatiana, and at Dimon's unnecessarily fierce defence of her. Thankfully, lunchtime finally arrived and I could wind up my fishing rod and head for the dining room. Otherwise, I'd certainly have got sunstroke.

Apparently, the entire time I'd been dropping breadcrumbs in the lake, I'd been under observation. As soon as I got rid of the rod, the director of the residence, an aubergine-haired woman about forty, trapped me in the corridor, wedging me against the wall with her flat belly. While we were speaking she never once took her hands out of her pockets, looking rather like an SS agent. It was as if she were barely restraining herself, worried that she might start choking me if she didn't stay on a tight rein.

"Sofia Arkadyevna, you are breaking the rules of this rest home," she told me in a cold and forceful tone. "You read the contract and you must be aware that starting fights, arguments, and creating an unhealthy psychological atmosphere are all forbidden in our community. According to the contract, we can ask you to leave in consequence of your recent actions, and without returning the fee you paid us."

"Somehow I don't remember reading a clause in the contract stating that I had to lobotomize myself and wear a condom over my head, that is, stop thinking critically and avoid expressing my personal opinion."

"We can all think whatever we like, but we must not stick

negative statements on the walls. Be aware that I am now giving you a formal warning."

Lunch was even more nerve-racking than my fishing trip. The tables in our institution were designed for four people. I sat next to Alla Maksimova, who was sitting alone, because as I saw the situation, we had both incurred our own boycott. But even this stupid fallen idol somehow considered it beneath her dignity to socialize with me. (Out of the corner of my eye I noticed enviously that Nata had already fully restored her standing in the community; she was sitting at the most central table amidst a big merrily-chatting group, clearly holding her own. How on earth had she managed that?)

Alla pretended for the entirety of lunch that I was invisible. She spoke not to me, but to a ghost standing behind me. She didn't even focus on my nose when she spoke; she addressed her words slightly to one side, into the air.

I said to her, "Alla, surely you realize that public opinion is just fluff. And that in reality, you have no way of changing whatever a bunch of clinical idiots are going to think about you after reading the newspapers? Now do you admit that a person's public image is just an illusion? Our community destroyed you through no fault of your own, without any real reason. And because I've stated a little bit of truth, they're already prepared to strangle me in a dark corner. You see how stupid it is to build your life around 'public opinion'; you might as well hide behind the wardrobe all your life."

"You made a big mistake," Alla fenced weakly, clenching her dentures, "and don't dream of getting any support from me. You're on your own with this thing. Even when my life is such shit, like right now, and they look down on me, I'm not going to team up with you because we live in different dimensions. You're translating the issue onto the plane of aesthetic values. But we're already living in a different world, the halfway-house to hell. And it's no place for opinions. Corpses crossing the River Styx are no longer measured by the size of their genitals. The only way they're assessed is by how fast they're approaching absolute non-being. And the slower, the better. If you want to stay on the right side of the threshold to the next world, you need to go and apologize to Tatiana, taking back everything you wrote. Then you'll still be allowed to live in this in-between place a little longer."

Alla spoke slowly and monotonously, like a cook in a vegetarian restaurant talking up her caramelized spinach. This made her words all the more unpleasant and painful. I somehow knew that this wasn't Alla speaking; she was a fighter. She was one of those people who never give in and don't accept a way of living that doesn't suit them. Instead, she was the sort to impose her own style on others. This submission to the majority betrayed some kind of self-lacerating suicidal mood.

"Personally, I'm not planning to die just yet. Far from it, I still intend to give someone a good sharp pummelling in the face, bottom and skull. This is no time to weaken!"

"Why are you doing this?" Alla asked. "It's not that I don't understand why you did it. In fact I understand why very well. I wanted to say: are you sure that this is what you need?"

"Hm, how come you've suddenly decided you understand my motivations and you know why I've taken up literary criticism?"

"Sonya, have you seen any children here?" Alla asked sternly and challengingly. "No, you haven't seen them? That's because they're not here! Everyone here has lived a long life and, trust me, understands something about people. And you're completely transparent and let yourself be read, just like those famous Japanese frogs with transparent skin which used to be bred specially for experiments, because scientists could see what was going on inside them without opening them up. So stop thinking that you're some kind of mystery."

"I'm not denying that you can perhaps see right through me. And perhaps then you can tell me something about myself, I'd be curious to hear!"

"Well then, come to see me this evening, I'll tell you."

Alla finished munching her lunch. She neatly crossed her knife and fork on her plate, wiped her lips with a handkerchief, not leaving the slightest trace on it, and melted away through the door.

How furious I got with these people who thought they understood everything about me! What could Alla, with her chicken brain, failing to handle the simple task of hanging onto her man, ever understand about me? But all the same, I thought I'd go see her that evening. It's always interesting to find out how one is perceived in the consciousness of the masses.

After supper, I glanced into our reading room in order to collect new textual targets for my thunderbolts of criticism. I was no longer afraid of starting a fight with anyone, because I already knew that nobody here liked me. So I had nothing to lose. As I was leaving the reading room with a pile of papers under my arm, my way was blocked by three would-be police agents. They were led by my friend, Dimon the fisherman.

"Put those back where you found them!" he ordered me.

"You again! Dimon, don't stick your nose in where you weren't invited."

"The lady's deaf," sniggered one old gasbag, shrugging his shoulders and glancing at his comrades. "We need to find another way of explaining."

And the trio started ripping the pages out of my grasp, freely poking me in the side and pushing me in the bosom.

I was prepared for any level of protracted and bitter moral struggle. I would have withstood any amount of emotional and intellectual opposition on the scale of the Trojan, the Hundred Years' or even the First World War. But I was completely unprepared for the tiniest physical confrontation. After all, I was used to living among a different sort of public, the kind that delivered even the worst insults verbally, and even fistfights took place in the clean field of LiveJournal, where the opponents dispatched regiments of words against each other. But here, as I realized, people were not too refined to indulge in the old-fashioned and brutal method of defending their position, like just hitting their opponents in the face and winding them with a fist to the ribs. Without respect for gender or other conventions.

To tell the truth, the last time I'd been in a fight was almost fifty years before, when I was still in school. A girl in my class and I failed to share a locker in the gym changing-room and, catching each other by the hair, tried at length and quite synchronously to push each other's faces into the tile floor. Since then, no-one had ever encroached upon my physical space, making this incident all the more shocking to my self-esteem. Naturally the guys managed to get my textual would-be victims away from me. However, I displayed a vitality that surprised even me, hitting Dimon in the face with a stack of papers a couple of times. I bit the hand of one of his vassals, and managed to scratch the other's face and pull out a hank of hair. They damaged me too: afterwards I found that during the struggle they even managed to tear one of my bra straps, bruise my arm and break a nail.

I was flabbergasted by the crude and archaic mode of combat they chose; I was so demoralized and felt so helpless that I couldn't breathe. I literally didn't have enough air. Possibly, precisely because of this state of hypoxia my brain behaved strangely and sent me not to my own room, the sensible place to go to wash myself and tidy up, but straight to Alla. Or possibly I went to see her because the last thing I heard before the attack had been her invitation.

I sat in front of her scarlet-faced, ready to burst into tears. Without saying a word, Alla filled her jacuzzi, sat me in the bubbling water, and placed a glass of cognac on the edge of the tub. I drank it off without tasting it. But five minutes later I felt better, my body relaxed and my legs involuntarily started jumping around in the bath under the massaging jets of water.

Alla noted the change in my condition with satisfaction,

slipped off her dressing gown and climbed in beside me. Probably under different circumstances our position – two naked women in a fairly small jacuzzi – would have struck me as somewhat pornographic and not really in good taste. But now, it was actually pleasant to have another human being, warm and living, close to me; very close indeed and with all its armour put aside. I could even accidentally brush her with my hip.

"So I suppose you've finally understood why they attacked you?" Alla asked, not in an unfriendly way.

"I guess they think Tatiana is a genius and a star of contemporary literature," I sneered. "The fools!"

"Any other explanations?"

"You can have as many explanations as you want!" I waved my hand, splashing Alla with water. "Maybe they just like her as a woman? That's even more likely. I've always noticed that the more neurotic and pathetic a woman is the more men want to defend her. They feel more brutal next to such fragile creatures, it seems. They wouldn't have defended a classy woman like you in that situation!"

"You're wrong! If you'd decided to criticize my work instead, then the whole residence would have rushed to defend me, and no less enthusiastically!"

"What are you saying? Ha, ha! They'd simply rush to your aid, would they? Yes, I seem to remember them all racing to comfort you with friendly hugs after the disaster with the will."

"The disaster with the legacy was one thing. But attacks on our creative work – that's quite another."

This was Alla Maksimova's theory about the peer support the pensioners gave each other and their fierce mutual defence of their writings: all these people, buried 200 kilometres away from their former lives, had for the long, long years of serious and responsible adult lives denied themselves any form of creativity or play. They had sacrificed this for the sake of someone else or out of fear of going bankrupt along the way. Here, at long last, they returned to childhood, and along with their childish recklessness they gained a childlike courage to write, compose music, paint or draw. They act just as little children do, not perforce, but with pleasure, not bothering their heads about galleries, literary prizes or other honourable mentions. Nonetheless they were just as sensitive as children. They already lacked the restraints which "every grown-up, well-educated individual" internalizes, obliging him to hearken attentively to every critical remark or thoughtfully examine every turd flung his way. On the contrary, they can now fling that turd right back at the person who threw it, with primordial directness. Hence they receive even the slightest cavil, every insulting word, as a vicious infraction of their sacred rights, a trespass on their final pleasure and sanctuary – the joy of creative freedom.

"That's why I advise you to stop throwing critical stones, or they can really make this place hot for you," Alla warned me in an almost friendly tone.

"Many thanks for explaining the local philosophy," I snorted by way of reply. "But if you don't mind I'll ignore your advice. If only because literary criticism is my version of their creative freedom, the same as all their little scribbles and doodles. And maybe I've wanted all my life to show up talentless artists and writers, in the same way they've longed to write and draw. Nor do I intend to limit my personal freedom for the sake of my or their comfort. In principle, I haven't got anything special to lose either. I've also reached that age when I'm not afraid of fighting for my happiness. I don't need to be a little ray of sunshine and please everybody all the time."

"It's your own business, I've warned you now. Whole-heartedly," Alla shrugged her bony shoulders, lifting them out of the water. Her décolletage really was wrinkled, just as I'd imagined. Liver spots were already spreading visibly over her skin like the oily yellow splashes on the kitchen wall behind the cooker of a slovenly housewife. Privately, I enjoyed the comparison; my own skin as it aged was taking on the tender, fragile rosy hue of dry rice-paper.

I realized I'd overstayed my welcome and stood to step out of the jacuzzi. While I dripped onto her rubber mat and wiped myself down with a thick towel, I suddenly had an absolutely ingenious idea.

"Alla, what if I make peace between you and the rest of our home? You'll be the literary superstar again! That wouldn't be difficult to do. These idiots will be carrying you around on their shoulders again and calling you the best writer in this poorhouse!"

Alla, for the sake of propriety, briefly opposed my notion, but I could tell by the blush spreading across her high cheekbones that she liked it. She really did want to once again be part of the geriatric gang and to shine amongst them like a prima-ballerina.

"Only don't take offence, OK?" I specified for the sake of caution, standing in the open door. "This is our secret, and no-one needs to know about it. Otherwise your situation will get even worse than it already is. Agreed?"

Alla nodded.

Resurrecting the general admiration for Alla really wasn't difficult at all. An insulting review of her talentless creations had already been pulsating in the belly of my laptop for quite some time. All I had to do was print it out and hang it up in highly visible places before breakfast.

As I strolled between the breakfast tables in my summer shift and narrow-brimmed straw hat I observed with satisfaction that my fellow diners had already tasted my verbal poison and worked up some spleen. I confess that I was expecting someone to hurl themselves on me in a hysterical fit right there, amidst the bowls of porridge and fruit salad. But everyone simply stared at me silently, moving their jaws, chomping their food thoroughly. No-one addressed a word in my direction. I was even mildly disappointed. Had I really managed to drive these pathetic predators off so quickly, with just the second crack of the whip? What a weak-willed bunch! They couldn't stand up to one little ringmaster! I left breakfast with the expression of a triumphant monarch, just like Elizabeth I. However, I'd rejoiced too soon; there was a letter waiting for me in my room. Someone had slipped it under the door, while I had been munching slices of banana in the dining room. The message was short, but impressively threatening:

Bitch!
You didn't understand the nice version, now for the nasty one. We warned you. Come today at 3 pm to the burned-out shop and defend yourself. If you don't turn up, either
a) you give up and admit defeat
b) or we'll come and find you later, but in that case you won't know the time or the place.
PS. We advise you to come at 3 pm prepared with excuses and sincere apologies. For your own good.

This little note really cheered me up. I even laughed out loud. And yet after my chuckle I felt an unpleasant sensation of real danger. Stealing glances behind me, I crept silently down the dark corridor. Light entered this cavern only from the windows in the end wall. And when they turned off the electric light in the daytime, my overexcited imagination made out a dark figure hiding in every doorway.

I cautiously knocked on Alla's door: no-answer. I slipped the letter into the pocket of my shift and, assuming a carefree expression, headed for the exit, keeping my shoulders rigid to thrust out my bosom, trying to assume the most nonchalant and dignified appearance. But inside my heart was juddering like a frenzied rabbit. I was more and more convinced that that letter's pathetic lines concealed a very brief message indeed: I was going to be beaten up! Again…

The cream of local society was reclining on sun-chairs on the lawn. My enemies had gathered in the shade of the poplars. Alla had settled herself in their midst, enjoying everyone's sympathy. I made big eyes at her, trying to lure her away for a tête-a-tête. I wanted to know the real reason why I was being summoned to the waste ground behind the burnt-out shop. Were they really planning to beat me up? But Alla had apparently already written me off as a person worthy of her attention, discarded me like used-up rocket fuel. She turned her face away and even demonstratively perched her sunglasses on her nose. What a bitch she was!

Nata was also among the throng of Alla's comforters, but off to one side with a pile of papers. She was reading and making notes in the margins. I sat down near her.

"What are you working on?" I asked.

Everyone nearby immediately hushed and fixed their rheumy, geriatric eyes on me and Nata, not even trying to pretend they weren't listening. Instead, they deliberately focussed their slimy, carp-like gazes in our direction, making it all too clear that I wasn't wanted.

Nata controlled herself well. She didn't turn a hair.

"Vagan has sent me a few different scripts to look at, so I can evaluate them from a professional perspective and give him my opinion."

I also peered at the papers.

"Oh, look at this, what a funny piece of dialogue!" I grabbed Nata's pen and scribbled in the margin, "We need to talk."

"Hmmm, you're right!" Nata drawled thoughtfully, taking back the page. "This script really deserves close reading."
"Thirty minutes, your room," she wrote under my scribble.

"Work away, I won't bother you," I stood up and headed back to the main building.

"Here, look what I got today," I blurted as soon as Nata came through my door. "Am I right in thinking that they're planning to beat me up?'

"Sure. Although they'll probably string you up instead if you don't publicly recant," Nata agreed, remarkably calmly.

"What kind of crazies are these people!" I was practically babbling from indignation. "What a barbaric method of resolving disagreements! This isn't the Stone Age, this is the twenty-first century! Differences must be resolved by dialogue and discussion."

"Don't even go there," Nata snickered. "Everyone here has seen life, they're experienced, they know the world. And they all know perfectly well that no dialogue exists which can fundamentally and instantaneously resolve a conflict. All these 'processes of discussion' and 'peace conferences' just give the enemy time to build up their muscles and buy more arms. And as soon as one of them is sure that he's ready for war, then he stands up from the conference table straightaway and starts pistol-whipping his neighbour's face. Leave these fairy tales about peaceful discussion to the kids. You've watched the news on TV, you know what happens after 'peace agreements'. Take Chechnya, Israel, Yugoslavia, even Libya – it's always the nastiest and bloodiest stage of the war, since the enemy gets a chance to build up all his reserves for the final attack. That's why it's better to attack straightway, before your opponents are completely mobilized. That way they won't manage to throw their whole force into the onslaught, and something will be spared for rebuilding peaceful life afterwards."

"That's the craziest thing I ever heard! Imagine, I came to spend my peaceful old age in the countryside and I find myself mixed up in this mess! I just can't believe it!"

I really was quite panicked about the battle to come. Nata poured me a few drops of sedative, urging me to breathe slowly and deeply. I felt a little better.

"My advice to you," said Nata, stroking my hair gently, "is to turn up and apologize. Tell them whatever you need to tell them: say, dear friends and neighbours, I had no idea how much you value what you write, how every letter in your short stories and novellas carries a sincere and deeply felt meaning that you've waited a long time to express. I now realize how petty I was to attack you so crudely. Please, keep drawing, writing, dancing, composing, and sculpting, with my blessing. I will write and dance along with you. Since creativity isn't a competition, where we have to measure ourselves against each other; creativity is an Eden for everybody, a corner of heaven for us all. It was made by the Divine Creator for everyone's pleasure, therefore it's infinite and open to everyone. Tell them that, and maybe even shed a tear or two; but not so pathetically that it looks like you're just scared. Rather weep a gentle, enlightened tear, as if you had just seen a holy flame rising from the Holy Sepulchre. You could even start hugging everyone in the group. Just throw yourself on them, plunge your wet nose into their necks, and hug hard. You've got the picture? It'll be great!"

"More lunacy!" I hopped angrily onto the sofa, tossing Nata's hand off my hair. "Indulge with these idiots in their pseudo-creative outpourings? Allow them to choke up the information highway with still more shit? And sacrifice my own pride? No way! I'd prefer them to break my legs, or at least convince me, prove to me, that they've got some talent, that they're chosen by God, kissed by heaven, genuinely entitled to single themselves out and become artists. I'm ready for an objective debate!"

"Sonya, you're all worked up! If only you could just talk this out, since the word is your favourite weapon. But they don't want to have a chat with you. If that were the case, the battle would stay on a verbal and intellectual level. But for your opponents the task is to suppress any resistance on that level. And that's why they have to attack you on a different plane where you can't, a priori, win."

"But it's so stupid, this isn't the way intelligent people solve problems!"

"Mrs Bulgakova, you're like a parrot! You harp on one and the same thing and you completely refuse to listen to me!

And yet you consider yourself someone gifted at dialogue? Well, you only dialogue with yourself and you only hear your own voice! Enough! I'm done! If you're not interested in my opinion, why the hell did you ask me here? Goodbye! Deal with your own problems."

Conclusively, but not furiously, Nata exited my room. She didn't slam the door, but closed it behind her with a firm, sure touch, like the polite but pointed way the turnstile doors close in the metro if you don't have a ticket.

I decided to face the fight. And I downed another swallow of sedative.

I stepped over the charred planks of the burnt-out shop in white sandals, almost unable to feel my own feet under me. I chose to be slightly late, in order to place my opponents at the disadvantage of wondering whether I would turn up.

What can I say? The encounter everyone had prepared so carefully happened in a rush. Everyone had gathered in the empty lot. Genuinely, ALL the pensioners who could walk, at least, all of those whose faces I knew, including Nata, Tatiana, and Alla. The last two, however, were noticeably uncomfortable and refused to meet my gaze. Nata, on the other hand, looked me right in the eye and sneered a little. That gave me courage.

They hadn't finished arranging their stage. I had imagined that the bullies would plant themselves in a semi-circle, with me placed at the centre, in a specially prepared "seat of shame" or maybe "execution block". But instead they clustered in random little groups, like the stuffing of a badly washed cushion, ignoring the theatrical effect.

"Well, are we going to get started?" I'd intended to shout, in a voice of command. But I only managed a whisper. I hadn't expected to sound so pitiful and helpless.

I wanted to sit down somewhere. I even looked around for a tree-stump or something. But there was nothing of the sort in sight.

I wondered who was leading this conspiracy against me, who would come forward to accuse me? Who was the billy goat leading the herd of rams? After all, everyone knows that rams aren't very good at organizing themselves or choosing a leader from their own flock. That's why shepherds, when they have to move a herd from one pasture to another, bring a donkey or a goat to lead the sheep. They calmly follow the stranger wherever he points his ears or his horns.

The ranks of my opponents rippled, instantly forming that semi-circle I'd been expecting. And in the foreground there remained... Nata! She still had the same provocative smile. I even think she winked. Two-faced bitch!

"Dear Sonya!" Nata sang out, sounding like a friendly but deaf milkmaid. "We invited you here to explain to you how cruelly and unfairly you've behaved to our babies. You see, our literary productions are our babies. We conceive them, give birth to them in agony, locking ourselves up in our lonely cells, and we love them no matter how they turn out. And we're even bold enough to show them to others, in spite of their imperfections. Just as a mother is prepared to defend a handicapped child, we cannot peacefully tolerate insults to our work. I think that, as a woman and a mother, you know that the more weak and vulnerable the infant, the more fiercely and desperately his mother will come to his defence. But a mother won't defend a strong, gifted child, because she'll assume that he can look after himself. We're not sufficiently deluded to imagine ourselves as great writers, or to think that our writings are capable of standing alone. But that's precisely why we can't allow anyone who comes along to poke our most vulnerable spots with a stick. We want you to cease your destructive actions. When you first came here, you and your son told us that your dream was to write a novel. So write it! Then you'll become one of us! Let go of your horror of other people's writing and of the writer living inside you. Let's all embrace, and from this moment on you'll be one of us, we'll be one family."

And Nata, theatrically throwing wide her arms, stepped towards me (the bitch was even wearing a loose tunic like the young Alla Pugachova to enhance the overall effect).

As Nata approached me, spreading her arms like fishing-nets, I shuddered like a goldfish tossed out of its bowl. It would have been awkward to run away from her. I simply didn't know what to do or how to escape from her repulsive embrace. I felt the same panic I'd experienced on that staff night out at my dear newspaper. On that occasion, our boss kept stealing olives off my plate and was making eyes at me as oily as those olives. Dispatching yet another shining dark-blue olive into his mouth, he screwed up his eyes like a woman, licked his bitten finger and shook it at me, warning, "Ah, Sonya! This could be very, very dangerous!" "Too right! Plenty of people have died from overeating," I'd thought, smiling sweetly by way of reply.

I'd got the boss's message pretty clearly and I tried to slip away from the party unnoticed. Not because I have any essential objections to sleeping with bosses, or because I advocate conjugal fidelity. I simply found the boss incredibly unattractive and I had no wish to sleep with him. I managed to vanish unnoticed from the party – unnoticed by everyone except him. He bounded after me as far as the elevators, spreading his arms wide, and started chasing me into a corner, pouting his greasy, blistered lips. He'd been telling the truth: that really was dangerous, and unpleasant. I considered my particular job too valuable to allow such liberties with my person. Fortunately, a quick dig into his groin and a none-too-well aimed spit in his eye served to interrupt his attentions. I didn't even get fired (I was quite good at my job), but I left of my own accord soon after. However, there was a lingering after-taste.

And right now, spreading her arms just the same way, and with the same despicable grin, Nata was heading for me. I already had a model for how to behave at such times. I even had a successful track record. So this time, my poke and my spit were considerably better aimed.

Nata, startled by my foot in her guts, gave a yell of surprise and backed off. And right away blows started to fall on me from all sides. I hardly had time to cover my bosom and face with my hands. Nina the lesbian was particularly ferocious. And, I thought she liked women! Perhaps I wasn't her type? I turned and ran, stumbling over the ancient, burned-out planks and barely warding off a fit of tears, even without the stimulus of punches and digs. I no longer heard running feet behind me. They weren't following me! I slowed down, turned around, and yelled, gulping down my spit and tears:

"Talentless bitches! Monsters! Idiots! Trash! Useless animals! Bed-wetters! Hopeless artists! You didn't even allow me to say a word in my own defence!"

"And we won't!" Nata roared back; her cheeks had turned an unhealthy crimson from excitement. "Actions speak louder than words!"

I noticed with evil satisfaction that, at least, the bitch had finally lost that sickening smile. I was about to yell another burning insult, when the crowd stirred and poured my way once more, like shit overflowing from a toilet. I turned around and ran for it again.

Within half an hour I was already speeding towards Moscow with my sunglasses on. No, I wasn't scared. I was thoroughly enraged, and I had to serve up an ice-cold revenge.

I couldn't return to my apartment – after all that's where the "really, really nice" tenants were installed. So I headed for my son's place; at least he had the basic male skill set to find himself a girlfriend with her own place willing to let him live in. As no-one was home, I sat by the door to wait. I didn't call Peter for fear of scaring him too early. I'd explain everything once he got here. Moreover, my watch showed it was already after seven, so the kids would soon be back. Dasha was the first to appear. She looked extremely worried at the sight of me. She didn't even take in my shabby appearance, she was so stunned by my arrival.

As soon as I stepped over the threshold, I realized why she was acting so tense: the apartment was a real pigsty. I decided to be a good mother-in-law today and not start telling her that a sloppy housewife was a bad partner for life. While Dasha rushed around the kitchen like a spring piglet, scooping left-over dinner off plates into the trash, flinging scummed-over cups into the dishwasher, wiping stains off the table with a grubby tea-cloth, I examined the state of the living room. Although I'm not particularly house-proud, my hands itched to start working; I began gathering the T-shirts, books, and papers scattered over the sofa into tidy little piles. When I'm fretting, some sort of simple work with my hands always calms me down, especially tidying up and washing dishes.

Sometime long ago I read about an experiment in which two mice were placed in identical stressful situations, exposed to blinding light, noise, and hunger. The one which survived the stress was the one with the filthiest fur. It simply started licking itself clean and managed to ignore all these exterior horrors; they didn't upset its little brain or its fragile psyche. In the same way I "lick my pelt", switch off from nerve-racking situations and thus gradually make myself feel better. But clearly today was not my day for calming down. When I had excavated the heaps of paper on Peter's sofa, I found a pile of old photos (from the days when they still printed them on photographic paper). Of course, even in my day every kid had a digital camera, but there were still places where you could only get printed photographs. I gazed at a picture of my younger self in a wedding-dress (for some reason, the registry office hadn't given us a disc with the pictures, but two packets of snaps printed on gloss paper). I blinked a damp eye at the sight of our happy family, strolling through a Spanish amusement park. I laughed at Peter's first passport photo. I riffled happily through my girlhood photos, taken before I met Sasha and before the age of digital photography. How amazingly pretty I'd been! Especially in that pink swimsuit on an Egyptian beach. I'd also looked very seductive in simple, but remarkably flattering dresses from Zara during a press tour of wine distilleries in France. And here was a piece of history: me in a very chic, rented, low-cut evening dress interviewing the vice-minister for natural resources at the "Energy" award ceremony. I was quite a beauty! It wasn't surprising that Sasha had followed me around all that evening, practically drooling on the floor, and constantly photographing me. And then he'd broken my phone by trying to insert the chip with the pictures. ("The files are too big, I can't send them by e-mail!") Naturally, I'd just teased this successful manager of a huge oil company a little bit, just pro forma, really. So that he didn't think too much of himself. He wasn't top class, of course, but he'd been an entirely acceptable candidate for the role of fiancé. Sasha thoroughly fulfilled the matrimonial hopes placed in him, and we'd exchanged rings within six months.

I smiled at my memories, smiling at myself and Sasha. There was no denying he'd been a nice person, it was a shame we hadn't managed to spend our old age together, as we'd always planned. We'd wanted to have a good time and travel in our old age. We said we'd take up ballroom dancing. And for our golden anniversary we'd leap from a parachute and get tattoo'd with each other's names. For after fifty years together it would be stupid to have any doubts about whether we'd stay together, and whether we'd need to get the tattoos removed. We'd also wanted to take up music. I was to learn to play the piano, he'd take up the flute (with his passion for tobacco, a wind instrument would have been very good for his lungs; he'd have benefited from the obligatory additional ventilation). And in the evenings we'd play duets, learning some not-too-complicated songs. We'd have argued, nagged, disagreed, gotten mad. I'd have banged on my keyboard, he'd have blown his flute. But, sadly, none of this was to be. Sasha didn't live long enough...

My gaze paused unexpectedly on an unfamiliar photo from an amusement park: four people sitting in a roller-coaster seat. A man, a woman, a boy and a girl. I wondered if I was losing my mind! Peter, who would have been about 14, seemed to be calling out to me through the photograph, making a funny face. Sasha had stretched his lips into an exaggerated kiss; he was in the back seat, holding tightly by the hand... that very same Tatiana the mouse, whose work I'd criticized, causing all my misfortunes in the old people's home. She was hanging on to the safety bar in a panic; her little face looked like a wax mask. In the picture she looked considerably younger than now, but there could be no mistake. She had the same trapped-looking expression, the same hairstyle, even the same sapphire earrings that she wore now! The seven-year-old girl sitting next to Peter was radiating happy fright. This had to be Tatiana's daughter Katya. They were the perfect image of a family on an outing. Bloody hell! This meant Peter had known Tatiana for donkey's years, and Katya too, and even my husband had known them well. Why, then, had I never heard so much as a whisper about my husband's friends: the retired librarian and her successful psychotherapist husband? I snorted to myself and sank into a seat. Immediately I jumped back up and slipped the snapshot into my bag.

I continued waiting for my son, all het up with impatience. As soon as he appeared in the door, I rushed to him:

"Peter! I've got some questions for you!"

"Mama, what are you doing here? Did something happen?" He blinked his tired, reddened eyes at me.

"Yes, something has happened. I ran away from the poorhouse. Because I got into a disagreement with this lady here," and I shoved the picture from the amusement park under his nose. "And now, I think, you might want to explain a few things to me."

"I just knew it wasn't a good idea to put you in the same home as Auntie Tatiana," my son flopped down, making the sofa's fragile metal skeleton creak. "It wasn't very smart of Katya to decide that it would be convenient for us to visit and keep an eye on both of you, if you lived close together; we could visit by turns."

"Right. That was, let's be frank, a pretty awful idea," I blurted, still not fully understanding the role played by Auntie Tatiana and Katya in my family's life.

As an investigative journalist and interviewer of no small experience, I professionally eviscerated Peter's memories, listening with masochistic fascination to a story I should have guessed a long, long time ago.

This story had begun more than 22 years ago. I had then been a brilliant 38-year-old, blessed by the goddesses Hera and Athena, with a stable, higher-than-average income, a good credit history, a smart seven-year-old son. I was recognized as a professional journalist and an expert on Turkish resorts, all of which proved my ability to balance my career and my private life. Overall, there was little to single me out from most of my peers. Perhaps I was unusual in my age group for still being in my first marriage. I'd become a wife so long ago, that it was difficult for me to remember that I'd ever lived alone. Our marriage had already lasted, terrible to say, for 17 years. And its length, unique among our generation, was just then its only virtue.

It's hard for me to say how it all began, but I remember clearly that when Peter started school, Sasha and I were already exchanging routine smiles in the morning and routine pecks on the cheek in the evenings. We'd lost our former passion and desire for each other. We'd even established lifestyles. He rose very early, around six in the morning, and spent the time until work doing his own thing. He jogged in the park, read books, watched the news, drank coffee over a newspaper, took our son to school. I only woke up after I heard the click of the lock in the outer door: that meant my husband had left for work. In fact, that click replaced my alarm-clock. I'd leap up gaily and begin to live my own, husband-free life. I cleaned my teeth, had breakfast, wrote something on the computer, rang news-makers. Or, if I had an editorial meeting, I'd get dressed up and go to the editor's office. Then I'd collect my son from school, do his homework with him, chat with girlfriends over a cup of coffee and on the telephone. In the evening my husband came home, and then we had something to fill up the lack of words between us: I'd fill him in on the meeting and my conversations with the people I was profiling; he'd nod and swiftly head off to bed. After all, he got up early: he was a lark (although when we married, we'd both considered ourselves owls and could sit up late in the kitchen of our rented flat talking over everything under the sun). Now everything was different. Sasha went to bed early, while I, after putting our son to bed, spent a long time messing on the Internet, reading LiveJournal, watching films, drinking wine, chatting on Instant Messenger. I felt a sensation of absolute comfort and at the same time of disquieting spiritual vacuum. I went to bed in the wee small hours, around three a.m., about three hours before Sasha woke up.

I suspect that we deliberately slipped into this way of life to avoid intersecting with each other in space and time. There were times when even I couldn't understand why we were still living together, when emotionally we were so distant. I wondered if I was living with Sasha because I simply didn't have any other offers. And I couldn't survive completely alone. It was essential for me, as I crawled under the duvet, to slither my cold heels against someone's warm, solid calf. And I started looking for other warm-blooded bodies to take Sasha's place in my bed. Quite soon, an entirely personable candidate for his position appeared.

Like everything else in my life, my lover appeared deliberately and according to plan. No, love didn't fall on me like a murderer striking from hiding. I wasn't entranced by someone's almond-shaped eyes, nor was I stalked by a mysterious, irresistible stranger. I couldn't excuse myself by claiming spontaneous abandon. I acted entirely consciously. Even while I was compiling a list of questions for interviewing a young director, Andrey Suvorov, who had staged a controversial, prize-winning play *Five Women, Four Walls*, which suggested that all modern women are criminals at heart, if one peels the surface layer of paint from their faces, I was already planning how to direct our conversation so that it culminated in something naughty, provocative and arousing. I was doubly excited by the prospect of sleeping with a celebrity and by the opportunity to direct a director: to conquer him on his professional territory. Clearly, my ambition outclassed my desire. Professional challenges have always tempted me more than sexual ones.

And everything happened just as I'd planned. Andrey, after all, was six years my junior, lacking the necessary life experience to play my game on an equal level. I skilfully led comrade Suvorov to the point where he felt compelled to prove to me that I was also a mask-wearing, self-betraying sinner, like the heroines of his play, and the majority of modern women. And when he failed to reveal any sins in my background, only a talent for committing them, he immediately tried to make up for my deficiency. I'm crudely re-telling our verbal sparring, which lasted for hours, and our sophisticated ritual dance. We fenced merrily, teasingly and lightly; the interview turned out highly successful and very lively. If my husband had taken an interest in my doings, this should have put him on his guard. A week later, I called on Andrey after his play to give him some hard copies of my piece.

I found him in his office, and perched on a chair to his left. We started flicking through the magazine by the dim light of his table lamp. I leaned in close, pointing out the relevant paragraphs and pretended to squint short-sightedly, in order to bend nearer still to his fingers. They smelled of tobacco – he affected a pipe. It all happened just as I'd pictured it. He finished reading the interview, studied the photos, then leaned backwards in his chair. I copied his movement and flung my right hand out towards him, palm upturned.

"Aren't I a good girl?" I asked challengingly, shooting him a provocative, sideways glance.

He had no choice but to give me a high five.

"Full marks!" he said, bursting into laughter.

I grabbed onto his hand and flung it upwards with a light smack from my fingers. In response, he high-fived me again. We struggled like children; he crushed my fingers in his dry, long-fingered hand, trying to bend it backwards. I resisted, with all my strength.

"That's not fair!" I protested, tossing my hair back from my face. "Pushing downwards is easier than holding a position! Plus you're a man and biology makes you stronger. Let's try the other way round!"

Now he offered his left hand palm up and I threw my entire 55-kilo weight onto it; I even began by leaning both hands on his, half-standing. But he held firm, and his hand stayed steady even under my entire weight. The strain on both sides was so great that neither of us had the slightest spare energy, even for speaking. We pushed against each other's palms, breathing heavily. Finally, my strength left me; I fell back exhausted and crumpled on my chair.

"Oooof! I give up," I managed to wheeze. My breath was panting brokenly. He collapsed into his chair in just the same way, chest heaving. I turned my face towards him. Our eyes met. He reached over abruptly and kissed me somewhere no-one had kissed me for a very long time, just under my ear.

I don't know how I managed to drive. That autumn in Moscow was very foggy, warm and damp. I had difficulty seeing the road in the murk. I swore to myself for the hundredth time that I would take those special drops that protect against fog-blindness, and yet I knew I wouldn't keep my promise. I liked the city in this intoxicating gloomy steam from the dozens of underground streams hidden under its asphalt layers.

Within two hours we had sunk back on the pillows of a hotel bed, just as earlier we'd collapsed back into our armchairs after our arm-wrestling match. We were breathing just as heavily. It had happened – I'd cheated on my husband for the first time.

"You know, you're right. Every woman in the world is a criminal, if you look hard enough," I uttered my first sentence since we'd burst like a whirlwind into that hotel on the outskirts of Moscow.

"Is that so?" he stirred. "And what's your secret crime?"

"A crime against myself. I live with a man I haven't looked in the eye for years." And, challengingly, I stared Andrey straight in his wide-open eyes. He wasn't embarrassed and held my gaze. That pleased me.

I never thought it would go so far. I'd planned, at the very most, to take a lover and see what happened next. I was curious to see how I'd change once I had a little emotional ventilation. The change turned out to be more far-reaching than I'd expected. I lost my head. Within a month's time I could think of nothing but him, when I could think at all. Most of the time I just smiled foolishly, failing to grasp the simplest questions. I gave my husband a fork with his soup and placed so many exclamation marks in my newspaper proofs that the typesetters gave me a warning. I was obsessed.

We walked the streets, holding hands, like students. I lacked even the wariness to look at the faces of passers-by, in case we met someone I knew. Yet I knew that Moscow was just a big village and how great the chances were of meeting some family friend, especially when strolling along the Boulevard Ring. I was so carried away by emotion that my soul had no room for alarm. We went to the cinema to see all the films in the program, sitting in the back row. As soon as the opening credits finished, he leaned his face over mine, and I sank my lips into the skin between his beard and ear. Quite probably we prevented others from watching the film, but no-one could touch us.

During that time I think I completely stopped seeing my husband. When I came home from my '"night work" and "evening interviews" he was already asleep. I suddenly realized that Peter was already old enough to come home from school by himself and do his homework on his own. Moreover, there was no reason why he couldn't consult his grandmother by telephone; under her alert guidance, the boy even learned to make soup for the whole family.

With growing urgency, I longed to break off at once with everything old, to crawl out from under my previous life, like a snake shedding its worn-out skin, and to throw myself into a new, beautiful life filled with joy. Something was pushing me to tell my husband that he'd lost his chance with me, that is, this amazing, bewitching, sexy, talented, cheerful woman, and that I was leaving him for another man. I wasn't even worried that this 'other man' had so far avoided making any firm proposals, hadn't spelled out the state of his heart or offered his hand. My relationship with Andy (I'd already given him a private nickname) seemed so firmly woven that I had no more doubt that all I had to do was hint, and an engagement ring from Tiffany's and a honeymoon in the Maldives with this famous director would be mine for the asking.

Every day my husband's face greyed and faded on my emotional map. And my marriage to Sasha increasingly came to seem like a watershed and a preparatory stage on the path to genuine happiness and the blessings of true harmony.

My husband, I think, also sensed that some kind of tectonic shift was in progress. But he gave nothing away and never tried to catch me out by digging in my email or text messages. I also hesitated to break a connection that had lasted for seventeen years. Both of us seemed to dread destroying a thing that had taken so much time and care to construct.

Our marriage had reached the stage where we were afraid even to have a drink together, because we each understood that if we softened our minds with alcohol, the barriers of propriety would fall, and we'd be swept away. We'd tell each other everything and get divorced the next day. So we became a pair of dedicated teetotallers. Although in the first years of our life together we'd boldly gotten drunk with gangs of friends, we'd also been able to drink peacefully together in our kitchen, while discussing the fate of humanity, building plans for the future, dancing, laughing, quarrelling, and then making passionate love.

In fact, if we'd always been as sober as we had now become, our son would never have been born. I would probably never have decided to ruin my life by becoming a mother. Eight years ago Peter had been conceived in some New Year's drunken passion and when in February I'd discovered, to my horror, that I was pregnant, it was too late to take the morning-after pill. Abortion struck me as a pretty nasty business, and I decided that having the child would be the lesser of two evils, if I had to choose between being scraped inside-out and buying Babygros. Clenching my teeth, I started to prepare for the feminine ordeal of labour.

While I was dreaming up plausible scenarios for breaking with Sasha, he wasn't idle either. To my surprise, he suddenly became an unbelievably affectionate partner. For absolutely no reason, five times a day, he started assuring me that I was unique, that there would never be anyone like me, that I was a wonderful person, his beloved. That I was a beauty, a genius, talented, the purpose and the joy of his life, the best mother ever, an amazing woman, an inspired cook, a snappy dresser and simply the best in every way.

This bewildering transformation in my husband intrigued me to no small degree. It intrigued me so much that I once even set my alarm for 6 a.m. to wake up at the same time as him. So we woke up, and we even unexpectedly took a shower together and kissed under the hot streams of water. And then I somehow wound up joining him on his morning run. At the beginning, we didn't talk. He ran with his earphones and music player, and I had my own music and my own rhythm.

Then we realized we were listening to the same radio station. We started laughing, and suddenly we were talking.

We discovered that while we hadn't been speaking, lots of important and interesting things had happened to both of us. I learned that he'd read lots of interesting books while we were separated, and he knew how to retell their contents entertainingly. He'd also read some books on psychology, and now he could entertain me with psychological tests and tell me the results immediately. I was suddenly enjoying being with him again. However, I hadn't been idle either, and I was able to tell him about the latest developments in contemporary art. We chatted so much on that run around the park, that it seemed astonishingly sad when the timer insisted we stop running and go home, so that Sasha could put on his business suit and head for the office.

Even though everything at home was going so well, I panicked. I couldn't break it off with Andy. Everything good in my life now was mysteriously bound up with him. I was afraid that if he disappeared, the bright, sparkling side of my life would come to an end. I still wanted to be with him; he made me feel truly alive, really me. And once again, with fear and trembling, I contemplated divorce. Only one thing stopped me: I didn't want to hurt Sasha. He showed such doglike devotion; he'd gazed at me so ecstatically when I ran over to him from the fitting room in a new dress; he so carefully and painstakingly chose celery, which no-one in our family ate besides me; he opened the door to me so joyfully when I came back in the evening, that I was convinced he loved me. To hell with it all, he loved me! And that meant he'd suffer if I left him. So I couldn't leave him; it would be a betrayal.

In short, we never divorced.

My affair with Andrey was stillborn. It needed its own space in my life, but I wouldn't make space for it. It couldn't develop; there was nowhere for it to grow. And what doesn't grow, dies. Within about six months this painful, unhealthy affair, pointless for everyone but us, came to an end.

When he told me it was over, he was sitting in that same chair where we'd wrestled so gaily at our first romantic encounter. He was leaving to undertake a project in Europe: he'd been invited to Prague. Nor was he leaving alone; he was getting married. What's more, they were having a child. And I must understand, because, obviously, he and I could never have children. And he wanted them.

I replied that I completely understood, that I was happy for him, gaining a wife and a child. It was wonderful. But that I also wanted to be with him, he didn't have to make me a proposal.

"I'm afraid the woman I have proposed to wouldn't be too pleased with that," he answered seriously, without a hint of playfulness or pretence. He spoke so gravely, that I realized he'd weighed his words in advance. He'd decided earlier exactly what to say, knowing that I would refuse to let go.

I got it: everything was really over. Everything!

We said goodbye, shaking hands. Like two business associates.

I'd been set free and I was to set him free too. A stillborn foetus cannot be allowed to poison living tissue. The time had come for a purgative miscarriage.

At first I sat around like a deep-frozen vegetable. Then I started feeling awful as if I really had suffered a late-term miscarriage. For a week I couldn't eat, but I still threw up: vile stomach juices, like rancid oil. Everything disgusted me, whether inside or outside. Then I stopped vomiting, but the nasty taste remained in my mouth.

While I was on sick leave, the magazine where I worked shut down unexpectedly and irrevocably. I felt nothing but pleasure: now I didn't need to force myself to get up and go to work. I could peacefully give in to despair. And I plunged into it. For weeks I sat at home by the computer, aimlessly searching the Internet. I'd weep for no reason, and carry on reading. The Internet bewitched me with its mindless infinity: on each web-page, twenty hyperlinks tempted me in various directions, and each of them led on to another hundred. I could click on any of them. So I used to click and click, changing the images in front of my eyes, but inside me nothing ever changed. I thought up a game for myself: I'd pick some random word on Yandex and follow up the first hyperlink on the page. When the new window opened, I'd click on the third link from the top. In the next window, on the seventh, then, on the fifth. And so on, endlessly. The goal was to click on a link that would bring me back to the first page where I'd begun, to close the circle. And then... then what would happen? Nothing. Then I found a new word on Yandex and began the whole thing over again. I could sit like this for hours, until my husband came into the room. He silently shut the hundreds of Explorer windows on the computer, turned off the light and carried me to bed. I would turn away, sink my nose into my pillow and start weeping again.

Then one day I realized that I hadn't had my period for two months. My worst fears were confirmed. I wasn't pregnant. The menopause had begun. This was old age. And beyond that, Death swung her inevitable scythe.

This finished me off. If, before, I'd been suffering from a fairly calm depression, now I succumbed to genuine hysterics. I lay in bed and sobbed out loud, tossing back my head and hugging my knees: "I don't want to DIEEEEEE! I don't want to DIEEEEEE!"

My miserable wails scared even me: that was how our alcoholic neighbour had howled in the summer cottage next door to ours when I was a child, when her husband secretly finished off a bottle which she had been planning to help drink. But I couldn't stop myself and carried on howling. At this point Sasha finally understood that I wasn't suffering from some minor complaint, but from a real psychological dysfunction. And he handed me over to the doctors.

The doctors helped. On my fortieth birthday which, defying tradition, I decided to celebrate quietly at home with family, I was already smiling bovinely at everyone. Behind my empty eyes, my brains, washed clean with special medicines, squeaked with sterility. I grinned and stroked my perfectly bald head. I'd had it shaved of my own free will.

"I haven't got the energy to wash these tangles every other day," I'd shrugged casually in response to my husband's stifled cry, when he discovered my new look. He stopped taking photographs of me. He suddenly fell out of love with his camera. It made no difference to me.

Everything gradually returned to normal. My hair grew out into a stylish hedgehog. A new magazine started up and, not without pressure from my husband, I was taken on as editor of the culture section. My husband's firm gave a lot of advertising to this glossy newsheet and they couldn't refuse him in such a small matter. Moreover, I was really coping quite well. I had genuinely come back to life. Even my periods returned. True, they lacked their former regularity and now followed some crazy timetable of their own, but all the same...

In a word, I didn't die. I survived, and I stayed married. In spite of everything.

And now I found out that at the very time I was dealing so painfully with my own issues, to spare him pain, while I was poisoning myself from within, Sasha was living it up. And how!

It turned out that our marriage's long survival was not my achievement alone. I hadn't saved it by sacrificing myself. Our fortress, apparently, had stayed standing only because that worthless Tatiana had not wished to destroy it! If my late husband had been alive right now, I would certainly have killed him myself.

As you've undoubtedly guessed, Sasha and Tatiana had had an affair. I'd figured it out too the instant I saw that cursed photograph. But the notion that Katya might be Sasha's daughter – that was just too much for me.

did good works and drilled their maids. Dr Rozhdestvensky's career went from strength to strength. He was summoned to solve the personal problems of the high and mighty; big companies hired him to boost staff morale. And his quiet, submissive wife listened to every word he said and never made any difficulties. But as she entered her thirties, Tatiana became more restless around her husband and his friends. She suddenly stopped staying at home, joined a dozen different clubs, and she even got her husband to let her assist with corporate team-building sessions.

At one of these sessions, she met the future father of her daughter, who by coincidence turned out to be my husband, Alexander Bulgakov, the manager of a big oil company. It all fell into place perfectly. Of course, Tatiana would never have decided to flirt with one of her husband's clients, especially not right under his nose. But it so happened, to everyone's surprise, that Tatiana and Sasha had known each other in the past; yonks ago, as kids, they'd been sent on holiday to the same summer camp and had even kissed after drinking a horrible bottle of cheap Madeira, before being horribly and multiply ill. So Zhenya was perfectly understanding when Tatiana didn't get in the car beside him to drive home after the staff training, but went off for a cup of coffee with her old friend instead. He wasn't surprised when she turned up at home in the small hours with unusually swollen lips – if people haven't seen each other for years, they'll have lots to talk over. You can't describe your whole life in two hours.

In other words, he calmly allowed his wife to get pregnant by my husband. When Tatiana did a pregnancy test and, like any honest woman, started packing her bags, babbling that she would take only the things she'd brought into the house, begging for understanding and forgiveness, and saying she understood the gravity of her sin, Zhenya urged her to stay. He promised he'd love her child like his own, all the more because he couldn't have children. He was delighted they were about to have a child, even in this strange way, a child they could raise together. And if she left him, he'd never find another woman to whom he could open up his true self. He'd remain alone, suffering miserably. Tatiana sobbed at the thought of his desolate future, but she still left.

She lived for seven months in a rented apartment paid for by my husband. And all this time Tatiana must have felt like the most fought-over pregnant woman in the world, because Sasha and Zhenya were competing for her child as if she were about to give birth to a Jesus or an Einstein, at the very least.

I don't know and, evidently, I never will know whether Sasha wanted to divorce me and live with Tatiana and her unborn child, or whether he was simply intending to spread himself between both his families. It was all happening just as I was struggling to decide whether to end our threadbare marriage, leap into the unknown and move in with Andrey. But there's no changing the fact that Sasha and I were simultaneously slipping away into parallel lives, greedily tasting outside air, and carefully concealing these parallel existences from each other. Incidentally, Sasha was extraordinarily crude and clumsy at this and only a woman as infatuated as I was could have failed to notice his ridiculous play-acting. At the time I was filled with other sensations, I was so childishly convinced of my own invincibility, that I took all his compliments like "You're the best" and "You're the only one I love" and that unexpected surge of renewed interest in me for the real thing. Now, however, it's obvious that was a masquerade of tail-wagging, the kind that a cat will do to distract its owners after it's made a mess. Yes, I was pretty much a gibbering idiot in terms of emotional intelligence.

And it all ended the way it had to: Zhenya took Tatiana home from the birth clinic, because he was the one she chose for the honour. He felt privileged and flattered beyond words. At 34, she became the mother of a charming little girl, whom they called Katya. For convenience, the child was registered as Rozhdestvensky's – after all, Zhenya and Tatiana had stayed married the whole time.

"The fact is that she got on very well with Papa and she loved him a lot," Peter told me with naïve but cruel sincerity. "But she still couldn't leave her husband for him, because she felt very sorry for you and she didn't want to cause you any pain. She believes very strongly in the law of cosmic equilibrium; she feels it's impossible to build happiness on the unhappiness of others. She thinks that if you do someone a bad turn, fate will inevitably punish you for it. And you know why? This is really a terrible secret, but I know what it is. Auntie Tatiana told me that her husband Uncle Zhenya had once cruelly dumped a woman after getting her pregnant. And fate punished him for that by taking away his ability to have kids. So don't think anything bad about Auntie Tatiana and Katya. They have a very positive attitude towards you."

Clearly I'd raised a perfect cretin with an infantile mind. Only a retarded child could tell me a tale like this, as if it was nothing out of the ordinary.

What other kind of son could you expect from my husband? Not only did he father a child out of wedlock, he had the wit to let his legitimate son meet his illegitimate daughter. "A brother and sister should know each other. When you grow up, you'll understand that it's important to have blood relatives, an extended family who will always help you out," Sasha had told him. Meanwhile he found it possible to show Tatiana my son, but I never met her daughter. He'd even managed to get Peter to stay quiet and keep his father's secret for all these years. Clearly, the biggest fool in this story was me. Now I was no longer surprised by the enigmatic glances Tatiana had sent my way in the old folk's home: I, too, stare with unhealthy interest at strange people and retards. But I'm terrified if they notice my interest and start staring back at me. My hackles go right up. Clearly, I had the same effect on Tatiana.

I'd never felt so startlingly worthless. Even back when I'd shaved all my hair off, I'd felt my life was more valued and meaningful than I did now, now that I knew that for at least

a third of my life I'd been deceived, that my husband, my
son, my family had lived a double life. They'd kept secrets
from me. At a time when I was shaking with pain, cutting
out everything alive inside me, without anaesthetic, for
the sake of something I didn't understand, some brainless
brunette was living in an apartment rented by my husband
and chuckling about me, meanwhile picturing herself as some
kind of Mother Teresa, forcing these dim-witted menfolk to
admire the generosity of her soul. What a bitch! Rage surged
through me; I couldn't even find the light switch, making me
even more furious. I was sure that somewhere here on the
wall there had to be the switch for the bathroom light. I had a
great longing to rip something up and piss on it.

It was after two in the morning and my hosts Peter and Dasha,
who had thrown me out of my own apartment by settling
those idiotic tenants in it, had gone to dreamland long ago.
It was just me who couldn't close an eye. I groped along the
corridor wall, thumping it wildly, in the hope of accidentally
finding the light-switch.

"Mama, what are you doing up? Why aren't you asleep?"
I heard Peter's voice and was promptly blinded by electric
light.

"Why aren't I asleep?" I asked in a dangerously gentle
voice, automatically slitting my eyes against the light.
"Because your old mama, my dear boy, wanted to take a
piss. But I'm not in my own apartment; I'm in a completely
unfamiliar one and I can't find the light switch. And the
reason I'm in your apartment is that you made me move out
of mine to live next door to a woman who has been looking on
and laughing up her sleeve at me all the time. You provided
Auntie Tatiana with a domestic pet she could watch without
stirring from her desk. I was her all-in-one performing seal
and poodle! Arf-arf!" I folded my hands under my breasts
and executed a little hop. "A big thank-you for placing
me in my old age in such an amusing position!" I tried to

make a formal low bow, but I miscalculated and banged my forehead painfully on the floor. My furious clowning ended remarkably clumsily: besides falling over, I yelled with pain and wet myself. After all, I'd been looking for that damned light switch for too long.

"Oh no, Mama, you're feeling ill again!" my son gasped. Apparently he still remembered my psychiatrically certifiable behaviour from twenty years before, because his immediate impulse was to call a doctor. But I swiftly grasped my danger and, gathering the remains of my strength, I stood up and assumed the calmest expression I could. Naturally, within the limits of my capabilities at that precise moment.

"Give me a cigarette!" I demanded.

"I don't have any," said Peter, standing there in his ridiculous boxer shorts that made his legs look like an undercooked chicken's.

"I said, give me a cigarette!" I roared. "Stop lying to me. Do you think I don't know you smoke? I've known for the last ten years! Doesn't it mean anything to you that you and your papa have lied to me all my life?"

Peter opened his bag and took out a pack of cigarettes and a lighter. I lit up, grabbed a dressing-gown off the hook in the bathroom and made my way to the kitchen. Peter shuffled after me.

"Why did you call a psychiatrist?" I asked him.

"You're feeling ill, you need help," he answered feebly, staring at the floor.

"I'm feeling ill, but I don't need psychiatric help. YOU need it to get me pronounced mentally unfit and incapable, so you have a legal right to dispose of my apartment and you waste no more time persuading me to do what you want. You'll lock me up in Kashchenko and will happily fuck your Dasha while a bunch of quacks stick needles in me. Thanks a lot, son! This is exactly what I deserve for suffering on that hard iron trolley, bringing you into the world. Go ahead! Bring it on! Maybe you'll cut my throat right now, so that I'm not in your way? Then you can peacefully tidy up my legacy. Although there's only enough to cover the funeral expenses."

I jerked open a drawer in the kitchen table, pulled out a knife and threw it over to Peter. He took fright and flinched backwards. I smoked, watching him. He stared at me, trembling. Then he picked up the telephone and cancelled the emergency call.

I stubbed out my cigarette. "OK, thanks for that. Thanks for your hospitality, I'm going elsewhere," I said, looking up from under my lashes at my son. "Well, don't think too badly of me." I went into the corridor, put on my shoes, grabbed my bag and started unlatching the front door.

"Mama, where are you going? You can't go anywhere in such a state!" Peter rushed to the door and blocked my way.

"I don't want to wait for the next time you take it into your head to get rid of me. I'm going to find somewhere safer."

"Mama, now take a look at yourself: you're wet, you're soaked, you're in a dressing gown, you've got a crazy look in your eye. Sleep a little, wait until morning, and then we'll think of something." Peter was shivering from cold and, more than likely, a little bit from nerves as well.

"No, my dear, I don't want to be taken away tomorrow morning in white handcuffs in a white van," I gave him a solid shove, leapt past him into the corridor and pressed the button for the elevator.

Peter ran after me, I made a dash for the stairs. He stood in the middle of the stairway and spread his arms, trying to restrain me. I ran right into him, pushed him, and he fell like a stone. There was a snapping sound. Peter groaned, and his arm was unnaturally bent between the wrist and the elbow – almost as if he'd grown a new elbow. He looked rather like a two-legged cricket.

I stood on the landing and stared with horror as, below me, he touched his broken hand with his whole one and at the same time used it to wipe big tears, like drops of September rain, off his face. Dear God, how sorry for him I felt! Almost as much as I did for myself. I crept down to him, sat beside him on the cold cement and wept together with him. I kissed his hands, his eyes, his temple, his knees, his back. I asked his forgiveness and hugged him so hard I thought his ribs might break. I was so upset and ashamed.

This lasted a long time, until Dasha and the paramedics appeared out of nowhere. Dasha tried not to look at me. She even made a special effort to look past me. But I could still feel the rays of contempt and hatred emanating from her eyes, destined for me. They ricocheted off the white ceiling, the floor, and the drearily painted walls, and rebounded on me. I wasn't offended. I understood: she was jealous. And, as a mother, this pleased me; it reassured me about my son's fate. It meant he had picked a girl who really cared about him. I even felt better, as a woman; if another woman felt jealous of me that meant I wasn't quite dead.

Dasha and Peter came back from the emergency clinic in the early morning. He had his right arm in plaster and she had dark circles of sleeplessness under her eyes. We didn't speak; we just stared at one another.

They went to bed straight away. I had breakfast, quietly gathered my things and just as quietly closed the door behind me. I couldn't stay there any longer. The fact that my son hadn't sent me to a lunatic asylum the night before didn't mean he wouldn't do it the next day. Moreover, they only had room for two in their lives: Mama Sonya was one too many. They hadn't planned to make room for me. I couldn't return to my own apartment; going back to the residence would be still worse. I had turned into a homeless tramp with my own apartment and a paid-up place in a poorhouse.

I rode along the Circular Highway round Moscow, feeling I'd reached a dead end. I had almost no money left. On my third circuit of the highway, I wondered whether to use the last of my money to buy a tent, go somewhere remote and camp by the side of a very calm and peaceful river, living on mushrooms and berries. I'd light a campfire in the evenings and gaze at the stars. And nowhere around would there be anyone who could hurt me, disturb my peace of mind or recall painful memories.

Fuelled by this fantasy, I went into a shop called "Your Home", and spent the last of my money on a cheap tent, cooking forks and a sleeping bag. With zero on my credit card and enough cash left to refuel my car a couple of times, I roared off down the most southerly motorway out of Moscow (I knew that a tent is a fairly flimsy habitation and therefore I set my sights on the south). I sped along the wide Simferopol freeway and imagined where I would strike my hermit's camp.

Evening drew in, the June heat died down and a chilly lethargy pervaded the air. The wind rushed through the open window, and on the car radio the ancient Alice Cooper was singing. My mood improved.

My son was probably not completely misguided in trying to commit me to a psychiatric clinic, since my thoughts had quite quickly switched from total despair and self-humiliation to inappropriately cerulean heights. I already saw myself living in a rural hermitage: a female version of Sergius of Radonezh. I imagined myself nursing and comforting the locals by my touch and through the power of my grief; that I would scare off wolves with one glance; and nourish myself on the scent of roses. In short, I was off my head.

After driving about fifty kilometres south of Moscow, I turned onto a side road and slowed down. I crawled along beside an overgrown clover meadow, studying the sparse grove on the other side of the road, and finally came to a halt at the edge of a pine wood. A wide field of bristling, stunted rye drove a wedge into it like a military formation. A country road dived into the edge of the wood. It circled the perimeter of the field, as if restraining it within borders that had once been agreed and preventing the rye from stepping onto the territory of the trees.

Not without a certain trepidation, I rolled down off the asphalt road on dusty, but well-sprung wheels. I understand why I'd always wanted to own a serious four-wheel-drive vehicle. Evidently, I'd always had in my subconscious the possibility of a flight into the wilds. As I'd never got myself a jeep, I now crept along carefully in my little sedan over the dangerous, untreated road. I drove another 200 metres and stopped. I got out of the car and discovered, under every tree, either an improvised toilet, or an equally casual garbage dump, or the blackened remnants of a campfire. Certainly not suitable surroundings for the hermitage of the future Saint Sofia. Clamping down on my internal fear and horror, I went on. Eventually, I found myself on a fairly even clearing about 700 metres from the asphalt road and 50 from the track road. Looking from the roadside, the point of my location appeared almost at the top left corner of the rye field. At the very least, in the thickening twilight, it looked clean enough, and no used plastic bags or rattling crisp or chip packets blew out of the darkness towards me. I walked around the clearing and discovered that its southern edge bordered on a small boggy patch with some sad crooked birches sticking out. I have always noticed that birches seem to choose the worst and least promising soil. It's very rare for pines or oaks to spring from a foul-smelling bog. I found this an interesting train of thought, highly symptomatic, since Russia traditionally considers herself to be the land of birch trees.

For all that I decided that the clearing was entirely suitable as a dwelling-place for that future star of the esoteric and spiritual firmament, Sonya Bulgakova, and I started building my Boy Scoutish camp. I fixed up the tent quite neatly – the result of childhood summer camps. I even managed quite confidently to light a little fire. I managed to drive my car right onto the clearing, winding my way with difficulty among the trees. It was good to have my car beside me.

Finally, I could order myself to stop fussing and calmly

surrender my soul to contemplation. I gave the order. My brain, however, refused to comply and continued creakily fussing, like an undercarriage after striking a high curb.

It was now completely dark, and impossible to descry anything beyond the yellowy aura of my blazing logs. My longed-for peace and calm never came. I felt cold and frightened. I leaped up and, panicking, stamped out the fire, for fear that marauders might be drawn to the flames. In darkness, I crawled inside my tent. There mosquitoes were buzzing around; it stank of damp and toadstools. The wet earth squelched under the rubber sheet. Evidently the boggy patch extended its sphere of rot considerably farther than I'd imagined. I started scratching, because of the mosquitoes and also from sheer nerves. I was now genuinely terrified. My familiar breathing techniques didn't help me to relax. The forest had somehow become full of noises. I kept hearing the crackle of breaking branches and imagining the sound of steps. The wind rose and seemed to be bending the crowns of all the trees right over my tent. They stooped like a tribe of cannibals over my roof, hissing viciously in a loud whisper: 'Eeeeeeaat! Kisssssssss! Kiiiiiiiiiiiiillll!"

Why on earth had I, a woman who had never in her life managed to spend a whole day alone, who feared solitude more than anything else, who dreaded being left one-on-one even with herself, suddenly decided to become a hermit and live alone in the forest? Where were my brains? Had they turned completely to mush?

Once again, something crackled and rustled. An object tumbled on top of the tent and my heart almost leaped into my throat. I sprang up, grabbed everything I could reach, and rushed to the car. I hopped into the driver's seat, locked all the doors and only then could I breathe again. From the car, everything already looked less frightening. Especially when, with trembling fingers, I turned on the radio and tuned in to light music. Now it all seemed once again like just an amusing adventure. I decided to spend the night sitting in the car. Driving out of the forest in the dark was unthinkable. I was amazed that I had managed to bring a car this far.

Thanks to the relaxing effect of pop music and perky DJs, I finally relaxed and slipped gradually into sleep.

I woke up freezing and groped for a blanket, trying to figure out what had happened to my pillow. Why was my neck so horribly numb? When I finally opened my eyes and remembered how I drove myself up against a brick wall, I was simply amused. The previous night's panic was gone. No doubt because sunrise was beaming through the dark canopy of pine branches, and the cheerful dawn chorus had even drowned out the chatter of 24-hour radio station.

I've always loved mornings. I wake up easily, always earlier than the alarm clock. Then, of course, I can spend as much as four hours idling in bed faking sleep. But that precise moment when it's time to leap out of bed is always a pleasure. It's like opening a new book by a favourite author, knowing that pages of enjoyment lie ahead; or like the opening credits of a film said to be spectacular; or like dressing up for a first date; or the successful interview for a new job. It's like choosing a new car in a show room, going out in a new dress, or driving down an unfamiliar road for the first time. It's a foretaste, a hint of what's to come, it's pure bliss! You're just about to start a new day and now, just as you emerge from under the duvet, the day's plan yet to be fixed, all your options are open.

There was time in my life when I got up quite late so as not to cross paths with my husband while he was getting ready for work. I sharply regretted my inability then to start the new day as soon as my eyes opened. And today I had the wonderful opportunity not just to step into a new day, but to crash loudly into it. After all, I was alone in a forest!

I flung open the car door, leaped onto grass still damp with dew and yelled: "Hurrahhhh! Good morning, Sonya! Good morning, world! Hello, sunshine, forest! And you, bog, hello as well!"

I skipped around and even did a sort of a somersault. What a wonderful feeling: to know that you can shout and no-one will hear you. And you shout not because you have to but because you can't help it as the joy of life fills you and pushes you on. My feeling that everything was painful, damaging and complicated was left behind, part of yesterday. Today a totally new life begins, and I'm free to do what I want with it. I can yell whatever nonsense takes my fancy, kiss the trunks of all the trees within my reach, fall on the grass face down, enjoying the scents of damp sedge, mud and worms. The smell of the earth… in a word, I can act crazy, because there's no-one around to make me act normal. And normality is all relative, anyhow.

When I had finally had my fill of romping, washed myself in dew, and brushed my teeth with bottled water, I decided I would stay in this place. I knew I could live here. For the first time in my life I would be alone, utterly alone, no husband, no son, no neighbours, no girlfriends to ring up, no online pals, no television chat shows. And I would enjoy it. I'd become a new person. I could make friends with this forest. The main thing was to work out the right plan for my days. I'd have to nap during the daytime, so as to stay awake during the scariest time, the middle of the night. And then when the sun was shining, I would feel wonderful again. I'd brightened up considerably. I walked around my new territory. I moved the tent to a higher and dryer spot. While I did this I realized that the tent would be my daytime home, even my office. Sleep would be possible only in the car, which I'd lock from the inside. I put down the back seat of the car and arranged it as a luxurious double bed. It even looked like a place for sex, if I found someone to have sex with. However, thoughts like these didn't suit my new self-sufficiency, and I quickly chased them out of my head.

I surrounded my campfire with lumps of turf. I piled up some firewood. I went to the rye field and further along the path to the nearest village. Far from a wretched slum, the village turned out to be a cultural centre with Chekhov's house museum. I bought food, water and vodka. And walked home with great satisfaction.

According to my new schedule, it was now time for sleep. As I was dropping off, I could hear my mobile phone complaining of starvation and insistently requesting to be charged.

"You'll get over it!" I mumbled to it and fell sweetly asleep.

I woke up, as planned, at twilight, fresh and energetic. I sat by the fire and snacked on some toast with fresh gherkins. Then I put out the fire and settled myself inside the car. I had to stay awake for about the next five hours. The radio got on my nerves quite quickly, so I pulled my favourite piece of technology out of the dashboard: a pen with a tiny light attached, and a notebook. And I started writing this very book. The words flowed surprisingly easily, the story gushing onto the paper of its own accord; I could already imagine typing up the text on my computer and then using it to blow the minds of everyone in our rest home.

But once I thought of the home and reception of my work, my hand was struck by paralysis. I couldn't write another line. Then I drank a gulp of vodka and forbade myself to think about the home, or about my son, in fact about anybody. Was it worth driving so far if even now, when all these people were hundreds of kilometres away, they were still holding me back? They could fuck off with their opinions of me! Ultimately, this text was the only thing which kept me from falling asleep in the fearful nocturnal forest, by entertaining me, keeping me alert, and cheering me up better than any jokes by DJs! It saved me from lunacy and hysteria.

I adapted quite swiftly to this strange rhythm of living; I even stopped keeping count of the days. I turned out to be fairly economical; my remaining cash was more than enough to allow me to buy half a kilo of gherkins and half a loaf of bread every day. I also gathered late-season wild strawberries. I really didn't need any more. I'm no glutton.

I got distressed at the end of the first week when after waking up in the late evening as usual and having my fireside supper, I was about to dive into the car with my notebook. and suddenly discovered that the car could no longer lull me with light melodies because the battery was dead. What's more, my magic pen with its little light had also stopped illuminating my literary path with its magic glow. Its battery was dead as well. My instruments had run down, but I was still full of inner fire.

That night I couldn't write. I simply sat in the car staring into the darkness beyond the windows, absorbed by amorous admissions of the nightingales. I held a conversation with myself.

"Sonya my dear, why, when you've longed all your life to write a novel, have you only managed to do it here and now, when there isn't a single reader for miles?"

"Because I was chicken. I was nervous, I wanted to please everyone and I was afraid of finding at least one person I couldn't please. I was terrified that that discovery would finish me off. And now, when there's nobody around to pat me on the head, there's no-one to spit in my eye either."

"Now you can see that writing isn't such a terrible thing after all, as long as you don't set out to make everyone happy. Even the greatest books, like the Bible, the Tao Te Ching, Harry Potter, don't please everybody. How could you have such big ideas about yourself and pretend to something the greatest writers haven't managed?"

"I wasn't consciously pretending. I was just afraid. Fear is not at all the same thing as megalomania. It was more like an inferiority complex."

"And why was it so important for you to please everyone, to have everyone admire you?"

"I wanted to make my mother happy. So that she'd stop thinking she'd wasted her youth by having me. I was more afraid of disappointing her than anything else. I knew that nobody would ever criticize me as much as she did."

"Your mother's been dead for five years."

"And now I'm sorry she's gone; she'll never be able to read my novel."

I diverted myself with this sort of internal dialogue until morning, and then, as always, I fell asleep. After waking up and performing my morning rituals, I opened the driver's manual and succeeded, with difficulty, in exposing the battery to the light of day. The damn thing was heavy. I dragged it painfully to the village, hoping to implore the local guys to charge it for me.

I immediately noticed that the locals were giving me strange looks. But nobody said anything unusual; on the contrary, they sorted out my technical problem pretty smartly. One of the men even helped me to haul the extremely heavy unit out to my car, concealed in the wood. We parted on friendly terms, although I cunningly ignored his broad hints about a generous tip.

As always, when I got ready for my afternoon nap, it was almost five in the evening. I had just laid my head on my cushion when someone rapped on the glass. Biting my tongue from surprise, I sat up so sharply that the blood buzzed in my ears. In front of me was a man in a police uniform. He was holding a photograph up to his face and comparing me with it. It was all soon explained.

My son, it seemed, had been most anxious about me. And when I vanished and didn't get in touch, didn't answer my mobile, and failed to turn up either at the residence or in my apartment, he called in the police to hunt me down. He recalled my former acquaintance with powerful political figures, immediately contacted some influential people, so that the hunt for me was carried out on a large scale. Photos of me were sent to all towns and villages. I even appeared on television: in the program "The Police Are Looking for These People" they showed my picture. Posters with my face and the headline, 'Have you seen this woman?' appeared online, announcing that I was a well-known journalist who had disappeared from her home. So it was no surprise that the villagers had been staring at me oddly; my face already seemed very familiar. And so they rushed to share their discovery with the police.

This pretty pickle had been organized by my old crony Fedya Vasilyev, with Peter's help. Fedya was a good guy; we'd become pals very quickly at a high-society ball. It was a charity function, and invitations cost a steep sum, which was supposed to be passed on to orphans. I got a free ticket, as a society columnist, and Fedya got a ticket as a bribe, to ensure that his soldiers kept an eye on things and guarded the guests' expensive cars. But besides that, he provided a dozen or so nice-looking sturdy young men, who flattered wealthy ladies of a certain age wishing to dance a waltz or a mazurka but lacking partners. So these handsome chaps in dinner jackets, radiating mysteriousness, entertained these middle-aged "girls" for a dance or two and sent them roses in tall sky-blue vine glasses. Naturally, they didn't reveal the real nature of their job, so that the ladies kept a pleasant aftertaste of lightly veiled mystery, enjoyment, and romantic excitement. Even before they'd left the dance-floor they were ready to buy tickets for the next ball.

At that ball Fedya and I – both smartened up for the evening – did our best to resemble birds of paradise. That is, two born plebeians pretended that they were pedigreed nobles, as more or less everyone did at this high-society reception. We differed from the other guests only in one thing: our relative poverty. When the guests bid for the privilege of choosing the music for the next dance, and the bidding ran to tens of thousands of dollars, we failed to hide our natural emotions and broke into identical grimaces of astonishment and contempt. It was frankly easier to conceal our genuine envy with mockery, and to suppress our bile, which would probably have drowned everyone in the room if we hadn't been such good actors. But we saw through each other immediately. Right there, we clinked our glasses of unglamorous vodka in token of eternal comradeship. We started swapping anecdotes, we even danced a little. But meanwhile we became friends. At last I had found a friend from within national security; every self-respecting journalist needs one.

Fedya always vouched for me, and I helped him out as much as I could. For example, when during the new Time of Troubles in the interregnum between Putin's presidencies, Fedya's territory was threatened by spontaneous meetings and pickets, I tried to ensure that our newspaper depicted his subordinates in the most restrained terms possible. And when a curfew was imposed in Moscow, Fedya wangled me a 24-hour pass.

My son went to this same Fedya for help when I disappeared, and Fedya, exploiting his government position and connections, turned all Russia upside down, forcing everybody to look for me. This meant I was speedily located and rushed to Moscow with an escort of official vehicles. However, the police didn't bring me home; instead, they fetched me directly to Fedya's office. What the hell, I had absolutely no objection to meeting my old comrade-in-arms and talking over our lives together. It even amused me that my disappearance had caused such a to-do. I'd had no idea that I was such a valuable old bird. It boosted the old self-esteem.

Fedya met me cheerfully and didn't even give me a lecture for causing so much fuss about nothing. He kissed me on the cheek, unceremoniously pinched my hip, and summed up: "Sonya old girl, you gave us the slip! I haven't seen you in ages. Come out to my dacha, I'll feed you up and we'll get drunk to celebrate your return! I'll hand you over to your son tomorrow."

"Too right!" I chuckled. "Let him fret another day."

"No, he's already done enough fretting. I rang him to let him know you had turned up."

We started celebrating my return to the civilized world in the back seat of his official jeep. When we spilled out onto the close-cropped lawn of his dacha near the Pirogov artificial lake, we'd recaptured that forgotten sensation of spiritual kinship. I was hamming it up, making faces to describe to Fedya the residents of our poorhouse; he guffawed and slapped his sides. We went inside; Fedya's pleasant wife nodded welcomingly, lent me one of her own gym outfits, and the three of us headed for the little pond on their land. In the pond, their lovingly fed fish were splashing around unbelievably loudly. In due time, they'd be caught on Fedya's rod to become a special treat for particularly honoured guests. One of the banks was set up like a patio, with a barbecue in the middle. Fedya's wife was making kebabs with sturgeon, chicken and pork. The delicious aroma dulled my critical faculties; the few remaining thinking parts of my brain were naïve, inexperienced, open and trusting. A rare Armenian cognac also aided the process of intellectual disorganisation and finally knocked out my grey matter.

While the meat was roasting, I amused my welcoming hosts with tales about Nata's crazy collection of children by different men, how Rafael's former wife, our local celebrity Alla Maksimova, was humiliated by being cut out of his will, and how as a result of all this our residence started going to hell. I even gave a colourful account of deep-frozen Tatiana, who'd turned out to be my own husband's mistress. And I didn't avoid spitefully mentioning my discovery that her famous psychotherapist husband was infertile.

The mistress of the house listened to everything with interest, but Fedya himself didn't look as if I were telling him anything new. However, he tactfully nodded at all my stories and didn't let on that somewhere in his official dossier all the complications of these people's biographies had long ago been filed and exhaustively described.

At last, I reached the moment of my embarrassing flight from the home; I had to describe our pitched battle.

"The way all these writerly wretches flung themselves on me! Like hungry fleas on a healthy dog," I waved my arms. "They started to bite and kick me. And you know who was the fiercest of all? Some woman called Nina. She's our resident lesbian; she thumped me harder than all the rest. I wasn't expecting it. I'd imagined a lesbian would treat female flesh with a certain caution, well, more tenderly than some. But she was ready to slay me on the spot!"

"You've actually got a real live lesbian there?" Fedya's wife raised her eyebrows.

"Alive and kicking!" I flung my arms wide. "And even very much in love. She's running after someone called Lena Moiseyenko. I don't know much about Lena, just that she used to be some sort of doctor."

"Fedya!" my hostess turned sharply towards her husband. "A former doctor called Lena Moiseyenko is living in Sonya's old people's home. Can she be the same one?"

"What do you mean, the same one?" I pricked up my ears.

"Surely it's not Andrei Moiseyenko's wife," Fedya's wife asked excitedly.

"It's possible," Fedya shrugged phlegmatically.

"Moiseyenko was Fedya's boss," Fedya's wife chattered, delighted that she could finally contribute her tuppennyworth to this conversation. "And Lena was his wife. You know, just a regular couple: he was an officer, she was a doctor. They were a really nice pair. Then she had some problems at work, and ended up becoming a housewife. She got fired and nobody else would hire her. Fedya, do you remember, we bumped into them in Novogorsk during the May Day holiday? That time when your favourite football team Dynamo got poisoned? She was already out of work then and very resentful about it. It made her very bitter."

"Yes, of course I remember," Fedya lazily shifted his

knees, which were spread far apart. "But that's Lena for you – what of it? Women are women. They get old as well."

Apparently today, as always, Fedya had risen early and was growing tired towards evening. He was already starting to snore, slumped awkwardly in his chair, while the meat was cooking. His wife and I tucked into the cognac and the sturgeon, which smelled of the fire, trying to speak quietly so as not to disturb Fedya's sleep.

"Oh, that was really the worst holiday we ever had," my hostess fluttered her artificial eyelashes, clearly recalling one of the most exciting adventures in her life. "I remember we woke up with someone knocking at the door, and straightaway we were interrogated. Fedya just had time to tell me, 'Alina dear, you know nothing'." (This was how I finally remembered that my old comrade's wife was called Alina and from then on it was much easier for me to chat to her.)

In a word, the pair of them had been thoroughly scared that they would both be taken to prison in connection with multiple infractions committed by Lieutenant-Colonel Fedya Vasiliev. But, strange as it might seem, he wasn't asked about any of those illegally distributed curfew passes, nor about the unavenged victims of his activities on behalf of the building and trading companies with which he associated. The couple were asked extremely strange questions: what had they been doing the previous evening, what had they eaten, and how well did they sleep, almost as if this wasn't an interrogation, but an interview with a polite but overly meticulous functionary from the public relations office of some international company.

Only when the interrogation was over (and they were interrogated by investigators from the highest ranks of the General Prosecutor's Office) did the couple learn that the previous evening the entire "Dynamo" football team had been fatally poisoned. The team had been living and training in Novogorsk. In essence the place was neither a guesthouse nor a holiday resort, but a training base for the police football team, where, thanks to extensive use of influence, cops who deserved the honour (and celebrities who were close to them) could spend their vacations 'living close up with famous footballers'. Performers were granted the same privilege in return for putting on free shows for the police. But now this elite of power-broking politicians and show-business stars came under suspicion, as did all the staff of this prestigious and exclusive recreation centre. Hard to imagine that eleven guys at the height of their physical powers had been dispatched to the next world by the most ancient of methods – poison. The police were working on the basis that the crime had been committed by their rivals. However, in the end all the blame was laid on an ordinary waitress from the local restaurant, whose motive remained a mystery. Possibly the footballers hadn't tipped her sufficiently, possibly one of the footballers had made an unwanted sexual advance.

"Just between us," Alina whispered in my ear, almost touching my earlobe with her warm, damp lips, "a lot of people thought at the time that it was some secret service operation. Because it just didn't make sense to poison the best football team in the country without a special sanction from them. No-one could have dared to do something so shocking."

"But why was it necessary? And to whom?" I gasped and then, remembering, returned to a whisper. "Why would the secret services want to poison eleven not very bright guys, even if they were very well paid for chasing after a ball?"

According to Alina (and, if she could be believed, Fedya thought the same way) the "Dynamo" football team had become a trump card in a high-stakes political game. It was rumoured that the footballers were poisoned in order to show the government up as completely incapable of controlling national affairs, and the police as incapable of protecting their own people in their own recreation centre, let alone ensuring national security. Not long after that case, the head of the police was buried, in the political sense, that is. The innocently slaughtered footballers became one of the bricks in the tombstone of his career.

"Only up there in the secret services HQ could they be so cruel," Alina whispered with drunken conviction. "Only they could murder eleven fine men just to serve their own ends."

Her version struck me as so monstrous that I had no doubts about its unreality. On the other hand, our politics were so crazy that it was difficult to relate them in any way to common sense. On the subject of politicians, I could believe almost anything, as if I were hearing about the behaviour of extraterrestrials. I can believe whatever they tell me about aliens, because I know just one thing about them: they are not of our kind. And politicians are the same.

Alina and I talked conspiratorially for a little longer. Then we called over Fedya's aides, who moved his sleepy, drunken body to his bedroom, and we all dropped off to sleep.

In the morning, I woke to the fragrance of real, freshly brewed coffee, which I hadn't had a whiff of in a long time. I stretched out on the snow-white sheets with pleasure, realizing exactly what I'd missed in my forest hermitage: real coffee, and white, starchy bed-linen.

I didn't luxuriate for long. Within half an hour, still hangoverish from the night before, I was loaded almost by force into a police car and driven off to be handed over to my son. He met me with an expression of genuine delight, and even a sort of repentance, on his face. He went so far as to throw his good arm around me, nothing fazed by the guys in uniform standing by. It looked to me as if he was ready to bawl. After assuring themselves that everything was in order, the uniforms left.

Peter and I sat down in the kitchen, and he kept fussing over me: "Will you have some milk? Some bread? A piece of cheese? Sugar in that, maybe brown sugar? Anything else? Will I warm up the bread in the toaster? Can I heat that up?"

He had already learned to deal quite deftly with all his household tasks using just one arm. The left arm was in plaster, bent at the elbow and bound up level with his heart, lending him a rather Byronesque appearance.

"Don't stress, Peter, everything's fine," I tried to calm him. "Everything's good. You're not to blame for anything. You're the most sinned-against person in this whole affair."

"I was so scared for you," Peter replied, looking at the window. "You have no idea how awful I felt when I couldn't find you. Not at home, not in the residence, you weren't answering your phone…"

"Forgive me, I behaved selfishly," I tried to take my son by his good hand. He didn't withdraw it, but he tensed up as if his whole self was concentrated in that limb. I imagined him breathing through his fingers, and I felt his heart beating somewhere under my palm. "My poor child," I sighed. "You really got lucky with your parents, didn't you? No daddy, and a lunatic for a mother."

"Mama, I'm the selfish one. I understand everything now. Forgive me for persuading you to go into that stupid old people's home. It was a mistake. I'll fix everything. Your apartment is free again and it's waiting for you. Come home."

"No, son, I want to go back to my elderly friends."

"Mama, what's the point of that? If you go it'll be hard and unpleasant for you there, I already understand that. And there's absolutely no need for such sacrifices."

"All the same I ask you to take me back to the old people's home. If you won't do it, I'll go there by myself."

"But, Mama!"

"Yes, it's hard for me there. But it's only through suffering that we find out who we really are and extend the limits of our capabilities. Only through pain do we discover what we're really able to do, if we can hang in there. It's very important for me. Pain means we're alive, you understand. If nothing hurts, you must be dead. You only know that your muscles are getting stronger if they hurt the day after a training session. If nothing hurts after you go to the gym, you've been wasting your time. I need to go to the home. Sure I won't have it easy there, but that's a kind of pain that I need right now. Through that pain, I'm becoming the real me."

"I want you to be alive and well. That's the most important thing for me."

"I will be, son, don't worry. I promise you."

"Just in case, take the keys to your apartment. You can go back there any time," Peter put the keys on the table. "You have your own home. And you have a family. Please remember that. And you're someone I really care about, Mama. And..." He broke off, finding words with difficulty; sentimental talk wasn't the sort of thing our family did. "I love you, Mama," my son finally sighed.

"I love you too. Very much," I admitted.

We finally hugged, as well as we could. I had the idea that I'd last hugged my son on a September day in front of the school door when he was starting school. At the time, I'd thought he was already too big for such calf-like nonsense. Only now did I understand what a fool I'd been.

I took the keys. They'd been given to me whole-heartedly, and I couldn't refuse them. If I had, I'd have been spitting on my son's generosity; I intuited that. Finally, I'd begun to understand my son.

Fedya's people had already delivered my car, which I'd left in his official parking space the day before. In certain cases, and for certain people, our security forces can be remarkably friendly.

I stood in the doorway with my suitcase.

"Peter, just one question," I asked, as if incidentally, doing up my sandals. "Does Tatiana already know that I know about her and Sasha, and Katya?"

"She knows," my son answered, looking embarrassed. "We had no idea what you were up to so, just in case, we warned her. Anything could have happened..."

"I get it. You were afraid that I would get hold of her and open her veins?" I sneered. "Don't worry! I have no plans to slap her in the face or beat her up. I've calmed down. To tell the truth, even when I was beside myself, I never wanted to hit her."

I really had calmed down. My thoughts had become utterly peaceful. I no longer had any desire to accuse anybody about what had happened in the past. Let bygones be bygones. If certain people, whom I'd considered very dear to me, got left behind in the past that meant that they belonged there. You don't let truly important people, as essential to you as breathing, slip out of your life.

I still didn't know how I was going to look Tatiana in the eye after all this, but I wanted to do it. I knew that our meeting, after all that had happened, would be one of the most important in my life. And I wanted to live through the real thing just once, rather than imagine it multiple times in my fantasies, winding up my already tense brain with contrived encounters. In a word, I had plenty of fairly solid, and mostly invented, reasons to return to the home. The truth was that I was simply being tugged back there by a very powerful force. It was where I really felt alive!

"Well, well, it's the runaway!" Nata rushed into my room before I'd even had a chance to change my clothes. "We didn't mean to scare you so badly that you'd hide in the forest and there'd be search parties for you all over the former Soviet Union. Looks like we laid on a bit too heavily with the stick."

"Typical!" I muttered. "Don't take credit for my escape. Your pathetic kicks and punches had nothing to do with it. I went into hiding for completely unrelated reasons."

"Oh really?" sneered Nata, as if she'd wanted to say, "A likely story." "Well, if that's the way it is, then I'm pleased, one less burden on my soul."

She glanced at me and smiled as if we'd been best friends at school who'd just pulled off a ripping but rather risky prank. She grinned conspiratorially.

I didn't want to yield to her cheap manipulation, but

against my will I found myself giving an answering smile. Then something gave way, and we both started roaring with laughter like lunatics. Nata grabbed a pillow off the bed and flung it at me. In response, I hurled a towel that had been hanging on the back of a chair right at her. She skilfully caught the towel in mid-air and launched it at me like a boomerang.

Pillow! Towel! Pillow! Second pillow! The balding stuffed cat! All at the same time – the pillow, the towel, and the cat! Nata seized the pillow which had just landed and collapsed with it onto the bed, as if I'd toppled her over like a bowling pin.

"You're cool!" Nata beamed at me.

"You're not so bad yourself!" I raised an eyebrow in reply, falling onto the bed beside her.

At this point, if one of us had been a man, we'd have made love then and there. At any rate, I was clearly reminded how my husband and I used to make up just that way, when we'd fought over some mutually irritating blunders for which neither of us was really to blame; that is, either each of us had to apologize immediately, or neither of us.

"Really, Sonya, I never thought that we'd frighten you so badly," Nata said quietly and very sincerely. "I really had no idea that Nina would show such unmotivated ferocity. I never suspected she was capable of it."

"Well, it doesn't matter, all water under the bridge," I brushed her words away. "You and your Nina had absolutely nothing to do with it. It wasn't your fault that I went to ground and acted a bit mad. I had other reasons entirely."

And, chuckling as if I didn't care, I told Nata what I'd discovered I shared with Tatiana. Just as if it didn't concern me at all. I told it like a screamingly funny, slapstick, foolish comedy. Nata listened without so much as blinking. I had impressed her. It was as if I had boasted to her, as if I were saying: "There you go! Even I have secrets! I also experienced something extraordinary in my life. I too have lived!"

"In a word, it was a pretty queer kettle of fish," I summed

up my tale. "When I wanted to bail out of our wonderful marriage, holding back purely because I felt sorry for my husband, asking myself how I could leave him when he loved me so much, when I was the light of his life, he actually couldn't give a damn about me. At that very time, he was fathering a child on the side. You know, this looks more interesting the more I think it over: look at how many times you've dumped the guys who fathered your children. How did you manage to do it? It's so hard, after all, to leave a man who's told you he loves you. It amazes me how easily you chucked your men. On the one hand, I understand you simply didn't allow yourself to fall in love with them. But did you really not feel sorry for them? Didn't you understand that you were causing another human being pain? They loved you, you know. Raf certainly did. Wasn't it cruel? How did you manage to suppress your pity?"

"When I broke off a relationship, I never looked at things that way. I never flattered myself that I was the only person who could make this man happy, or that I meant anything unique to them. I never had any doubt that each of them could cope without me. Of course, some of them would howl: 'I'll die without you!' Well, if only one of them had – as it turned out, not one even came down with a cold." Nata laughed nastily and immediately turned gloomily serious. "No doubt I did act from some compulsion to be cruel. It was probably some kind of inferiority complex that allowed me to walk away from men so easily. I couldn't believe that I might mean something to them, that they might regret losing me. Only after turning forty did I accept that men were human too. Not in the way they say about women: 'women are human too', meaning that even women have some rights and can think. I never doubted that men have rights and an intellect. I didn't believe that men were human because I didn't think guys experience emotion the way we women do. That a man can weep from love, and not just because his favourite team lost a match. That he can go out of his mind when the woman he loves isn't around; or because he can't hold his own child. I thought that only women felt these emotions, just as only women have periods, labour pains, or the menopause. Yes, I realized that I meant something to each of them. But only in the way that a particular brand of beer was important to them; I was just the woman they happened to prefer. If their favourite brand wasn't available, they'd drink a different one just as happily. I felt that they loved me just the same way: they just happened to prefer me at the time. When I met the kind of man who made me believe that he could really love, and not just 'prefer', for the first time I wanted to stop and to have only his children. Maybe I really fell in love for the first time?"

"And who was this man?" I was genuinely curious.

"You know him, but you don't know that it's him I mean," Nata crinkled her eyes mysteriously. "I'll tell you sometime. But my story won't be as interesting as yours."

We both fell silent, thinking over all that we'd heard.

"Well, I'll be damned! Shocking stuff!" Nata finally spoke up. "So Katya isn't Zhenya's daughter…"

"Well, of course not!" I felt rather offended that, out of my entire story, Nata was chiefly struck by this detail. For some reason, she felt Zhenya and Katya were the stars of the narrative, when the main heroines were really Tatiana and I. Nata seemed to be deliberately whittling down my triumph as holder of the most exciting real-life experience and engrossing plot. I was right to be wary: to counter my queen of hearts, Nata unexpectedly pulled a trump card out of her sleeve: and it was the queen of spades. I don't think she would have told this story if she hadn't noticed traces of boastfulness and self-glorification in my tone as I recounted my adventures. In any case, she was also a pretty outspoken type of person; she'd lived her life rather like a performance, a theatre play, making up the plot by herself from day to day. She deserved credit: her play was certainly more powerful than mine.

"For me, if you'll forgive me, the biggest news in your

story is that Katya isn't Zhenya's daughter. He and I used to be rather close..."

It all began long ago, in 2003, when Natasha Sokolova was as fresh as a pot-plant and as innocent as a snow-white seal-pup. The pretty daughter of an exemplary single mother, an engineer, she'd graduated from the Literary Institute, wrote avant-garde short plays, which enjoyed massive success among her eighty or so online friends, and which, strangely enough, no publisher or theatre ever wanted to buy. And her degree from the Literary Institute was useless for convincing money-hungry publishers that she was the real thing, a promising female writer. None of this reduced Nata to despair: as far as possible, she enhanced her karma through the creative use of body-piercing and mini-tattoos; she had faith that the future would lead to better things. Less than a year after she had finished college her mother finally persuaded her that at this rate, there soon wouldn't be a tattoo-free patch on her body, and that her karma would still be in the garbage, where every morning her mother dumped the mountains of empty beer bottles from Nata's room. Nata's mother was an inexhaustibly kind woman, but old-fashioned; she wanted her little Natasha to pay her own way. Encouraged by her mother's light hand (dealing a heavy clip around the ear), Nata completed a doubtful screenwriting course, for which her materialistically minded parent shelled out almost one and a half thousand dollars. During this period she virtually ceased to give Nata pocket money, allowing her no more than access to the family refrigerator. She wanted the best for her daughter, not an early death from starvation.

Having no other choice, Nata started off as a dialogue-writer in the screenwriting group in Rafael Oganesian's newly started film-production company, and frenziedly set about building a career. The adrenalin of terror proved an extremely effective stimulant for creativity, and soon Nata was being trusted to write entire episodes. Filling in the details of other people's scripts rapidly palled on her. Nata was desperate to become the leading scriptwriter and to promote her very own, personal series based on the life of psychotherapists. As a beginning scriptwriter, she wanted to show real life on screen, to write from nature. So she went off to get to know psychotherapists in person. Ivan Pavlov's ideological heirs had cast a spell on her. In no other profession had she encountered such a quantity of nutty people. At that time she still took any kind of deviation as a sign of being special or chosen. She didn't know where to look: every shrink she met was more eccentric, and more interesting, than the next. She was fascinated by them. They treated her like an important person and asked her lots of questions. She didn't yet know that asking lots of questions, while avoiding answering any themselves, is a professional quirk of psychotherapists. Nor do they give away any advice on life or reveal their carefully constructed worldviews. Their professional ethics obliges them to treat clients in this way. Many of them, even outside of work hours, can't switch off their inner doctor; they live in character. In this way, Nata was overcome by the sense of her own unique significance: she felt important, she reached far-ranging conclusions from meaningless premises, she learned to rap her knuckles on the table at the end of every sentence, as if placing a full stop after each thought. Even before this, Nata had considered herself exceptionally clever and experienced, much smarter than her mother and her girlfriends. This unrecognized author measured experience by the quantity of beer and vodka drunk in the OGI and Bilingua literary clubs. By this scale alone, she left her mother far behind. Moreover, the girl had already tried smoking pot. In short, she knew almost everything about life.

She discussed profound matters with the psychotherapists rather like this:

"And so," crossing her legs and lighting a second cigarette from her first, Nata was asking the doctor who was best-disposed towards her, Zhenya, who supplied therapy to well-heeled women and even had advertising billboards on a national motorway, "Which psychological problems are most widespread among our population? What do people usually come to you about?"

"And what do you think the answer is?" asked the specialist, narrowing his eyes.

"Well, I think there's nothing that affects people on a greater scale than love. The most destructive and merciless psychological battles today take place by email and in the bedroom."

"And what role do you feel you play in this total war?" Zhenya asked.

"Well, I'm a soldier who's been shell-shocked twice, transferred to war reporting and is now observing the battle from a bunker," Nata said flirtatiously.

"And from your bunker, can you see how combat tactics have changed today?"

"Today psychological war, just like ordinary war, has naturally changed because new kinds of weapons have appeared. Just as in ordinary war, psychological tactics are now carried out at distance. In order to destroy enemy forces on one half of the globe from the other half, you send out drones and bombs, and the combatants never see each other's faces. It's the same thing in the love wars: the cruellest, most destructive blows are struck from a distance thanks to new technology: the Internet, mobile phones and the like. You can send a single text message: 'You idiot, I never really loved you, ha-ha,' and turn off your phone. That's it! The poor dumpee takes Valium and rushes off to a clinic to heal her spiritual wounds. This way, after all, she can't even slap your face in revenge, or get in a response strike!"

Conversations like this one could go on until the early hours. Nata felt that each of her observations deserved being carved into the marble of the Taj Mahal, as if all the world's wisdom was concentrated inside her skull. But nonetheless Nata still remained a sweet, fluffy, 22-year-old seal-cub. And the sight of a defenceless seal-cub, as we all know, arouses a man's predatory instinct. It wakens a desire to smash that cute little pinkish nose to bloody fragments. (It has to be the nose so as not to spoil the pelt). Then to skin the body and hang the pure white skin above the chimney-piece.

And while Nata was revelling in ergonomically designed leather chairs, showing off her cleverness, storm clouds were gathering over her head. Naturally, Nata didn't then understand that her imperturbable naivety was the main cause of this irresistible desire to thump her on the nose. People, especially us Russians, are destructive by nature; when they come across a virgin white snowdrift, they are instantly impelled to jump on it, stamp on it, and just to finish the job, piss "Here was Vasya" all over it. Bubble wrap similarly inspires people with a craving to crush all the bubbles, letting out the air inside them. It's perfectly acceptable to drown newborn kittens all at once in a pail of water. And the one that scratches, wails and resists most fiercely is taken out of the pail with respect: "Well, look at you, you cheeky fellow. You can live!"

As for Nata, she was drowning with pleasure and enthusiasm, happily out of touch with reality. After waking up one morning on the psychotherapist's couch completely nude, she considered herself victorious. She was convinced that she'd long ago captured the soul of the psychotherapist Zhenya, and now he'd given her his body as well. The young scriptwriter imagined that since they had already spent so many hours talking about love, the soul, eternity, people, private matters, and about her, there must naturally be a deep and genuine link between them. After all, one doesn't have such quality conversations with just anyone. Somehow she failed to notice that she was really the only person speaking during these long hours, and that she knew hardly anything about Zhenya, besides the fact that he was good at intelligently formulating open questions.

She wasn't even remotely surprised or afraid when her

pregnancy test came up positive. Instead she was joyful and started listening to her body, searching for changes and new sensations. She only grew wary when, instead of the ecstasies and dramatic euphoria she'd expected, Zhenya reacted to the news of her pregnancy with a fairly dry (and typical for him) 'open' question:

"And what do you feel about it?"

"What do you mean, what?" Natasha responded in surprise. "Why are you asking a question like that? Aren't you pleased?"

"What makes you nervous about the idea of pregnancy?"

"Zhenya! It's your child!" Natasha playfully threatened him with a finger. "Quit this playacting! I want to hear that you're as pleased about the child as I am."

"You say you're pleased about the child. What does it mean to you if someone else is pleased about it or not?"

"Are you making fun of me?" Nata became furious. She no longer felt like the all-powerful know-it-all, completely in charge of her own life, that she'd been just a couple of weeks earlier. She didn't understand what was happening. "Why do you keep asking these idiotic questions? What do you mean by it?"

"Why do you consider questions about the child idiotic? Do you think a child is not suitable grounds for questioning or consideration?"

"Give me a simple yes-or-no answer! Are you with us or not? Are you really not happy that we're going to have a child?"

"Is it really so important to you that other people should be happy about the arrival of your child? Or would you give it up, if you find a man who doesn't want the child?"

"What is this nonsense you're talking? What do I care about other people, as long as this child is important to you and me?"

"Why do you consider this unborn child only as an extension of yourself, assuming that it won't have meaning for other people, and that its role in humanity will be to become your personal plaything, to amuse you and me? Why do you refuse it the right to be meaningful for, let's say, humanity as a whole? Do you think that you are incapable of giving birth to a significant, noticeable, talented individual?"

"Zhenya, what are you talking about? What has humanity as a whole, some abstract 'everyone', got to do with us? This is about us!" Nata was still putting her faith in words, but she already understood everything perfectly. She could hear behind all of Zhenya's profound questions five simple words: "I don't need this baby". She already understood that he would do everything in his power to escape the situation and to pretend that it had nothing to do with him. He would ask even more questions and act clever. Let him go fuck himself. This psychotherapist, someone people went to for spiritual help, was himself gravely pathological.

"You must answer one simple question: do you want this child as a child, or do you want him as a 'means', as a 'twig', which you can use to attach the father to you?"

"That's enough, Zhenya, I can see through you."

"If your child has independent value for you as a being in his own right, can you really give him up under any circumstances? And if you only want him as part of a 'set' with a husband, then is it worth giving birth? If the man disappears, leaves you, dies, won't the child lose all value for you?"

"That's enough sophistry." Nata understood that she wouldn't get any more from him than a headache.

She was left alone in her interesting condition. Zhenya expertly got rid of her, trying to convince her that however her pregnancy ended was her personal choice. Other people's opinions should count for nothing beside her genuine wish. And only she could say whether she wished to have this child. Zhenya juggled words so cunningly that somehow or other she was left wholly responsible for the fate of this foetus, as if she'd gotten pregnant without any help.

A womb carries the inevitable curse of responsibility.

How convenient it must be to be the culprit, but always be able to justify yourself and wash your hands of the affair, assuming that you'd never dreamed of getting someone pregnant. You could say, "Ultimately, I have nothing to do with this – she was the one who went and had the abortion!" And that would be true. The right to decide means real power. That was how Nata realized that she was now her own mistress.

A conviction that she could shape the future through her children was not the only lesson Nata took from this personal disaster. She realized that once she had accepted the right to control her own life, to live at her own risk and by her own responsibility, she also had power over those not yet alive. However, much time had still to pass before she was to put this power into practice.

"As you've probably already guessed, because of all this I never did write my independent series about the lives of psychotherapists. I gave birth to Oleg instead. I didn't really have a choice: my rhesus-negative blood group narrowed down my room for manoeuvre. You're not allowed an abortion with that blood group, all you can do is give birth. So I did. Although I'd probably have had the child in any case. I wasn't intimidated, and I was afraid of absolutely nothing. And I did the right thing. My mother helped me. In fact, everyone helped me. When I understood that it was my choice whether to give birth to this little person or not, I took a step farther. Realizing that the destinies of future beings depend on you makes it easier to deal with the present. If you already have the right to decide on behalf of lives not yet lived, sorting out those that already exist gets much easier. All the more so if you're dealing with a person whom you find wanting."

Nata hadn't been seeking a way to ruin Zhenya's life, or nurturing schemes for revenge. But when she suddenly had the opportunity, the temptation was enormous, and she couldn't resist. The chain of coincidences was almost as if someone had intentionally planned to provoke Nata. Had she deliberately planned the whole thing, it couldn't have gone more smoothly.

Nata had only just finished maternity leave and was finding it difficult to re-adjust to the rhythm of working life. She had even caught a stupid cold, which she used as sufficient excuse to take sick leave and spend a little more time at home. In fact, to get this meaningless piece of paper she'd even gone to an exclusive medical centre, which was covered by insurance she'd bought two years previously. It had been strongly recommended to her by none other than Zhenya, who had registered there long ago. The centre really was of the highest quality; what's more, they had no queues. But when Nata got to the office of the therapist she needed, no-one was around, either in the corridor or in the office. For some reason the office wasn't locked, and the computer monitor on the desk, still switched on, was shining alluringly. From sheer feminine curiosity (possibly not entirely innocent), Nata swiftly pulled up on-screen the medical history of her child's father. And she discovered, with interest, that he was suffering severe problems with his male organs. More precisely, testicular cancer. Prompted by a wicked impulse, as if someone were pushing her on, Nata swiftly changed the word "right" to "left" in the case history and shut the file. She scurried out of the office and left the medical centre in a hurry.

"I never doubted that sooner or later someone would notice this ridiculous mistake, this falsification, and that the only harm Zhenya would suffer would be the effect of the joke on his nerves," Nata justified herself. "So he'd suffer a little, but he'd survive. It would do him good. It would do him no harm to learn to fear destiny sometimes. That was exactly how I rationalized it. And when I learned that he and Tatiana had had a daughter, I assumed the mistake really had been caught and I even forgot all about it. But it turns out that this time fate really wasn't on his side."

"You talk about this so calmly," I said, horrified. "Do you really feel no regret at all?"

"Me? Regret?" Nata gave me the contemptuous stare of an Indian goddess. She was sorry for nothing; she believed in her right to direct destiny. I felt disgusted. But I tried hastily to clear my mind. I needed a woman friend.

"So you pretended that Oleg and Katya weren't suited to each other and needed to split up, because you assumed that they were brother and sister?"

"Well, of course," said Nata. "Just so."

"Then this young pair should be very grateful to me for removing any obstacle to their union. But you're a pretty cold-blooded mother. Even when you thought that there was incest going on, practically under your nose, you kept quiet! And you didn't say anything to Oleg about his father?"

"You know they weren't over-keen to ask my advice," Nata started getting annoyed. "By the time I knew what was going on, they were well past the stage of eating ice-creams in the park. And believe me, if you hadn't revealed these extra details today, I would have sorted it all out pretty sharply, and so that they wouldn't have been able to stand each other any longer. I'd have managed everything. And I'd have resolved the situation a lot more elegantly than by dropping a bombshell on them, like: 'Hey, lovebirds, you're brother and sister'. If I'd come out with that kind of announcement, things would be much worse for my son. And think of the psychological trauma they'd suffer! Fear and guilt would have taken root in their subconscious minds, plus resentment against me. And hundreds of questions! Try to think two steps ahead of yourself!"

"And does Tatiana know that you're the girl her husband threw over because she got pregnant? That you're the one who caused him to sin against karma?"

"Until today I had no doubt that she knew nothing. I figured that if she knew that Oleg was Zhenya's son, then she wouldn't have looked the other way at Katya's relationship with my boy. But now I have my doubts."

"But don't you want to tell her everything, to make it all clear?"

"What's the point? And don't you even think of shooting your mouth off!" Nata gave me such a serious stare that I realized this was less of a request than a threat. Perhaps I'd been over-hasty in accepting her as a friend. I decided I'd be less open with her in future; I'd tell her nothing about the literary inspiration that had descended upon me in the forest, or about how I was now overwhelmed with ideas for a mockumentary novel. After all, she was a pretty dangerous lady.

Already in the police car driving me from Fedya's dacha to my son's Moscow apartment, I'd felt the beginnings of this quasi-documentary text taking root in my mind. As I turned over in my memory all the events and conversations of the previous evening, I caught myself thinking that I needed to find out more about the strange case of the murdered football team. It suddenly struck me as a good subject for a book: the sort of para-documentary prose, where the author brings in mysteries, builds hypotheses that can't be proved, and makes significant suggestions, writing as if he'd been there in person to eavesdrop on everyone. Biographical sketches in glossy magazines always make me laugh, when the journalist tells his story as if he'd been a third party in every celebrity's bed at the same time. Stuff like this:

"Alain Delon kissed her lips and recoiled abruptly. His nostrils flared, but his pupils narrowed: 'Did you sleep with him? I'll kill him! It would have been better if he'd robbed my house!' Alain roughly pushed the half-naked Nathalie back onto the silk bedsheets, jumped into his trousers and rushed out of the house. That same evening the body of his rival Stefan Markovic was found in a dump in the back yard of his house, with a bullet in his head. When Alain came home, he met Nathalie at the door. She was carrying a suitcase. Alain threw himself on her and started kissing her passionately. But now she shoved him fiercely away: 'Never! I will never let myself be held in the arms of a murderer!'"

That was the sort of style I imagined for my detective novel. I realized in a flash that this kind of text attracts publicity simply by virtue of its topic; the media would attract the public, the public would bring in cash. Hurrah! In old age I would finally become rich, like that Rowling woman who sold her soul to Harry Potter!

Just as soon as I had shown Nata out, and, finally, changed my clothes and unpacked my suitcases, I flung myself on my computer and settled down to read whatever I could find on this case online. I already pictured myself travelling to that ill-omened Novogorsk within the next few days and finding out all the details on the spot. The Internet provided me with biographies of all the innocently slaughtered footballers; their murderer, I read, had been sentenced by the courts to 25 years' hard labour, which meant she would be free within a year. Well, wasn't that an excellent factual background for the plot of my future book! I would have to hurry and get it written as fast as possible.

Next morning my little car's engine was turning over while the cook was still warming up saucepans of milk for our morning porridge. This way, nobody could bother me with stupid questions. I told only the girl at reception that I was heading off for the whole day on a car trip.

I didn't reach Novogorsk until lunchtime. I needed to find one of the waiting staff who could still remember the events of more than twenty years ago; someone elderly enough, but not yet senile. Quite quickly I came across a very well-informed and with-it old lady, who had spent her whole life living inside the Novogorsk town limits and sincerely considered it the centre of the world. The local food and air were, clearly, very helpful for human organisms, since this 80-year-old grandmother was completely compos mentis and even very sharp in her recollections.

"So tell me, this poor girl, who went to prison in the end, what was she like? I suppose she was a very poor, simple, ordinary kind of girl?" I led up subtly to the question that interested me.

"When it all happened, Nina was already far from being a girl, but a woman about thirty, and maybe older than that," the old lady settled into her tale. "And it'd be hard to call her simple. We never could understand why she was working with us as ordinary waiting staff. She was such an interesting young woman, with a mind of her own, and she'd been quite well educated. She was single, that was the only thing, that's probably why she joined us, in the hope of catching a nice man. After all there were mostly men living at the hotel, and the best sort, too! Former, future and present athletes – a good selection box."

"So the problem was that she became bitter because none of them wanted to marry her, and she decided to send all of them to the next world at the same time? A sort of 'if I can't have you, no-one will'?"

"I think the investigators thought the same way you did. But that wouldn't have been at all like Nina. The truth is that she was a very gentle person. She was even a vegetarian."

"Well, so what that she was a vegetarian," I shrugged. "Hitler didn't eat meat either. And was she good-looking? Do you have any photos of her?"

"As if I could still find them after all these years!"

However, the old lady did find some photos after all; I just had to insist a bit harder and project enthusiastic interest.

From the old computer monitor, a typical girl from Central Russia looked out. Perfectly pleasant-looking. Only her gaze betrayed a sense of weakness and confusion. Her smoky grey eyes brought to mind a newborn kitten. The snap had been taken at a New Year party for the staff, somewhere in their quarters, clearly clandestinely. All the girls had on identical dresses with high starched collars. They'd pushed their hair up high, in tall bouffant piles, as waitresses often must. There were no fancy party costumes, only ribbons of multi-coloured tinsel draped over their shoulders. There was one bottle of cheap champagne between all of them, and identical blue aprons over the white dresses.

I studied Nina's face again. Damn it! It wasn't an accidental resemblance. There was the same small, slightly turned-up nose, the same high forehead, the same T-shaped figure, which not even the waitress's uniform could soften. And the same unmanicured hands with short, strong fingers. In one hand, Nina was awkwardly holding a glass of champagne, extending it in the direction of the camera. She did this so clumsily that the simple gesture betrayed she wasn't used to drinking champagne. Her hand was obviously more accustomed to heavy, thick-bottomed glasses. She had hooked the index finger of her other hand into the pocket of her apron, the way men usually hide theirs in their jeans pocket, leaving most of the palm exposed above the fabric.

"Tell me, did this Nina by any chance have an odd habit of carrying in one of her pockets blank pieces of paper, cut to about the size of your palm, scribbling on them, and then popping them into the other pocket?"

"What's strange about doing that?" the old lady looked at me over her glasses. "All waitresses get that habit. In the left pocket you put the clean sheets for orders. When you've filled them out, you put them in the right pocket."

"I get it," I nodded. Everything was making sense. "And did you ever think that perhaps this girl wasn't married because she wasn't interested in men? That she might have a non-traditional sexual orientation?"

"Nothing of the kind! Nina had a perfectly normal orientation, like everyone else. She even had a lover: one of the guests. He didn't visit too often, and of course, they tried to be discreet, but everyone knew that she was hopping into bed with him at night. But she can't have been so hot between the sheets, because he only came once every six months or so, and he never took her away with him."

"Really?" I was genuinely surprised. "And what was this guy like?"

"A very well-known individual," the old lady arched her brows significantly. "That's why I can't say anything about him; we're not allowed to talk about the guests, how they behaved here, how they train and how they relax, we're never to talk about that to anyone. That's just the kind of place it is. We look after our own."

"And he was holidaying here when that incident with the footballers happened?"

"Well, I really can't remember now. But afterwards, when Nina had already been imprisoned, he used to come here. And you could see he was troubled. He was boozing heavily. Maybe he loved her after all and he'd made plans for her?"

It already failed to surprise me that the heroine of my projected book had coincidentally turned out to be a fellow resident at the old people's home. I even suspected that this was unlikely to be freak chance. Sooner or later, I was sure, I'd discover a logical explanation for this unexpected connection.

Just as it wasn't a coincidence that I'd found myself living side by side with my husband's lover, so it wasn't simply a whim of fate that Nata had followed Tatiana into The Mounds. People are like cranberries; pick up one, and all the others follow like beads linked by fine threads. As they say, there are no coincidences or chances in life, just things we haven't fully understood yet.

I still had to find out who this mysterious guy was. This would obviously explain a great deal. The perfect method of discovering his name would be dosing Nina with a truth drug and forcing her to disclose everything. A splendid idea! Where could I get hold of the necessary pharmaceuticals? After all, the secret services used them. But they'd hardly share a drop of their magic potion with me.

My search for clues led me to examine the photo-archive of honoured guests at the resort's training centre. But there I found an entire gallery of venerable and famous men; picking out any one face was completely impossible. I was stalled!

One faint hope still remained: it was just possible that those scraps of paper, tirelessly scribbled on by Nina, might provide some sort of hint or clue. I would have to steal them! Theft is a fairly risky business. I'd need a confederate, preferably a man, since our lesbian friend was physically pretty well developed and could certainly do me some damage if she caught me in the act.

For the first time, I regretted not acquiring a single suitor at the home. I urgently needed to fix this omission. Of course, I wouldn't immediately confide to him all the details of the business. People make much less fuss when you keep them in the dark. Moreover, when they think they're doing no more than joining in some jolly prank, rather than an important investigation, they don't expect to gain anything special from the outcome.

In a word, what I needed was a strong, enthusiastic, brave and not excessively bright guy, who wouldn't ask unnecessary questions. Over supper I examined the faces of all our menfolk, trying to imagine how well each of them matched this description. In principle, every other man could have done for the role. Evidently, this type of man is particularly likely to live to a moderately advanced age, the kind who isn't inclined to over-deep contemplation, never undermining his brain with a mass of unnecessary questions. Those who live to a ripe old age are cheerful types, always ready to launch into some merry whim: eternal children.

"Even here one can have quite a good time," I admitted, for the first time since I came here. And my thoughts drifted off in a rather naughty direction.

I took a chance and chose my Sancho Panza on the basis of a game of mental eeny, meeny, miny, moe. I finished the game; the random result pleased me. This old man could be considered handsome without too many disclaimers and objections. He was tall, not at all bent, with a thick head of grey, but still glossy hair. He had entirely unobjectionable dentures, and his loud, infectious laugh rang out at all the jokes his friends were cracking at dinner. In a word, I liked him. I made my plans for the evening: I set off to catch myself a man.

That evening, typically for early June, was warm, mosquito-ridden, and windless. Our lake had blossomed with algae, making it look like cream of spinach soup. The sun was reflected in the far side of the lake like an egg-yolk. A sense of well-being and satisfaction prevailed.

The pensioners were picking the remnants of dinner out of their teeth with toothpicks, combing their hair and changing into clean clothes. They were gathering in the wood nearby for a campfire party. This was the first time I'd gone to one of these evening get-togethers. Expectations ran high. My light-blue jeans worked extremely well with my velvet turquoise blouse from Victoria's Secret. Perfume in weather like this would have been excessive: I simply rubbed a spoonful of scented honey over my lips, to give them an alluring shine. I slipped into my brassiere some rose-petals I'd gathered from a bush before dinner. I went into the courtyard, where the usual gang had already gathered for the party. And off we went.

We quickly reached the "ceremonial glade". While the men tramp around it like bears, charging through the naturally decayed birches which had sprung up higgledy-piggledy in the pine wood, the women coquettishly strolled wide of them, raising their knees high with every step. It was as if they were trying not to damage the tall but still succulent grass with their elderly shuffle. They gathered brushwood, so I did too.

At last the bonfire blazed up; a thick pillar of smoke rose from the pine needles. The pensioners froze expectantly, staring into the flames, as if trying to feed it energy by the power of collective meditation. At last, beer and plastic glasses appeared.

We began with the traditional games played in such situations – "Crocodile" and "Contact". Gradually, people started paying less attention to what was going on and split up into smaller groups. I continued to sit by myself. I was in seventh heaven from the unexpected sensation of calm and peace with the world. I completely lacked either the strength or the desire to start actively attracting attention. But life and the gender balance (or rather, imbalance) in our residence were such that in order to be noticed by the male minority, a woman had to be extremely conspicuous. I sensed my body was gradually relaxing and filling with warmth as the fire crackled. My body was becoming a balloon. I didn't even want to talk, let alone use body language or chuckle enticingly, tossing my head back, over the jokes the men were passing from group to group. I know that men melt when women laugh at their unfunny jokes. But this time I abstained.

From time to time, somebody passed me a plastic glass filled with various fluids (to judge by the fragrance, perfectly nice). But I refused, taking the ever-changing odours as an additional aroma-therapeutic bonus to my relaxation. I gazed into the fire. Voices hummed all around. I half-closed my eyes and stared down the bridge of my nose. The world had become enchantingly fuzzy. All the sharp lines between objects had vanished and everything blended softly. Then I closed my eyes completely, but through my lids the dancing flames were still visible and alternating shapes of light and shadow crossed my internal eye. Thus I experimented, meditated, and got completely distracted from my mission.

When I returned to reality and half-opened my eyes, I realized that, naturally enough, I'd drifted off, collapsed against a pine trunk. Around me a cluster of my more responsible comrades had gathered. I managed to spot the most important detail: the handsome guy I'd picked out was among them. I made an instant mental calculation of all the advantages of my position and immediately pretended to be deeply asleep. But I eavesdropped attentively. I knew they'd start trying to wake me up at any moment. I'd need to do a good imitation of waking up. Damn! Yet it was also a stroke of luck: I hadn't even had to make a spectacle of myself in order to get everyone's attention. I'd have to add a new law to my psychological profiling of the male sex, such as

Rule No X:

In the Brownian motion of women it's not the most bright and active one that draws male attention, but the most immobile. Stillness is a challenge.

If only I'd known this earlier, how much energy I could have saved myself. Now I finally understood how Sleeping Beauty had created a sensation despite lying there like a log. Meanwhile, the high-level conference on how to restore me to consciousness continued.

"Sonya! Sonya! Wake up!" different voices were calling me. But I only curled up sleepily.

Everyone in turn leaned over me and tried shaking me by the shoulder. I snuggled more securely into my velvet blouse, clinging limply to my tree-trunk. Finally my handsome guy also decided to try his strength as an alarm clock. And when his hand touched my shoulder, in order to rouse "slumbering Sonya", I turned my head to one side as if half-asleep – but in reality I was on full alert – and smartly pinned his hand against my shoulder with my ear. At once I innocently opened my eyes, gazing straight into his, as if I'd taken fright and been reassured by seeing him.

"Oh! Did I fall asleep? Is everything over already?" I displayed charming incompetence and confusion. "Goodness, why am I sitting here?"

I started to stand up and held out my hand to the handsome guy for support. Once I'd taken his hand, I had no plans to just let go. I slipped my arm through his, and leant my head on his shoulder: "Oh! I really am sleepy! Isn't it so cosy here in the wood! But it's cold! Can I snuggle up under your coat? I feel chilly after my snooze."

Without waiting for permission, I slipped inside his coat, like a chick hiding under the hen's wing, and slid my arm round him. We walked all the way back like this. I know how to hook myself on to people. It's one of the great journalistic talents, you can't get anywhere without it.

"How amusing, here we are walking along with our arms around each other, and I don't even know your name!" I giggled up at him, from somewhere under his armpit.

"Yuri."

"What a marvellous name! I really like the name Yuri. It has special meaning for me."

"You don't say?" he drawled distrustfully.

I brought us both to a halt: "Wait! Say that again!"

"What?"

"Well, whatever you like!" I put my ear to his chest. "You've got such a great voice, when I listen from here, beside your heart. You must speak from the heart. Say something else!"

"Sonya, are you coming on to me?" he started laughing.

Things were not going quite as they should in my planned scenario. I tittered in embarrassment, but maintained my grip on his sweater.

"Well, maybe I am. I fancy you. I'm making eyes at you, flirting a bit. Yes, I like you. You're cool. You're so handsome and good-humoured. I really want you to like me."

He took a deep breath, ready to reply. Hastily, I put my finger to his lips: "Shhhh! Hush, don't say anything. Not a word, not now! Let's go on into the village and steal a carrot from the local farmers? Or go skinny-dipping? Do you know how warm the water is right now?" I carefully removed my finger from Yuri's lips, waiting anxiously for his reply, looking him in the eye. Hurrah! His answer was even better than I'd hoped: "I've got a better idea. I'll show you a special place. You'll like it."

It turned out we had a long way to go, about three kilometres. And I was very pleased that he dragged me to such a distant place; it meant that he had no intention of making a quick getaway. We walked along in just the same way: I kept my arms around him, he covered me with his coat.

"You smell so good!" I said, sighing loudly, and thrusting my nose into his chest.

"So do you, like a rose," he replied.

We walked along the road to the village. It was soft with dust; the sky was brightening, and the turn-ups of our jeans became damp with dew. Finally, we got there. Yuri led me onto the raised bank of the river.

"This is the river Nerle," he said.

The stream turned here abruptly towards the rising sun, as if the river had suddenly realized it was flowing in the wrong direction and commanded itself to go left. And there, in the new direction, the new day was beginning.

"How gorgeous!" I crooned.

"Humph! You ain't seen nothing yet." Yuri pulled me away, onto a low hill, where the ruins of an old church stood. It was strange that unrestored churches still remained in this area. I'd thought that in the 2000s, the Orthodox clergy had reconstructed all the ruins with crosses that it could get hold of. But this one stood in a completely abandoned village without a paved road leading to it. Probably even clerics had failed to see any point in the project. We crept through the old churchyard, passing rusted crosses thrusting out of low mounds that were almost level with the ground. Yuri confidently led the way to the church itself. We climbed up by a narrow spiral staircase, which trembled alarmingly under our feet. In places we had to step over gaps where two or three rungs were missing. We clambered up to the belfry. There, where we stood, a hundred and fifty years ago people had gone in black robes to ring the bell. Now it was overgrown with wormwood, rough grasses and even small birches. Instead of an onion dome, the dilapidated roof yawned over our heads, here and there pierced by blinking stars. It was getting noticeably brighter. The horizon was a molten line, while there was already a hint of the heat of the coming day in the chilly air. From this height, the earth looked like a living being, thickly furred with forest, through which the river cut like a vein.

"I come here in the evenings to sketch the sunset," Yuri said, as if to himself.

"Why not the dawn? Surely the dawn must be just as glorious here!" I clapped my hands ecstatically.

"Just because it's the sunset."

He pulled out a picnic blanket out from somewhere. We sat side by side on it. I slipped downwards and laid my head on his knee. We silently watched the sun swimming straight towards us. When its shining edge stood clearly above the horizon, Yuri bent down and kissed the hair on my temple.

"Let's go," he whispered.

Yuri turned out to be a truly nice guy. I occasionally even had rumblings of conscience, knowing it was questionable to use him while keeping him in the dark. When the following day, blue with cold but glowing with pride, he laid before me the last surviving crab from the Nerle, I almost thought of abandoning my scheme. When he harrowed half the sandy lakeshore with his body as he headed and passed completely hopeless goals in a game of beach volleyball, and then victoriously glanced my way, I wanted to hug him and pat him on the head. I saw the envious glances of the other women who sought his attention, and I realized that I'd been ridiculously lucky, that I'd picked up the man coveted by most of the female population of The Mounds. How had I failed to notice before that we had such an attractive man in our residence? Most likely, if I'd realized earlier the value of the prize and the level of competition, I would never have decided to go after him so casually and spontaneously. And even if I had decided, nothing would have come of it. We always solve problems more easily when we think they're going to be straightforward and manageable, even if they are in reality considerably more complicated. As soon as you imagine something is going to be almost impossible, that's what it becomes.

When Yuri knocked on my door after supper and

invited me to come to a "little campfire, just for friends", I melted. Nonetheless I resisted my sentimental feelings and methodically set about grooming Yuri for his predetermined role as a blind tool of espionage.

The "little campfire" was quite impressive. When Yuri and I, as a pair of late-ripening young lovers, showed up at the campfire considerably later than the others, everyone regarded us understandingly: Nata, Alla, that dreadful Dimon and two of his companions, the same ones who'd first assaulted me physically over my literary critique. Nata was fussing over a bag of food, ordering us all around in her low, chesty voice. Dimon was paying court to Alla, rubbing her with anti-mosquito lotion and pushing the driest log under her bottom. It must have been precisely his jealous defence of her art that had earned Dimon this post with the former literary superstar, now newly restored to her position. My Yuri and Dimon turned out to be friends, it was pure chance that Yuri hadn't been among the guys who'd used their fists to make me surrender the manuscripts of our local writers. Now all of this had, of course, become grist for jokes. Nobody was afraid of me any more. Everyone understood that my days as a critic were over. And although the incident had been smoothed over, it still came up in conversation.

"Now tell us, Sonya, were we really so terrible and did we really scare you so much?" Dimon laughed drunkenly, winking at Alla.

"How did you manage to live for a week in a wood without any comforts?" Alla joined in.

"I had a wonderful week," I laughed. "During that week I became a completely different person. Word of honour."

"You don't say," Nata drawled, cutting up some meat into strips for the grill.

In an unnecessarily candid impulse (I probably wanted to stay the centre of attention for longer), I immediately admitted, that while I was parked in the wood not far from Chekhov's house-museum, I'd never put down my pen; I'd also started scribbling. I also admitted that I finally fully understood the pensioners' urge to compose. And I owned that it wasn't worth insulting their genuine desire for self-expression. And that if it was worth criticizing writers at all, then only those who aspired to be included among the Classics with a capital C and therefore demanded serious analysis and criticism. Only this kind of writing deserved critical scrutiny, although even that wasn't true every time. But if a person wasn't aiming for a paragraph in a textbook of literary history, then let him write, as God inspired him.

"Overall, the most important thing I've learned is that I won't find a better place or a better community in which to write my book. Only here can a writer feel at peace, knowing that the guys here will be supportive and protect them from mean-spirited criticism. So Nata, Dimon, and all my other friends, I ask you to take me under your wing and protect me."

"We've got to drink to that!" growled Dimon.

Nata was smiling. She looked completely satisfied with her double victory.

"Won't you tell us what you're planning to write?" she enquired, rotating the strips of meat. "That same story about yourself, your husband, and some others?" she winked meaningfully.

"Of course not! You underestimate me," I flared up. "I told that story just to you." I pronounced the last words with particular emphasis, so she understood not to spread it. "You think my imagination is so poor that I can't write about anything other than my own sexual problems? Life is full of other stories. I've already been attracted by one and I'm going to include all the participants in the drama. I've already taken a reconnaissance trip to gather material and ideas."

"Really?" Now everyone was staring at me with interest. "So where did you go? And what's the story about?" Questions rained on me from every side.

"This is a story about death for the sake of dedication.

And my fact-finding mission was to a private sports and recreation centre called Novogorsk."

I was so intoxicated by my moment of triumph that I missed the way Nata stared at me just then. Yet she must have given me a very strange look. I regretted afterwards that I had concentrated all my attention on how I was presenting myself, and not on how my audience was reacting to my speech.

No matter how my fellow drinkers pressed me, I decided not to reveal any more that evening. I had to torment my public a little, pump up some tension, in order to guarantee continued success. I hadn't even noticed the way Nata tried to change the subject by starting to bustle about:

"Right! Who wants some meat? The bird's done already, hand me your plates!"

We tucked in. We chatted desultorily, telling unfunny stories and laughing at them loudly. Pot appeared from somewhere, which I virtuously refused. When everyone was stoned, I had another impulse to cajole them:

"Dear friends! I understand that our tiny literary circle doesn't need a critic. But positive reviews, in my opinion, are actually highly desirable for any creative artist. Let's write eulogies for each other and put them on display!"

Right there, around the fire, we began composing songs of praise for each other. They turned out to be highly comic. At one point I was standing on a stump declaiming dithyrambs in praise of Alla Maksimova. I only remember that I managed to rhyme the "counter-spelling" and "compelling". Or something of the sort...

While the guys collectively pissed in the campfire (to extinguish it), we girls slowly made our way along the forest path in the direction of the home, giggling for no particular reason. Fortunately, the men caught up with us fairly quickly and Dimon drew Alla off somewhere to one side. Yuri and I also very conveniently fell behind. I hung on his sleeve and kept talking, in a rush of inspiration: "No, I really think that we have to set up an institute of 'benevolent literary criticism' in our residence. And I'm willing to provide it. I've dreamed all my life of being another Vissarion Belinsky.[1] I want to reveal new talents and draw attention to them. That's why I tried to be a critic as soon as I got here. By sheer stupidity I got the wrong end of the stick. Instead of immediately acting the way I wanted to, praising people, I decided to set myself up as an authority and be critical. Although, in my heart of hearts, I don't think either Alla or Tatiana are without talent. They write very sincerely, and that's valuable in itself."

I fooled Yuri as cunningly as I could. It looked like I'd pulled off my main goal: I made him believe that the only reason our geriatric community wasn't familiar with Nina the lesbian's work was that she was terrified of criticism, extremely shy, in dread of corrosive meltdown, and that was why she carefully concealed her writings in the right back pocket of her trousers. That was why she'd attacked me so fiercely – she saw any kind of criticism as a threat to herself.

"I think she's writing wonderful, very affecting poetry, love lyrics," I brought Yuri to a halt by hanging onto him with my whole weight. "Poets are particularly vulnerable. They're so much more thin-skinned than prose writers. And while novelists and short story writers eagerly distribute their works to the masses, poets are very reserved. I think that Nina is writing verse. And she's terribly afraid that they'll start laughing at her and scribbling graffiti about her. That's why she can't make up her mind to share her work. That's it! I've got it! Goodness, just listen to what I've come up with!"

I quite naturally gave the impression that the brilliant notion of thieving Nina's scrawled-on scraps of paper (on which poems of genius were written) had just come to me. I convinced Yuri that Nina was longing for enthusiastic reviews of her poetry, and that we would be doing her a huge favour if we broke into her room, filched a few pages, and printed them with gushing commentaries.

---

[1] 19th-century radical literary critic who famously became the first to discover Dostoevsky's talent.

I inspired him to such a degree that he was ready to go and blindside Nina right then, if only to purloin her poems. I persuaded him to wait until tomorrow.

The next thing was to lure Nina out of her room, if only for forty minutes. I had promised Yuri that I would come up with a solution. I had no doubt that my inventive brain could think of something. However, not a single worthwhile idea entered my head when I was cleaning my teeth in the morning, nor over breakfast. I started to worry.

"Well, when shall we do it?" Yuri, finishing his morning omelette, cocked his chin inquiringly.

"After supper," I nodded confidently, and hurried off to my room in order to peacefully form a plan in private.

But everything seemed to conspire against me that day. I had hardly shut the door behind me and switched on my laptop to check how people were lured out of their homes in detective novels and true-life criminal tales, when someone knocked. It was Nata.

"Listen, last night you really intrigued me with that story about this book you're going to write. Own up, what are you writing about?"

"About death in the name of duty, like I said yesterday," I replied evasively.

"Who dies? From what?"

"You'll find out everything when I write it," I had no intention of discussing this; I had other things on my mind.

"And the action happens in Novogorsk?"

"Yes, like I already said," I answered, slightly irritated.

"So it's about the footballers who died?" Nata said, as if spontaneously guessing. Although there was little enough to guess: there couldn't have been so very many high-profile deaths in Novogorsk.

"Clever girl, you got it! That wasn't too difficult. After all, deaths aren't so common in that health resort."

"Have you got some inside information?"

"Well, I might have something," I wanted to look

mysterious, and I wasn't about to admit that apart from the drunken theories of the wife of my old friend from the security forces I had absolutely nothing up my sleeve.

"Did that friend of yours in the police tell you something?"

"Well, he happened to be on holiday there when it all happened. But I have other information too."

Nata started pressing me rather angrily, insisting I tell her everything. I wanted to get rid of her as fast as I could. Our conversation grew uncomfortable.

"You know that that woman who poisoned them will be out of prison within a year?" Nata wasn't giving up.

"Of course I know," I said, and here I finally realized that Nata was showing more than an idle interest, in fact, she knew the subject very thoroughly. I was instantly eager to know what lay behind her questions.

"Come on, admit it, do you have something to do with this case?"

Nata just compressed her lips.

"And did you know that that Shalimova woman was already free long ago?" I deliberately prodded Nata by getting Nina's surname wrong.

"Shalamova," she corrected me automatically. "How did you know she'd been freed? Did your friend tell you that? Do you know where she is?"

"I know, but I won't tell you," I was cheered by the knowledge that I seemed to be the only person in the home who knew Nina's secret, since she had settled here under the surname Tretyakova.

"I need to know where she is," Nata said very meaningfully. "I need to meet her. It is absolutely vital that I see her."

"And what makes you think she wants to see you? Perhaps you're a secret Dynamo supporter, thirsting for revenge?"

"It isn't funny. I have to give her something that I'm sure she needs."

"I'll think about it. I need to consider everything."

I saw Nata off with difficulty and sat down, exhausted, on my bed. I no longer had any doubts that Nina and Nata were in the same home for a reason. That they'd arrived here in pursuit of each other. And if Nata Sokolova wasn't aware that our local lesbian was none other than Nina Shalamova, whom she needed to meet, it meant Nina must be following Nata, not the other way round. Clearly Nina knew that Nata possessed something she needed, and was waiting for the moment to steal it from her. But why hadn't she stolen this thing before now? Both women had already lived in The Mounds for some time. I couldn't figure it out! To hell with it! How complicated everything had gotten. The pieces just didn't fit together, and time was rushing away. And I still hadn't found a solution to the day's main problem: how were we going to lure Nina out of her lair?

In the end, having failed to come up with anything cleverer, I ripped a sheet out of a notebook and, disguising my handwriting, scrawled:

"Come this evening at 7.30 to the burnt-out shop. This is important."

I crept down the empty corridor to Nina's room and slipped the note under her door. At supper, I couldn't taste my food. I was constantly looking from Nina to the clock. Nina was obviously on edge, and that reassured me; it meant she was planning to meet the mysterious stranger.

Yuri and I ate our meals rather hastily, evaded our friends and, putting on a show of being overtired from the sun, ran off to our rooms, having planned to meet at Nina's cell at precisely 19.20. We even synchronized our watches, like they do in spy films.

As I'd flung open my door, ready to go and carry out the theft as planned, I started in fright. There, outside my door, stood Nata. She was just about to knock. Her other hand held a small parcel.

"Can I come in?" Nata pushed me to one side and marched in as if she owned the room. "Here's what I've got to give Shalamova. Have a look and you'll understand how important it is. She genuinely needs it."

Nata handed me a very heavy envelope. I peeked inside: it was full of papers, a printed-off text.

"Read it!" Nata ordered. "Just don't ask me any questions about it. There's more than enough written there to make everything you need to know perfectly plain. And not a word to anyone!"

"I'm sorry, but I can't read it right this minute," I hopped from one foot to the other anxiously, realizing that I was already quite late. "I'm in a rush, I have a date. Leave it here and I'll read it tonight."

Reluctantly, Nata placed the envelope on my table; clearly, she'd imagined that we would arrange everything on the spot and that she'd leave with contact info for Nina. But now I was calling the shots. We left together, and I locked the door. I had to pretend that I was on my way out; as soon as I could I rushed back into the building, to the corridor, where Yuri was already tapping his fingers on the wall impatiently.

Fortunately, he was dependable and had already dealt with his share of the job. He'd extracted the spare key to our local Sappho's room from the warden on duty.

We glanced around us like criminals, unlocked the door and rushed into terra incognita. We rushed to the desk and started wrenching the drawers open. We found what we were looking for immediately. A mass of sheets bound with string into solid postcard-sized bundles! They looked just like a library catalogue. We each grabbed a packet and began eagerly reading.

I turned over the first page, the second, third, fourth. I couldn't make any sense of it. What was I holding in my hands? The very same words had been entered on every page:

When you love somebody, that person can't die.
Love is a force that conquers everything.
It forces cities to grow.

It sends rockets into space.

It inspires; invents; creates; leads; gives life a new beginning; and that means it can bring people back to life.

The person you love can't die while he's alive in your heart. All you have to do is refuse to forget.

Repeat these words every day, believe, hope, and wait. And one day you'll see how true this is.

The one you love will come back to you. And he'll tell you how much he loves you. Even if he didn't manage to do this in his first life.

Copy this message a thousand times and when you copy it for the ten thousandth time, something will happen.

Every page was numbered. I looked through my bundle quickly: 8125, 8126, 8127, 8128…

The paper changed, so did the handwriting and the colour of the ink: only the text remained the same.

"Do you understand what this is?" I asked uncomprehendingly. Yuri's eyes were wide open; he was still ruffling the sheets.

"Seems like somebody she loved died."

"Right. And now she's writing a chain letter, believing she can bring the person back to life this way."

"She's even crazier than we all thought," Yuri whispered loudly, with a trace of horror.

"I'd like to know for whom she's driving herself mad? The answer to that question must be in this room!" My brain suddenly seemed to switch on. "Let's find it, quickly!" I slipped my packet of chain letters into my pocket and started opening as many drawers as I could.

"What are we looking for?" Yuri was giving me a look I didn't like; he put his brick-sized bundle of recipes for resurrection back in the writing desk.

"I don't know! Some photos! Letters! Diaries! Something that will help us to understand to whom these eight thousand notes are dedicated!"

"No, Sonya, we're not going to do that," Yuri sternly grabbed my hand, already rooting through the wardrobe. "You're going to put back the papers you stole right now, and we're going to beat it out of here."

"Not likely!" I hissed. "Not if I have anything to do with it!"

"Sonya! This isn't what we agreed. We came here to get poems. There aren't any poems, so we have nothing more to do here. There's no need to get involved in people's personal, very personal, affairs."

Yuri roughly put his hands in my pocket, trying to pull out the papers I'd appropriated. I howled and slapped his hand. He grabbed me firmly and started searching me. There are certainly disadvantages in keeping your confederates in the dark. When they don't understand all the subtleties of the task facing them, they try to spoil everything at the last minute.

While we were grappling furiously, our precious time was melting away.

"This is important! You don't know everything that's involved! Let's get out of here, and I'll explain it all to you later!"

Yuri didn't give way. We had wasted too much time: Nina could appear at any moment. As, indeed, appear she did. She didn't even seem very surprised to catch us out.

"I knew I was being decoyed on purpose," she blinked her stubby eyelashes tiredly, taking in our rumpled appearance. For some reason she didn't fly into a fury. "Want some tea, sneak-thieves?"

I realized she wasn't planning to beat me up this time, and my courage and confidence returned.

"I wouldn't say no," I tried to look as if nothing out of the ordinary had happened.

And that idiot Yuri immediately started to ruin everything, launching into stammering apologies. What a useless fool! And I'd expected masculine support and protection from him! I glared at him, signalling him to shut up. I realized I had to get rid of him rapidly, dump him. It looked as if he wanted to leave but didn't know how. I made it easy for him:

"Yuri, I dragged you into this. You don't even know what you got involved in. And I think it would be best for everyone if you leave now. I need to sort out this situation alone."

The old guy resisted a bit for form's sake, putting on a show of chivalry and high moral principles, but not too much. Then, with a sigh of relief, he shut the door behind him. The last thing he did was shoot me a meaningful glance.

Finally, Nina and I were alone.

"You can carry on looking for whatever you need," Nina offered, not without a hint of mockery.

"Sorry," I finally judged the time right to apologize. "Tell me, who is this person you write about in your letters?"

"Why should I tell you about it?" Nina was looking at me in a way which made all half-truths, games, and coquetry seem out of place.

"Because I really want to know. I even think that it may be important for me to know. I know a lot about you. And I don't believe that you poisoned those poor bloody footballers." Nina tensed her whole body just noticeably, then got herself under control. "What's more, I have something you desperately need. And I need a reason to give it to you."

"What's this thing you have?"

"I don't yet know myself what it is. It's a bunch of papers, and they're for you; and by all the signs they've been waiting many years for you."

When she heard me say this, Nina reacted as if she'd just taken a nip of spirits: she relaxed and sank back in her chair. It seemed she really had been waiting anxiously for some documents. How neatly everything had come together!

"Have you read them?" Nina frowned at me. I shook my head.

"Well, why shouldn't I tell you? I have absolutely nothing to fear. I've done my time."

"Don't you mean, you've done someone else's time?"

"We'll get to that!"

I realized I didn't need to persuade, distract or pressure her any longer. If you want water to flood out, all you have to do is make one hole in a dam, and the water does the rest by itself, bearing away the fragments of the barriers that held it back. As a journalist, I knew this very well. When a person has kept silent about something for a long time, concealing a secret, and then suddenly decides to tell all, he'll tell his tale minutely, emotionally, sincerely, not leaving out a single detail. You can only tell a story this way once. It's crucial to be beside such a person with a recording device when the dam breaks; then you've got an excellent shock-horror article.

"I know there are rumours here that I was a copywriter in a big advertising agency," Nina began. "I started them myself. And they're true. I worked in advertising and had some pretty major clients. I was responsible for naming products and services, texts for street posters, radio and TV advertising reels, PR memes, publicity events. Everything was really going well. All my emotional and mental energy, all my life-force, was pouring into this media tunnel. You can imagine what it was like: jumping up in the middle of the night in order to scribble into my bedside notebook some rubbish like: 'Video: baby born, walk in the park, first snow, ankle-deep in waves and so on. Voiceover: the best moments in life are free. Sony lets you turn them on whenever you want'. After writing this down, you suddenly feel a wave of extraordinary pride in yourself for being so creative, and then right afterwards, like a hangover, you're engulfed by a feeling of existential meaninglessness and emptiness. The emptiness of everything, including your nocturnal inspiration, and your 'creative' yesterday and your 'productive' tomorrow. Probably, from the intellectual point of view, my work was no worse than hundreds of other jobs, like being a bank teller or a caretaker. Perhaps if I'd been married or I'd had a child, I wouldn't have had time to tie my brains in a knot. But for whatever reason, I lived alone. Have you noticed how many brilliant, beautiful, successful females of our generation have never been fulfilled as women? I remember how at the start of the 2000s, you'd walk into any sushi-bar on a weekend, and there'd be dozens of women in their late twenties wielding chopsticks at every table, either alone or in single-sex couples. And I'd sit down as well and dig into some rice with my chopsticks, read a fashionable book, then I'd go get a manicure or a pedicure, I'd go to my Spanish lesson, then I'd call on another unattached girlfriend or even go to a concert or a nightclub. Sometimes I even woke up with some guy. But I'd still feel completely cut off from whoever it was, totally alone. It was as if I were missing the organ you need to make emotional attachments.

"Loneliness, creative work, when you have to be in a sort of shallow trance all the time, part-immersed in a different state of consciousness with a different logic, or better still with no logic at all, but pure distilled emotions – that was the way I lived. The ability to capture particular conditions and moods and to find the right words to plunge listeners into that mood – that was my work. After all, people buy emotions, atmosphere, not just a bunch of carbohydrates in cholesterol glaze. People buy a different life. You seduce them, you entice them, you distract them, you're a witch, a shaman, a magician.

"All of this makes you stop feeling the ground beneath your feet. It's as if you're living in the eye of a whirlwind, suspended above the earth. And then downshifting came into fashion. Suddenly everyone was writing about it everywhere, it was the fashionable topic for conversation. And then one day I just lost it: I left my job in a hurry and went off to live a simple, natural life in the lap of the land. I found a job which made minimal demands on my brain. I started working as a waitress in Novogorsk. But, as you know, an unquiet mind always finds something to worry about. Even in a vacuum it'll find a subject for reflection and a topic around which it can wind a thread of thoughts. I found my 'mental spindle' quite quickly.

"At the start, I read a lot, went for long walks, kept a diary, and even got interested in handicrafts. Basically, I lived just like a typical old maid, some impoverished noblewoman stranded in the countryside. The only thing that spoiled my resemblance to, for example, Pushkin's heroine Tatiana Larina, was my lack of any secret passion, any unlucky romantic history. I hadn't had an unrequited love or an 'elevated passion' or a Messianic eccentricity. I could hardly endow any schools for peasant children, found a hospital for the poor, or eat my heart out for a state councillor. But things didn't continue this way for long. Quite soon, it all changed. I found a man, who immediately came to mean everything for me... More than likely, at that time it could have been anyone, because I was looking for just such a man. For someone, who could become the centre of my universe..."

Nina spotted her man as soon as he arrived at the resort. He clearly wasn't an athlete: his delicate build and constantly fuddled expression gave him away. But his eyes didn't wander aimlessly. Quite the opposite: he looked deeply into the eyes of everyone who spoke to him. It was as if he was looking for something in another's eyes, practically demanding by his look that his interlocutor immediately and without any prelude reveal their whole interior life to him. He was searching for a somebody inside everyone he met. He was looking for someone who was much more nervous, fragile and defenceless than they wanted to let on.

He was far from being your typical adrenal-driven, life-loving athlete. Nor was he an injured sportsman, constantly surveying his own body for signs of recovery. He gave the impression that he had completely forgotten about his body, and that he lived quite separate from it, carried along by inertia. He even walked in a rather ungainly way, as if all he could control was his legs' forward movement, and how and where they moved was none of his business. He seemed to toss his feet away from himself. His movements resembled those of a wooden puppet. His arms were the same. When he lit a cigarette at the bar, he literally dropped the lighter right on the table; he had only occupied his mind with it for just as long as it took to start the task, without actually finishing it.

Every morning he woke up looking as if he'd had a rough night. In fact, there was no "as if" about it. It was obvious every morning that he'd been drinking the night before. He always kept his mobile phone in sight, as if expecting an important call at any moment. He fiddled with it, felt to check it was in his pocket, like a rookie cop with his freshly issued pistol. If his mobile did ring, he would shudder, stare at the shining screen for a long time, then finally answer, speaking very fast. He spat words familiar to Nina: press-release, press-conference, PR-message. After hurriedly wrapping up the conversation, he'd drop the phone, like a heavy dumb-bell he'd been holding for half an hour.

He chose his meals carefully, standing at the buffet table with an empty plate for a long time. He'd size the food up, sniffing it; but as soon as he'd carried the plate to his table, he lost all interest and ate without looking at or savouring the food. He tossed mechanically down the hatch all those things he had just selected so scrupulously.

Nor did he resemble the company bosses who turned up in large numbers in Novogorsk, luxuriating in their well-being and relishing the process of filling their stomachs. He was a different type, rare in that setting, but quite common in others, especially advertising agencies. In her former life, Nina had seen plenty of such types. Expectedly, she was drawn to him, from sheer curiosity; she wanted to know what this scarecrow was doing in a temple dedicated to sport.

"So how do you like our chicken cutlets?" she asked him in an acidly cheerful tone, snatching his empty plate from under his nose. She spoke as if she were interested in the strength of the joint which was smoked at both ends, and not the taste of the reconstituted chicken legs.

"Cutlets?" He cocked his head and glanced around, as if

the cutlets might be floating somewhere in the vicinity. Then he gave a stoner's squeaky giggle and looked at his plate. "Oh, the cutlets, of course! I think they provided me with all the protein I need and stuffed my arteries with permissible levels of cholesterol, so today I hope to avoid having a hypertonic crisis or whatever you get from excess cholesterol! So you can be reassured that until tomorrow you have made this body of mine relatively assured of continued existence, as long as no nuclear reactors blow up tonight in Obninsk or some other closed town, causing a mass outbreak of mysterious deaths in the Moscow region."

He'd gotten carried away, and interrupted the flow of words with an effort.

"Well, if that's how it is, I advise you to have some seaweed salad for supper. They say iodine helps you survive radiation poisoning."

"You're right, I should have considered that too. I'll definitely follow your advice."

"Make sure you do! Our guests have to be the winners, whatever it takes, even when nuclear war breaks out. They have to be Citius, Altius, Fortius!"

"That's a rather limited slogan."

"Well, that pop group Viagra might have added to their song 'the higher the love, the deeper the kiss' a chorus in Latin: slower, lower, softer."

"Now what do you know, you've got a real chance of writing a new unforgettable hit and wrecking the brains of 90% of the population with those lines. You'll get rich and you can buy yourself a big house."

"I'm willing to let you use those words in your novel."

"My novel?" He tensed up so much he even seemed taller.

"Well, didn't you come here to write a novel?" Nina risked everything on the question.

"No, I'm not writing a novel," he giggled again and ruffled his hair. Clearly, Nina had hit the nail on the head. It wasn't difficult: old Dovlatov got it right; the majority of journalists, PR workers and advertising sloganeers really do dream of writing a novel. And they live their whole lives in expectation, savouring in advance that special day, when some supernatural sign or unique configuration of stars will suddenly take them by the arm, lead them to the keyboard and whisper the opening lines of their first book. Nina decided to play the role of this "finger of fate". Ultimately, this was the only interesting emotional or humanitarian entertainment which had remotely stimulated her in recent months. She decided to play Cassandra:

"So you're not writing? That's a real waste. I think you should definitely write a book. It'll work well for you. Honest Injun, I can see it all: you've got the right face for a literary encyclopaedia. So why aren't you writing?"

"That's a good question, but I'm afraid I don't have any good answers," he answered flirtatiously.

YES! Nina exhaled, adding aloud: "I think you could make an interesting tale out of anything, even Homer's catalogue of ships or who begot whom in the Old Testament."

"But various senile old men already told those boring stories before my time. It's all been done." He automatically took his cigarettes out of his pocket and reached for his lighter. At the last moment he remembered he could only smoke at the bar or on the street, not in the restaurant.

"Shall we go for a smoke?" Nina suggested, putting the tray down on the table. And they went outside.

Her intuition hadn't played her false: this character really was an artist in a state of creative paralysis. He worked for the police press department and was sick of the boredom and routine of daily work, dreaming of doing something big. He really was suffering the agony of creativity, trying to fashion his personal Text, which he couldn't quite bring to birth. He'd made an effort, but he'd had no results for so long that he'd even started to doubt there was anything inside him worthy or willing to be born. He'd begun thinking he was empty, creatively sterile.

"Well, as they say, if you can live without writing, don't write. Isn't that so?" he asked, concentrating fiercely on his shot of whiskey in order to bring it to his lips. "And it looks like I'm not compelled to write. It goes further: I can't write. That's the crux of the matter."

This conversation was taking place five hours after they'd met over his lunch; they were already in this untypical holidaymaker's room. It was late evening. The air from the street had breathed a wave of semi-transparent mosquitoes into his room; they were buzzing their aboriginal dances around the lamp. Nina and her new friend had to turn off the light. In the darkness, the alcohol they'd had made itself felt more boldly, even in those parts of the brain it shouldn't be able to touch. Like a horse-thief in the night, it silently and cleverly undid all the locks and opened all the doors.

Nina felt as if she were back in Moscow on the traditional office Friday night out, the kind the Japanese rather charmingly call 'nommunication' from their word nomu: a drinking spree where everyone begins by confessing their own talentlessness and insignificance, and, after getting steadily more drunk, crawls onto the table and yells that they're unacknowledged geniuses. She'd done it herself. It was a familiar, accustomed mood. She suddenly felt that what she missed more than anything else in her hermit-like existence were these Friday night bar crawls.

"Who taught you this stupid idea about not writing if you can live without it?" Nina asked. Alcohol had infused her with authority and aplomb. "Do you know how Victor Hugo wrote his most successful novel, *The Hunchback of Notre Dame*? Did you know that his wife took away his clothes and his food and locked him in his bedroom until he'd finished the manuscript? Once a day she opened a little hatch, just like in a prison cell, gave him his rations and collected his waste in a pail. Did you think he wrote because he couldn't get away from ink and paper? No, it was just because his wife believed he had it in him, and that this was the best thing he could do.

As for him, I bet he could have got by without writing; he had other interests. Do you see that 'don't write if you can help it' is the wrongest of all the phrases people say or think? It's a false truth, which people say deliberately to get off the right track. The same way they deliberately place a false wardrobe with a fake hearth beside a door leading to a perfect parallel universe or to a treasure. They do it so as to prevent you from falling into another, magical reality. People who have already been there guard the entrance, so that it won't get too crowded. Cowards say it, worried about their space at the real hearth. They don't know that everyone who gets there brings their own bundle of logs to the fire. And without these new people, the fire on the enchanted hearth will quickly go out. They think they can keep the fire burning with their own couple of logs. But in truth, the fire only continues because of these fresh newcomers, who won't accept anyone's word on face value, who pierce through the denials and the false hearths and reach the real thing. Only from the warmth of these fresh logs is a new blaze kindled in the dying coals of the old folks who have fallen asleep or even died around the chimney."

Nina had pretty much exaggerated herself into a Muse, a Margarita, a Gala Dali, and a Lily Brik rolled into one. Fiercely, with all her stored-up oxygen-starved energy, she devoted herself to playing this game. She literally ordered her Master to write. He submitted without demur. People usually submit very easily when you order them to do something they wanted to do anyway. They even start to love you a little for giving the order they wanted to give themselves; for opening the dam of their personal reservoir.

Nina and her Master developed a peculiar routine. Collecting the athletes' plates after breakfast, she'd remember what she and Misha had been writing together the night before. And she felt surprised that she'd been drawn into such a strange, unhealthy, and utterly genuine process. She felt as if right now, while she was smiling and wheeling her trolley between tables, she were really asleep. And that she would only wake up that evening, when she was once again sitting by Misha's laptop, and he'd started to pace the room, glass in one hand and cigarette in the other, and she would begin to visualize a different world. She would write to his dictation, without understanding how she could exist in that other world among the people he had invented, while her fingers continued to hit the keys on the pad without missing a letter. She lived over again the words she had blindly typed at night. Only in the mornings, as she collected plates smeared with the remnants of porridge, could she see his text in perspective, and not like a fish flung into the aquarium of his fantasies.

Towards lunch she felt slightly freer; she was able to watch the news and think about the outside world. For example, she could worry that the money in her purse was running out while there was still a whole week till payday. Or that the manager was watching her suspiciously. Or that her fellow staff were crassly persisting in offering her facial toner and powder and tactlessly reminding her that Guerlain "Happy Lodge" cream worked wonders for bags under the eyes. She genuinely could not understand what all these smirks and shuffles meant. What was the point of this petty hassle when right here in the resort, every night, a marvel was being created! Growing up between two plasterboard walls was a whole parallel world, so much greater, meaningful and genuine than all these fake-ceramic bowls and miserly wage packets. This night-time wonder made it ever more difficult for Nina to pretend to be an ordinary moo-cow, grateful for her glass of processed milk and clump of free hay. And all the time life was being created right there! Life! Although imaginary, this new life was so much more vital and sincere than any of the life she had lived before that she longed to shed her physical body and transmigrate into this fantastic world, which offered greater emotional honesty than all the petty things of this world taken together.

Nina was horribly divided. Sometimes, while she revolved in her mind scenes Misha had dictated to her the night before, she dropped glasses or froze in ludicrous positions, or gave answers that didn't make sense, or simply turned away from customers who had asked her about the number of calories in their meals, and walked silently away. She had become odd, unreasonable. She had fallen in love.

Towards suppertime she completely lost herself. She wanted nothing: not to eat, not to smoke, not to comb her hair or laugh or jump or fidget. She wanted only to sit at the computer, to channel her whole body into her ears and fingers, to listen and record. To melt away completely. As a born midwife forgets herself during her patient's labour, and begins doing breathing exercises and sympathetically clenching her empty belly, so Nina completely forgot her own self and entered another's subconscious.

At lunch, he'd appear in the dining room, and they'd pretend that the previous night hadn't happened. But they only looked into each other's eyes as into an abyss.

After supper, like terrorists planning a bomb attack, they'd nod to each other and meet when it was already dark in his room, where she would immediately sit down to the keyboard while he lit up and began pacing.

They didn't talk. In fact, that first conversation they'd had on their first night remained the only one they'd had. They knew nothing more about each other. But every night they grew closer.

Nina still hadn't quite grown into her role of Muse; she would try to tell stories about herself, complain about life, display the complexity of her own character. She even got a little offended when Misha responded to her attempts at openness by waving her away unceremoniously: "No, no! Not now! Can't you see you're dragging me out of that world into this one. I'm trying to get inside someone else's skin, to become him, and you're chatting with me, the ordinary me. Trying to answer you is as difficult as jumping out of a train, transforming back into myself, and then scrambling into the next train after waiting an hour and a half."

The text grew spasmodically. Sometimes Misha would get carried away, and Nina could hardly type fast enough; the keyboard would be groaning with pleasure under her fingers' energetic massage; at other times, prolonged silence would hang in the room, and Misha would stand by the window, staring into the violet gloom his hands crossed behind his head. Nina would remain silent, fearing to interrupt his thoughts. She hoped that he would soon pluck the thread he needed out of the surrounding darkness and move on, bringing her with him. Sometimes it happened just like that, and Misha would energetically spring up and once again run around the room, scratching at his three-day stubble and dictating furiously. And sometimes the opposite would happen: he would step towards the bed on wooden, unyielding legs, topple onto it and say: "That's it! No story. I don't know what happened next. I'm all out of words."

Then Nina would start gently dragging out of him all the details, question by question. He would answer reluctantly, with irritation, with frequent hysterics, "Well how would I know? How can I know when they met there? And fuck knows what he said to her! What are you asking me? What nonsense! How should I know what happened? I don't give a fuck how it all ended!" After the first explosion of irritation, he would grow quiet, as if his entire body were sinking into the mattress, disappearing into it, merging with the sheet. And then, even more nastily, but already with an air of confusion at his own behaviour, he would force out some words: "Well, more than likely, that couple were only pretending not to know each other existed. But in reality…" And once again he would start telling his tale. And once more he would step into the real world, like an inflatable doll gradually filling with air and swelling from the inside out, gorging itself on space. At first his story was schematic, dry, lacking flesh. But as he went on, it filled with details, scents, flowers, sounds. The text gained weight, filling with life and blood, like a mosquito drinking from an artery.

In this way they wrote two books, which were even published by a decent publishing house, but failed to excite much response. Critics reviewed the books coolly and readers were not in a hurry to rip them off the shelves. After the second book failed to earn either the praise of eminent critics, or the affectionate enthusiasm of ordinary readers, Nina's writer fell into a depression, which, however, he tried hard to ignore. Like an athlete who had counted too much on Olympic victory, he strove to reach the red ribbon at the finish line and the victors' podium, even overcoming the pain from muscles and breaking limbs. He was prepared to resort to any kind of drug, just to get where he wanted. And Nina didn't always manage to confiscate the things he temporarily mistook for elixirs of strength, and which she saw as mindless dope.

Nina never doubted that Misha succeeded in overcoming his creative uncreativity only because he was writing these works with her, rather than alone. She tried to take everything negative on herself, all the digs and sneers, and for him she chose only those words from the reviews and Internet forums which would give him strength and faith in himself. It was probably only because Nina had taken on the role of a living shield that Misha even came to the resort a third time, planning to write a third book.

"I've spent too long on this business to stop because of a few foolish consequences," he laughed nervously.

Nina was still carrying trays, waiting for him in the same place. More than two years had passed since they first met. They had been through a lot together. And they had the strength to admit to each other that what existed between them was already more than symbiosis. That it wasn't just an ordinary companionship or a productive way of spending time together. But, in spite of this, they lacked the spirit to admit out loud that this was love.

Their relationship still was not physical. This wasn't because neither of them thought about it. But each one was afraid of losing the spark that kept them together if they took a step further. Nina had even worked out quite a tidy theory about how the relations between a muse and an artist could not, had no right to cross over into the material world. Despite all the LOVE in the world.

"Although I loved him so much, I couldn't just get him to marry me like an ordinary woman, have his kids and make him walk with a pram in the park." Nina, both inspired and regretful, was carving out a platform of words to stand on. "The role of artist's muse excludes any kind of physical connection. Muses don't have a body as far as their masters are concerned. Just think of Turgenev and his Pauline Viardot, or Balzac and his Ewelina Hańska, both married to other men. As soon as they grew close enough to squeeze each other's hands, the writers died, both creatively and in real life. Even the materialist Mayakovsky could only love another man's wife, Lily, who was restrained by the chain of her marriage to Osip Brik."

What kind of love story fails to get gory sooner or later? Love calls out for blood sooner or later. If love isn't infused with at least a drop of someone's crimson lifeblood, then it can't be the real thing. Or else one party must defend or rescue the other from deadly danger. Then their love is proved through the blood-stained conflict. Or possibly the bloody drama of jealousy must be played out. Although, of course, the most natural test is that of whether their blood can be united, the test of children. Love without blood is like untested iron, fragile and bendable.

Fate, clearly despairing of waiting for Nina and her writer to make a serious decision, had taken the task upon itself. She arranged such rivers of blood to achieve her purpose as if there were an abattoir upriver, processing its pre-Christmas orders.

It all happened as if in a bad detective novel. As ever, Misha came to Novogorsk with a crate of whiskey in his luggage and plans for a new novel. Nina gladly sampled both. They went on a creative and alcoholic spree, completely oblivious to the rest of the world, when suddenly a pair of handcuffs snapped shut on Nina's wrists, where she sat drumming on an empty table in the waitress' staff room as if on a keyboard. She was led out of the building and placed in custody. She thought it was all a misunderstanding, and that the same day or the next everyone would understand that she had nothing to do with the terrible crime – the murder of eleven players from the Dynamo football team – that had taken place in the sports resort, where all she had done was carry plates around.

Nina didn't even think it was necessary to get a lawyer. It was all so crazy! She thought it was silly to start seriously worrying about her fate and hiring a good lawyer. Like it would be silly to go about in a fur coat in summer. Couldn't everyone see that it was summer and no snow could possibly fall? Couldn't everyone see that she wasn't the sort of person who could kill? That it was all nonsense?

She didn't even worry much as she sat in solitary confinement. And she should have done. In spite of all her transparency, good references from colleagues and her obvious absence of any inclination towards serial killing, the investigators collected a mass of evidence against her, which the judge found more than sufficient to declare Nina guilty and sentence her to 25 years' hard labour. They would probably have given her life or even the death penalty, but by then the latter had been repealed in our country, and life was set at 25 years.

Only at that moment did Nina truly feel the realness of the real. She suddenly grasped that all these exterior events were not shadows on the wall of a cave, not phantoms or illusions without power to touch her life or her internal world. She suddenly realized their terrifying power and force. They had smashed her artistic and emotional cocoon, scraped her out and shoved her into a grey cell with strange, barely female creatures. Nina was so shocked that she couldn't take in the reality of all that was going on, even as she climbed into her convict's uniform. She imagined she was taking part in some over-extended practical joke from a reality TV show. Of course she wasn't famous enough to be on such a program. But perhaps television had started including ordinary, un-famous people in its show, just for a change?

The story of the writer and his muse had turned from a romantic tale into a tragedy. And despite the horror of the deaths of the eleven murdered footballers, in this fairy-tale they were no more than extras; while the laws of any tragedy demand the death of the protagonists.

"I can't stop thinking that I killed him. All those years I was beside him like a midwife. But I took on the job without any experience of midwifery. You see, when he was staying in our hotel and swilling down vodka, I felt so sorry for him. I lost my sang-froid. And a doctor has to keep a cool head, take a remote, clear view. I was like a trainee in a panic, giving him an epidural on the spot and doing a Caesarean. I dragged his text into the world artificially, defying nature. The tactical goal was achieved, the book was born. In my euphoria I didn't realize straightaway what I'd done. I forgot that someone who has had a Caesarean even once will always need intervention.

"A good midwife doesn't grab the scalpel right away, doesn't cut her patient open to scoop out the baby. She assists, suggests the necessary positions, massages the patient's back, teaches her how to breathe. She helps the miracle happen, but she doesn't take over the show.

"Perhaps I knew then that, having operated once, I had denied him the chance to give birth by himself? Perhaps I really wanted him to be powerless, unable to complete the most important thing in his life? Could it be that I acted deliberately, so that he'd come back to me every time? After all I'd wanted him to return over and over. It would have been better still if he'd never left me. So just when I thought I was saving him, all I had done was prepare him for death.

"They arrested me just when his new story was taking shape. He was in a frenzy – the words bursting out of him, and, naturally, he returned to Novogorsk. I know he'd been attempting to write independently, without me. That he was trying his hardest, but whatever he did, he spent more time drinking than working on his text. Every day he drank himself into a worse state, and once he hadn't emerged even by lunch (it was a long time since anyone had seen him at breakfast) or supper. He didn't show up at all. The next day the staff grew concerned, forced the door of his room and found him dead. His heart hadn't stood up to the alcohol he'd swallowed. They said he'd taken other stuff besides alcohol."

Nina finished telling her tale. There were just two things I couldn't understand: how Nina came to be free, when she still had more than a year left to serve, and why she still wrote those strange chain letters. Did she really believe she could bring Misha back to life if she copied out this set of words so many thousands of times? The answer to the first question turned out to be very simple: Nina's sentence had been reduced for good behaviour and by an amnesty.

"I understand that, but where do the 'chain letters' come in?" I asked.

"That part of my work in the advertising agency always gave me a lot of pleasure. Of all I did at work it was the only thing I really believed in," Nina shrugged.

All my life I'd wondered where these endless, stupid letters come from, sent by friends as well as people I barely knew to jam up my inbox. After all, so that idiots could send this saccharine, dribbling spam, someone had to write it first. But who did it, and why? There were never any ads in these letters, just a few words about love, faith, luck, health, hope, and happiness that all went straight into the cerebellum. Did someone really write all these crude texts for disinterested reasons? And in this day and age, when any scribbler with a modicum of talent could sell his rubbish and get paid some sort of a fee? I'd been right: chain letters were not in fact entirely as simple and disinterested as they might seem.

"The reality is, chain letters are simply a technique for

finding weak spots in society," Nina spoke as if she were explaining the multiplication table, rather than illuminating one of the biggest mysteries of our times for me. "For an ad to be effective, we have to make it touch something sacred inside an individual, the most sensitive threads of the personality. Millions of dollars are invested in advertising. And you've got to know in advance exactly where to probe, where to find society's most tender, sensitive spot. Chain letters help us to find that spot. You see, even if a person refuses to believe in chain letters and gets furious when he receives them, if the text mentions something that is genuinely important to him, if the words in it are really sacred for him, he'll forward it all the same. He may surround it with a thousand smileys or curse words, but he'll forward it. But if the letter mentions something that's insignificant or irrelevant for him he'll delete it and forget about it.

"Thanks to chain letters we've figured out new signals, and created accurate 'emotional maps'. The more people react to the letter and the more it's forwarded, the greater the relevance of the ideas and emotions we've formulated. If we use these same signals and emotions in an advert, they will almost certainly stimulate desire to buy the item being advertised. In fact, a hundred years ago programmers invented invisible meters, which the user never notices, but which track every message he forwards. This is incredibly interesting, it shows how society's priorities have evolved. It shows how, for example the fantasy of 'wealth' has been superseded by fantasies about love, and love fantasies by dreams of self-realization and self-fulfilment. And this is extremely cool, since you know where to press, you can sell the same item first as a thing that will bring the buyer wealth, next as something that will guarantee love, and finally as something that will allow him to be fulfilled and discover the real 'him'. Or become famous. Or acquire a family. The thing to be sold never changes, only the emotional 'outfits'. It's sweetened high-calorie water all over again, successfully parasitizing on people's eternal emotional famine. The key to correctly determine, at the right time, what people are dreaming about now: a love potion, a genie in a bottle, an elixir of youth or something else.

"Of course, our department spent money on 'the science of happiness' strictly for pragmatic, research-driven reasons. But I always enjoyed this part of my work. I found it interesting to guess the unsaid part of a story. After all, a person doesn't open up about his innermost desires even to himself. Thanks to chain letters he can suddenly find out his real priorities. And then I still believe that when people forward the same text, genuinely believing it, it becomes sacred, emotionally enhanced. Did you know that chain letters about love have the most consistently high ratings? Not those about money, or health, or career, or success, but the ones about love? I find this statistic very reassuring; it gives our species hope. It means things aren't so bad after all. However, money is the second most important thing, and that's depressing.

"I want to tell you something: don't get angry, when someone you know sends you a chain letter. Just read the letter, and you'll understand what is currently most important in your friend's life. If you don't want to forward it, well, don't. But you should respond sincerely to your friend, wishing him with your whole heart whatever the letter was about, because he needs it. Behave as if that friend has opened himself up to you. He's asked for help, for sympathy."

Nina and I had talked all night; it was already dawn. But I still had questions for her. Why had she attacked me so violently at the burnt-out shop? If she wasn't a lesbian, why was she following Lena so obviously? I still wanted to know if she really believed that by copying out all those ridiculous chain letters another couple of thousand times, she'd bring a dead man back to life. And what was in those strange sheets of paper that Nata had given me for Nina? And where had Nata gotten them?

I realized that I could answer the last three questions myself by looking inside the envelope Nata had brought. I simply had to slip away from Nina without her following me and trying to take her parcel there and then. I started speaking more slowly and stupidly, more intimately. I left long pauses, with yawns. This way Nina soon succumbed to the sleepy mood and dropped off in mid-sentence. Everything worked in my favour: that it was light outside, and also that Nina had expended too much mental energy by re-living the most tormenting episodes of her life. So I made the most of my chance when Nina's eyes closed, and let myself out, silently closing the door behind me.

To tell the truth, my own eyes were already closing. And, although I wanted to read the documents Nata had given me right then, I fell asleep as soon as I had sat down on my bed with the papers.

I was woken by a knock at the door, and immediately heard the rustle of papers flying off the bed; I remembered everything that had happened the night before, and decided not to open the door to anybody. Whoever was on the other side, Nata, Yuri, or even Nina. I wasn't ready to talk to any of them, I had to read that manuscript before Nina took it away. I checked my fridge: well, a couple of yoghurts, some coffee, and some dried fruit should hold me until evening without having to go to any meals. I closed the blinds, so that nobody looking in could tell whether I was there, switched on the kettle and settled myself in bed with a heap of papers.

They turned out to be exactly what I'd been expecting: the last novel by that same guy whom Nina was hoping to bring back to life with her letters. I'd guessed this because the text began with a dedication, stating that this book was written for her sake and with her.

I'd never encountered a book as upsetting as this one. It revealed too many of the things that had never been spoken between Nina and her Master. Everything he hadn't managed to say to her when everything was going so well was now expressed in his characters' words to each other. This was almost certainly the sincerest of his books, although I hadn't read the others. I think a person can only write such a penetrating text once in this world; after that, all he can do is die. The book contained so much tenderness, grief, feelings of guilt, ecstasy, dependence, gratitude, and love, that I would have expected him to die of these emotions somewhere half-way through. The whole book was one long confession of love: the scale of the admission matched the depth of his feelings.

It was that rare sort of book which makes you a different person after reading it, when you want to call someone, own up to something, implore forgiveness, or even fall in love.

As soon as I had turned over the last page, I knew I had to pass the manuscript on to Nina without delay. I couldn't torture her with suspense even one minute more. She had waited too long for this message.

Nina opened her door straightaway, as if she'd been sitting behind it all day waiting for my knock. I didn't know how to begin.

"You were right. You haven't been writing those thousands of stupid chain letters in vain all these years. I don't know how, but it worked. Here, take it. This is his unpublished book. He's pretty much come back to you, out of nowhere, in order to say how much you meant to him. Can you imagine? I think he died from love, and not from…"

"What nonsense! People don't die from love," Nina interrupted me. And, in a lower tone, she added, "They die from lacking it."

Although she was trying to act unmoved, the papers were trembling in her hands. She held the pages very close to her eyes for some reason, although she usually held a newspaper at the same distance as anyone else.

I wasn't surprised that Nina only had to read a few words written by the man she hadn't seen for a quarter of a century, whom she had already mourned long ago, to be overcome by emotion. Only when I was very very young had I thought that feelings don't live long, that they diffuse into nothing like perfumes, to be replaced by new ones. When I was 16, I thought that at 26 I wouldn't even remember the name of the boy with whom I danced at our graduation ball and greeted the dawn afterwards. Adults always told me: "You'll meet a million more guys like him; wait until you get to college and you'll see." And I'd believed them. But then it turned out that at 26 this boy was more in my thoughts than he'd been when I was 16. And at 56, still more than at 26.

The truth is, emotions are our most tenacious part. A person always returns to the place where he experienced his most powerful sensations, in order to live them over again. Even murderers, creeping around the sites of their former crimes, exemplify the general rule. In a news story about a hospice, I read an account of a wealthy man who kept a private bodyguard in his ward, who knew that he didn't have long left to live. But he didn't weep or gnash his teeth; he wrote his will in a businesslike way and made sure everyone knew how to dispose of his business after he was dead. He read a lot, watched the news, and then asked for a baby goat to be brought into his ward – he'd grown up in the country. He stroked the baby goat and burst out crying. After sixty years (!) just the smell of the little goat and the feeling of its rough coat under his fingers had plunged him back into all those emotions which he must have believed long since quenched and scattered against the background of hundreds and thousands of impressions from the rest of his life. But the reality was different.

I wasn't surprised by the way Nina seized those pages. I left her, quietly shutting the door behind me.

Nata was marching up and down like a sentry outside my room.

"Well then, do you see now that those papers are really

worth passing on to the person who's meant to have them?"
she asked me.

"Yes. It really is a very powerful and important piece
of writing. You can't imagine how she felt when she started
reading it."

"What!" Nata turned pale. "You already gave her the
papers? Without me? All by yourself? Who gave you the
right? And when did you manage it?"

"I drove there today and handed them over."

"Come on, your car's been parked in the parking lot all
day!"

"I can use buses too, you know," I managed a fairly quick
comeback.

"Sonya, I should have been the one to give her that text!"

"But why you, of all people?"

"That book has to be published. I can't do it until I've
met Shalamova. And besides, I just really want to meet this
woman. Sonya, what a malicious, hard-hearted person you
are. You understood long ago how important this was to me.
And you deliberately acted so as to frustrate me. So what do
you get out of this? Are you happy now?"

"I'll arrange for you to meet," I was struggling to retain
my dignity and not slip into a harangue, although Nata's tone
called for one. "It's just that Nina had to read this text as soon
as possible. Can I ask you one question? Don't answer if you
don't want to."

"Go for it," said Nata.

"Which of your kids is Misha's?"

"My daughter," Nata sighed; clearly, she couldn't
simultaneously think about Misha and pick a fight with me.

"She has an amazing father. She's a lucky girl. I'll come
to see you again, but later. Okay?"

Nina called over when she'd finished reading. But she
didn't look transfused with light, happy or comforted, as I'd
expected.

"What's wrong? Why the gloomy expression?" I looked her in the eye. "Didn't you like the text? You think that he couldn't do it without you?"

"It's a wonderful book, but it's horrible," Nina shook her head. "It's all incredibly wrong."

"What?" I almost choked from rage. An exquisite book had been dedicated to this woman, and she turned up her nose at it. "Look, girlfriend, don't you think you're being too critical? You're stricter than the harshest critic!"

"I didn't say it was a bad book," Nina rebuffed me, weakly. "It's a very talented book. But it's fatal for me."

"But what's upset you so much?"

"Well, he killed me!" Nina yelled, starting to cry. "He killed the heroine, who was me. He didn't want me alive. That's the horrible thing!"

"But it's only a story, after all!" I was astonished by Nina's irrationality.

"You can't understand," was all she answered, continuing to cry quietly, and handing me the manuscript. "I don't need this book. Give it back to Nata."

"So you knew Nata gave me this text?" I started with shock. "All these years you've known that she had the book your Misha wrote, and you were waiting until she gave it to you of her own accord?"

"I didn't know this book really existed. I didn't think he'd finished the novel. But if the book did exist, then the keeper had to be Nata, the mother of his daughter."

"So you knew all about Nata, and about their daughter?" Nina was sufficiently weird for a dozen crazy ladies.

"Of course. But that doesn't change anything. I loved him with all his wives, children, illnesses, defects, doubts. I loved everything about him. I never thought he'd respond by trying to kill me off."

"You know you're Nina from the book, but Nata doesn't. She thinks that you won't get out of prison for another year. But she's longing desperately to see you. She says that the book is far from everything, that it's only a part of what was saved up for you. Are you ready to meet her?"

"Sure," Nina shrugged, rather indifferently. "Right now, if you want. I don't think anything she could tell me would be worse than what I've just read."

"So shall I call her?"

Nata came immediately. She and Nina stared at each other for a long while, as if they were meeting for the first time. I really should have left the room and given this pair the opportunity to sort out their relation to the dead man without any bystanders. But my curiosity overpowered my sense of tact. I decided to stay in my chair and sit very quietly until they chased me away. After all, you shouldn't deprive yourself of unique life experiences or leave the places where you really want to be. In extreme cases, you always find others who are willing to kick you out of the situations that interest you most. You don't need to do it for them.

The writer's ladies began talking straight away, without any preamble, as if continuing a conversation that had started long before. Maybe they really had been waging conversational duels with each other in their heads, for more than twenty years.

"So are you in shock?" Nata asked in a businesslike way.

"Yes, it was painful for me to read," Nina agreed, honestly.

"I also thought that it wouldn't be right to release this story into the world just the way he wrote it. That's why it's been in my desk all these years, why I've never sent it to a publisher. You've got to rescue yourself, to rewrite the ending. It's only fair, it's the right thing to do."

I almost jumped out of my chair yelling that this was an insult to creativity, and that neither Nata nor Nina had the right to decide on the writer's behalf how his creation should end. If he'd written in a death, that meant death was the only possible ending. But I caught myself in time: one squeak out of me would ensure I'd be popped out of the room like a cork from a bottle, while the ladies would continue working things out without me, and I'd miss the most interesting part. So I bit my tongue and sank deeper into my chair.

"It would be stupid, somehow, to rescue myself with my own hands," Nina shook her head doubtfully. "Of course, a princess can always save herself from evil wizards and dragons. But then the point of the story is that the princess wants to be saved. She wants someone to try to save her, to care whether she lives. That's exactly why she sits and waits for her prince and doesn't try to sort out the problem by herself. And it turns out that my prince didn't want me to live. He wanted me to die. Now I understand why he didn't come to see me after I was sentenced. Sure, it would have been difficult, but with his connections – he worked for the police press service after all – he could have reached me, if he'd wanted. Instead he abandoned me. On my own. In prison. It was the scenario that worked best for him."

"And what did you want? Of course, he had to kill you. It was the only way of freeing himself from you and finally trying to achieve something independently. To feel completely himself and to have faith in his own ability to create without chivvying, without guiding hands. And, as you can see, he pulled it off brilliantly. But at the start he had to kill you, by proxy. You put yourself in the way of the blow. You need to understand what you're in for when you start playing with forces that are greater than you can understand."

"I know all about those forces," Nina growled. "Whether or not I did it well, I played my role. Thanks to me, Misha wrote three perfectly decent books."

"And if instead of interfering you'd let him develop of his own accord, then there would have been more than three, and he'd still be alive," Nata parried coolly. "Believe me, I know this about him for sure. Any silly bitch can put pressure on a man and push him around. That's why the majority of stupid women, deciding to play at being Muses, see their role just the way you did: to stand behind his shoulder with a stopwatch, bullying the artist and urging him on with kicks. Shoving and pushing. Idiots! Women like that should be punched in the head. A person must control his own work, and that control must be allowed to mature. But I'm not the type to pass judgement, even on you. People only experience what they genuinely desire. Evidently he wanted to experience creativity by compulsion more than he wanted the free variety. I'm sure you had the best, purest and most constructive intentions. There's no doubt that you loved him, and that excuses what you did."

Nina had become angry; her eyes glittered like a wild beast's. She was struggling to hold herself back, but for some reason she didn't interrupt Nata, simply chewed her lip nervously. I was worried that at any moment she might jump up and fling herself on the other woman. But instead she sat still on the end of the bed like a dark, heavy cobblestone.

Finally, Nata seemed to have said everything that she had been storing up for so long; she stared expectantly at Nina, waiting for objections. She craved them. And, evidently, she had saved up both spite and counter-arguments for further discussion. For some reason, Nina didn't rise to the challenge. She studied Nata with silent curiosity, and only her compressed lips and slight scowl revealed that she was neither crushed nor paralyzed; that, on the contrary, a stern decisiveness was maturing within her. It was unnerving, because there was no predicting which way this wound-up aggression might explode. Finally, Nina spoke in a tightly controlled tone:

"Is that all you wanted to tell me? Can we consider this meeting closed?"

"I know this is difficult for you," Nata said in a velvety voice. "But think over my offer again. You can still rewrite everything. This manuscript has been waiting for you."

"You can publish it as is. I have only one request: that this episode remain between us, if only for a week. I don't want the whole residence to know more about me than they already do, before I have a chance to leave."

"You want to run away?"

"It has nothing to do with you."

"Nina, you're an astonishing person. I don't want to say goodbye to you this way," Nata switched on her super-feminine persona. "If only because you were able to see the real person inside Misha and because you wanted to drag him out of his shell. I'm not kidding, I genuinely respect you."

Her last words were spoken to empty air, as Nina had already walked out. The door slammed behind her.

Nata sat in silence for a long time after that, crossing her arms and gazing straight ahead. Finally, she remembered I was still in the room. She straightened up awkwardly, like the Queen Mother settling herself on the throne for a formal photo, and tilted her head in my direction. She needed to play this scene to the end, even if she was acting in front of a half-empty theatre and chance audience.

"She shouldn't have rushed away like that," Nata said, unsympathetically. "After all, she had a chance to find out the secret of genuine muses. Would you like me to tell you the secret for nothing?"

I shrugged.

"People unfamiliar with religions should never get involved in these games," Nata started waxing metaphysical. "Because they don't understand how such powers work, although all of it was described long ago. In Eastern philosophy, the masculine essence is associated with a white light, the female essence with black. White symbolizes total purity, the subtraction of all colours, total peace. Black is the unity of all the colours that have ever existed. Total absorption. A black hole is the most feminine of all the symbols ever dreamed up in the universe. Nina is right to say that a man without a woman's influence won't move from his spot and will never attempt anything, like a sphere placed on a completely level surface. But you can force this sphere to move by pushing, rolling, leading the motion. And that's the wrong way. A sphere pushed along by the direct application of blind force will stop as soon as the hand pushing it also stops. A Muse shouldn't push. Instead, you have to create a whirlwind on this level surface, so that the sphere voluntarily chooses a unique trajectory towards it, attracted by the power of gravity, just as black holes drag in the matter around them. That's how a Muse encourages her Master, without pushing him."

The next week passed in a sort of echoing, strained silence. No-one was talking, but our eyes spoke volumes.

Yuri made a point of not noticing me. I gave the impression that I couldn't give a damn about him. For some reason he was keeping a low profile and was little to be seen.

Alla gave me neutral little smiles, but no longer invited me to visit her jacuzzi. She looked rather depressed. Clearly, her return to popularity among the pensioners hadn't made her happy.

Ever since my return to The Mounds, Tatiana had tactfully tried not to enter my field of vision. Even in the dining room, if we arrived at the same time, she tried to sit somewhere I couldn't see her from my table. So there were none of the explanations between us which I simultaneously wanted and feared. Evidently, we were both too cowardly for this to happen. Peter let me know that Tatiana was looking for a different old people's home.

Nata and Nina shot glances at each other like duellists. They also pretended that they were perfectly indifferent to each other.

I felt like a human Switzerland, struggling to stay neutral.

Although Nina had never been one of the most outgoing pensioners, she was now neither to be seen nor heard. I paid no attention to her demonstrative pose of "I want to be alone", and cheekily called on her in her room in the evenings. I'd already told her I wanted to write a book about the eleven murdered footballers, but that now my idea had changed.

Now I wanted Nina herself to be the heroine of my novel. Therefore I spun my ideas out for her, trying to win her over and gathering details. Nina resisted me weakly. I felt as if, before my eyes, Nina was wilting into a shadow, dissolving into the air. Now and then she went for a drive. She admitted that she was looking at different old people's homes.

"Where are you running, who are you running away from, and why?" I kept asking her. "You've no grounds to fear that Nata will give your secret away. And I'm going to write a book which will rehabilitate you, and only then will your incognito be revealed. In any case, I won't say a word to anyone without your agreement. Are you afraid of Nata? No need! I think you and Nata are similar in a lot of ways, you have a lot in common. If you drop this running away right now and try to be open with her, then you two will be great friends."

"Sonya, stop trying to get inside my head and quit pretending that you understand everything about me!" Nina shook me off. "You know nothing, absolutely nothing, about what I'm really like. You can't imagine, for example, why I chose this home. There's no way you can figure out why it's time for me to get out of here."

"Oho! The mystery of the seven seals again! You came here to follow Nata, because she had a stronger connection with the man you loved than anyone else living. That's all there was to it. I think you were hoping that sooner or later you'd find something like the book which has finally wound up in your hands!"

"As if that needed proof! You're only able to come up with the most superficial reasons. But my motives, trust me, were different. And now they don't matter any more; my plans have changed. Incidentally, that's mostly thanks to you."

Nina had become even more enigmatic than before. The pensioners had noticed that something was happening to her. Many of them were trying to guess why she was no longer scribbling on those scraps of paper, but nobody could offer an explanation that would be remotely logical. Given that my neighbours were coming up with completely absurd scenarios, Yuri had judged what he'd discovered about Nina's secret too personal to reveal. That was a consideration in his favour. I even started to respect him again and was ready to forgive him his petty behaviour the other evening, when he and I had broken into Nina's room to steal her conspiratorial poems. I decided to pardon Yuri and condescend to pay attention to him again.

Once at supper I sat down near him and hinted that, for the sake of his outstanding chivalrous qualities, I was prepared to forgive his panicky behaviour. But he didn't seem to want an amnesty from me. He acted rather coldly. He seemed slightly disgusted with me. Well! I felt the same way about him! Who did he think he was? Did he think that if he behaved like a stuffed turkey for another couple of weeks, I would realize what a hero he was and beg to go back to being friends? Not likely. If the guy didn't know how lucky he was, good luck to him. I would fill the vacant space he'd occupied in my brain with more interesting things. For example, I still didn't understand what Nina had had in mind when she announced that she'd come to The Mounds not chasing Nata, but with some other notion in mind. Why had the appearance of the unfortunate Misha's manuscript upset her plans? I read and re-read the copy of the unpublished manuscript that I'd far-sightedly taken. But I didn't find any answers there.

The week Nina had allowed herself to find a new bolthole had ebbed away. But her intention to leave had lost none of its firmness. She had even found a bolthole. Surprisingly, this quiet lady didn't choose to slip away invisibly; instead, she decided to bid farewell to The Mounds by throwing us a goodbye party. I think this was the longest and most intense evening of my life...

There was a buffet and a pair of barbecue grills in the courtyard of The Mounds. Two amplifiers protruded from the open windows of the dining room. Some New Age racket was playing. Everyone was wandering around the buffet with paper plates, hoovering up the various kinds of grub and arranging themselves wherever they happened to be, on seats or on the grass. No-one was expecting anything in particular to happen. They started drinking before Nina's official farewell speech began. She was also wandering around, answering all questions only with an enigmatic smile and a promise that there wasn't much longer to wait, she would tell everyone everything any moment now.

The day hadn't been particularly hot. And as soon as the sun had started to disappear into the clouds lining the horizon, a chilly dampness blew in from the lake. The already mildly intoxicated pensioners were fetching warm coats and blankets from their rooms. Now the lawn, scattered with sitting and standing people wrapped in blankets, resembled a drifting ice-floe crowded with the survivors of a shipwreck. It was still sufficiently bright to see who was who. But you already had to step close and peer nearer to make out people's expressions and guess what they were feeling.

Nina finally decided that the time had come. People formed a group around her and she said a few words, as expected on such occasions. How much she would miss us, how great everything here had been, but all the same she was leaving and hoped that we would all continue to enjoy life here. In short, she finished without any excitement.

The excitement came after her speech. My Yuri suddenly appeared beside her (possibly, he'd been there earlier, but until he spoke I hadn't noticed him). Yuri asked people not to go, saying it wasn't over yet, there was a second news item this evening: he was also leaving in the next few days. So this party was a farewell for him as well.

"Whaaaat! Are you two leaving together? Are you a couple? Are you getting married?" questions broke out from all sides.

"No, we're not a couple and we're not getting married.

But we're leaving at the same time," my former companion explained briefly.

"That's news, did Yuri dump you?" I felt cold but strong fingers grip my elbow, as I glanced over my shoulder. I looked around. It was Alla.

"What are you on about! As if there was ever anything between us!" I snorted.

"And was there anything between you?" Alla raised her brows, indicating disbelief.

"Did we look like we were pledged till death do us part?" I said bitterly and walked away.

To be honest, I was shocked by this unexpected plot twist, and I wanted to figure out what was going on. If I went up to Yuri with questions, he'd imagine I was jealous. I wasn't about to let that happen; it would be better to hear everything from Nina. But I was not the only one who had questions for her. I noticed that Lena the medic, whom we'd long taken to be Nina's secret lesbian love, was moving towards her uncertainly. Evidently, Lena was disappointed at the loss of her devoted admirer and also wanted to say something private to her at parting. Ha ha! Perhaps she was even about to offer herself to her for the night? Of course Lena would have thought and fantasized about this at some length. She'd had expectations. How can you give up fantasies like that, if every day there's at least one idiot reminding you that you're the object of their homosexual passion?

Meanwhile the party went on. Through the gates rolled an extraordinary stretch limousine, painted all the colours of the rainbow. Out of it, and into our midst, spilled people in brilliantly coloured outfits, carrying rattles, gongs, trumpets and drums. The air filled with noise, vibrations, hoots and whistles. Overcome by the wave of unaccustomed sounds, I fell into a trance. I don't think I was the only one affected by the music: the party, which had been fairly lacklustre up until then, suddenly re-ignited with mounting enthusiasm. People got sucked into the dancing. I came to my senses for just long enough to realize I was being borne right to the middle of this ecstatic whirling. And Nata was in the centre of it all, spinning around and bouncing up and down. She puffed out her skirt, bent right over and sprang into the air, throwing out her legs. It was as if she'd become that very same black hole she'd described to me about a week before, and was trying to absorb the entire world into herself. The world, including me, was certainly drawn directly towards her. I was so dizzy that to avoid toppling over, I had to hang onto Nata's shoulders. Her crazily wide eyes were laughing, she kept on dancing, and by some kind of miracle, held me upright. I hung on to her, unable to take my eyes from her laughing face.

"I think they slipped magic mushrooms in our food. Something's not right, I'm telling you. Drink never has this affect on me," I whispered loudly. "Amazing! I had no idea our Nina could throw a party like this!"

"It wasn't Nina," Nata answered. Only instead of answering audibly, she seemed to blow pearly-velvety word bubbles from her lips into my ears. They rolled around inside me and tickled, raising waves of inexplicable gladness and making me laugh with my whole body.

"Who acted for her?"

"I didn't want one of our craziest ladies to leave us without a fuss. So I asked Vagan to put up some kind of show – he knows how to do it."

I suddenly felt a chill. "And you don't feel that you might be taking over her party that way?"

"I'm just making her little tea-party into a real par-tay."

"So you're still competing with her? Well, you've got your revenge! God, how awkward!" I relaxed my arms, which I'd kept hooked around Nata's shoulders. It no longer felt as if something was dragging me along; nothing was sweeping me away; the vortex was plugged, the whirlpool that had snatched me up had stopped spinning.

I made my way out of the general excitement, although I was forced to admit that even from outside, it looked strikingly beautiful. But I wasn't alone in failing to be drawn into the bacchanal. Yuri was also observing, from a little distance, the goings-on. Put more accurately, he was observing me, rather than the dancing. He was waiting for me! Had he decided to say a personal farewell?

We walked towards each other; silently offering his arm, he led me towards the lake-shore. Our trainers bounced lightly on the boardwalk. The planks underfoot were slightly damp from the evening dew and Yuri spread out his wind-cheater. The music, drifting over from the lawn, didn't scare the fish; they jumped out of the water with a splash and dropped back in, almost as if the lake were taking rapid breaths.

"You really love me that much?" Yuri asked me.

"Me? Love? You?"

"Have you lost your nerve again?"

"How do you mean?"

"Are you afraid of yourself and your feelings again and now you want to pretend that nothing happened between us?"

"Did something happen?"

"Sonya, that was one of the most astonishing, touching, and beautiful letters I ever received in my life. You have to be truly strong and sincere to write like that. Do you really believe I might think you look silly for writing that letter? Do you really have such a bad opinion of me? How can you love me so much if you think I'm such a bastard?"

Love? I was thinking. A letter to him? From me?

"Have you got this letter with you right now?" I had to keep a straight head, and not betray emotion.

"Yes!"

"Let me see it."

Yuri started groping around somewhere under my bottom and pulled a sheet of paper out of the pocket of his wind-cheater.

"You want to take it back and make both of us pretend it never existed?" he asked warily. I didn't answer: my eyes were flying over the lines.

Yuri! I am no longer ashamed of letting myself be the person I am. Who knows how much time we have left and it's probably stupid to act a part and wait for a special occasion. So I'm no longer too embarrassed to admit my love. I love you. Please don't leave. Please stay.

All my life I've been afraid of looking foolish and vulnerable. And what's more foolish than a woman in love? That's why I've never said these words to anyone before. But now it's all the same to me how I appear to others and what they think of me. After all, who says that love is something to be ashamed of, a thing to hide? I don't think anyone ever made me believe that. I just realized it by myself – realized it or made it up.

I used to think this rule protected me. Now I realize that I built myself a prison cell. But you've helped me tear down the wall around me. And that's why I'm asking you to stay. You're the first and only person I can tell: I love you.

I finished reading.

"Unfortunately, I didn't write this."

"You didn't? Then who did? I haven't been seeing anyone else here."

"She wouldn't have written if there had been something between you. Think for yourself: which of our local ladies has never admitted being in love to anybody? Do you keep up with the local literature? Think about it!"

"It can't be!" Yuri frowned sceptically and bit his lip, looking pleased with himself.

"Exactly," I nodded. "Alla's your girl. She probably only started hanging out with your friend Dimon in order to get closer to you. It's got to be her."

We fell silent.

"So this means you don't love me?" Yuri enquired, already sounding playful.

"Quit with the love thing. You're a pretty greedy guy," I sniggered in reply. "I'd rather hear why you've suddenly latched on to Nina."

"She's amazing."

"Are you hoping that if you die, she'll remember you too for ten years and bring you back to life by writing letters?" (I hung onto my smile, as if nothing I said meant anything to me).

"Yes. People have this idea that if someone is capable of feeling real love once, then they'll be able to manage it a second time too. When I understood just what sort of letters we'd found, and how many years she'd been writing them, I was impressed. And the next day I went to see her again."

"May you live happily ever after!" I slapped him on the back as I got to my feet. "Do you want me to send Alla over?"

"No, no need. If she really wrote this, she'll hardly be thrilled to discover you know about her letter. I'll find her myself." Yuri offered me his arm as we stepped off the boardwalk.

"And what are you going to tell her?"

"Oh, nothing special. I'll say, well done for confronting your fears. There's nothing more natural than admitting your feelings to people. People need to know, it makes them feel loved, they like to be liked; they love to feel loved; they need to feel needed. Something along those lines…"

"Well… wow… I like your style!" I laughed in reply.

I'd thought that Yuri and I hadn't been missing for long, but in our absence the mise-en-scène at the residence had changed completely. There was no music, no jollity, quite the reverse: some untidy rushing around, a lot of anxious whispering. Only then did I notice the ambulance parked alongside the party bus. Inside it, Lena was being strapped to a stretcher and fitted with a tube down her throat. Lena, whom everyone had forgotten during this leaving party, including me!

"What's wrong with her?" I hurried over to the doctor who had just slammed the ambulance door.

"Looks like poisoning," she snapped crossly, and as the pensioners watched, the vehicle rolled straight out of the courtyard.

To hell with it! I should have seen this coming. I shouldn't have taken more than a step away from Lena today! Only now I understood that this was the way it all had to end. The jigsaw pieces, which had lain for so long unhelpfully in different compartments, suddenly sprang together into a glaringly clear picture: Lena Moiseyenko was the reason Nina had come here. Fedya's wife had seen her in Novogorsk. She was behind the poisoning of the footballers. And for all these years, Nina had been preparing her revenge…

I found Nina inside the summerhouse in the most distant corner of the courtyard. She was peacefully sipping a cocktail, watching the panic outside with inhuman calm. She was enjoying the spectacle!

"Why did you poison her?" I demanded as I arrived, flinging myself down next to her, as if putting a casual question about the weather.

"She knows why," Nina smiled.

I couldn't get over her calm. It wasn't surprising that she'd once been blamed for the murder of the footballers. If she'd reacted to their poisoning as she did now to Lena being borne off in an ambulance, I'd also have ordered her arrest without thinking twice.

"So you came to The Mounds to follow her?"

"It's the other way round," Nina corrected me, with exaggerated gentleness. "She followed me here. I knew she'd come after me wherever I went, so I brought her right here. Can you guess why, Miss Marple?"

"I have an idea, but I assume yours is more accurate," I passed the challenge back to Nina. She took me up on it.

By herself Nina could never have figured out the person who poisoned the football team, however desperately she wanted to. But she was positive that Lena had to be responsible, because Lena did everything to make her think so.

When Nina was in pre-trial detention and later in a prison camp, everyone forgot about her. Even Misha, whom she'd trusted so much and whom she longed to see more than anyone. Only one person did not forget her. Nina didn't immediately suspect that the parcels and packages she received regularly from different addresses came from one and the same well-wisher. At first, stunned by her new situation, she simply accepted the unexpected gifts from the outer world as a continuation of that surreal, grotesque and tragic absurdity into which she had somehow stumbled. By the time the fifth parcel arrived Nina began asking herself: who was this mysterious benefactor and why were they helping her regularly, carefully concealing their identity and never using the same courier twice? There was no doubt that one person was sending these parcels. When they contained biscuits, it was always the same kind of Belgian cookie. When they contained accessories, such as stockings, underwear, handkerchiefs, it was clear that they had been chosen by the same female hand.

But who? Why? And why the anonymity?

Nina didn't wonder who or why for very long. No matter how much she wanted to believe in the best and think that somewhere on earth there was someone who really loved her and cared about her fate, common sense always led back to the most unpleasant version: clearly, the real poisoner felt guilty and was trying to soothe her conscience with these packages. This person's conscience was not particularly demanding, and was easily pacified by the thought of a few pairs of panties or stockings dispatched to the women's prison.

Nina spent a long time trying to imagine what sort of person this was and what was going on in their head, but she could never compose a satisfactory psychological portrait of this monster. She couldn't get inside the soul of a woman who could commit such an act (and Nina was growing more convinced it was a woman who administered the poison and framed her). Since she couldn't figure out what sort of person this might be, Nina decided simply to proceed by elimination. The task was neither simple nor swift, but since the very thing

Nina possessed in quantity was time, she was able to write long letters and send them over and over again, entering into drawn-out correspondences with all the intermediaries who had posted her parcels, persuading and convincing them, gradually gathering nuggets of information about the person behind it all. Water wears down stone, and questions asked endlessly will eventually find answers.

Towards the end of her fifth year of intensive correspondence, Nina actually managed to form a composite picture of her benefactress. It took her a little longer to remember where she'd seen this face and to trace the people who could help her put a name to the stranger.

It's difficult to collect information when you're locked up in high security, and when all the letters you send to the outer world are stamped with a prison postmark; it's difficult to find answers to the questions posed in such letters. But it's not impossible. So by the time Nina marked her tenth anniversary in the prison camp, she already had a fairly good idea who Lena Moiseyenko was; she'd even obtained her home address. Stranger yet, she had, somewhat belatedly, learned about the private life of this woman who had followed her from afar all these years.

On the anniversary of the day the Dynamo team was poisoned, when every TV channel in the country was once more broadcasting the details of the tragedy – already a part of history – Nina allowed herself some troublemaking. She wrote Lena a letter. No, of course she didn't tempt fate by writing openly, "You unbelievable bitch, were you trying to salve your conscience with parcels? Did you really hope I would never find out it was you who poisoned eleven men and framed me? And wouldn't you like to come and sit out the last 15 years of my sentence?" No, of course Nina weighed every word. All she wanted to do was scare her addressee a little. Fully aware of her own hopeless position, she wanted to lure Moiseyenko into a protracted, nerve-teasing game. Therefore her letter was extremely distant and correct, allowing

Lena to keep her dignity and even show surprise and non-comprehension, should she so wish. But it would certainly create the necessary effect in her tiny conscience.

Nina wrote Lena along the lines of "you don't know me, nor do I know you very well. I live in this prison camp, everything is going OK here. Some well-meaning people gave me your address, knowing that you're an extremely kind-hearted woman who can't ignore others' misfortunes. The world is not without good folk ready to sympathize even with people like me, and I know this well because I've always received very nice presents from various addresses. The parcels are great, only I'd love to have some Swiss chocolate for old times' sake. And there's no way these secret parcel-senders can know that. I can't tell anyone. I'd also like to correspond with somebody, so I'm writing to you in the hope that something might happen! I kiss your hand. Forgive me if I've written anything rude. Sincerely yours, and so on."

It was a typical prisoner's letter; notes like these are sent in stacks to every address the convicts manage to get hold of: newspapers, charities and social clubs. But the wording was deliberately provocative. Naturally, Nina didn't receive an answer to her letter (she hadn't expected any, although sometimes she wondered "what if..."), but in the next parcel, arriving right on schedule in the middle of the month, there were several bars of delicious Lindt chocolate in various flavours. That was already complete victory for Nina, vindicating the accuracy of her speculations. Undoubtedly Lena knew that somehow or other she had been found out. But, for some reason, this hadn't frightened her off.

Nina didn't write to Lena again. She continued gradually stockpiling information, following Lena from afar and waiting for her chance. The chance that would come when the gates to freedom opened.

Of course, all this time Nina had wondered what had inspired an apparently normal, perfectly nice woman, and one who had taken the Hippocratic oath, to commit such an unusual crime. Her research had turned up two curious details. First, someone told her that, long ago, Lena had suffered a terrible personal tragedy. More precisely, her grief formed a drop in the huge sea of unhappiness which flooded a hundred football-supporting families on the day of a certain match between Locomotive and Dynamo teams.

Lena's husband was a passionate football fan. He supported (as one did in an era of total corporate loyalty) the Dynamo team which all men of his type admired. And he raised his son in true masculine style, that is to say, he brought the child to the stadium, taught him football chants, gave him team scarves and watched football on TV with him. The boy could shout abuse at a referee before he was potty-trained.

Of course, the father and son couldn't watch an epochal match like the clash between Locomotive and Dynamo on television like couch potatoes. This was the kind of match you had to watch in person, yelling "off-side, off-side", stamping your feet and blowing hooters. Everything happened just as it should: the new Locomotive stadium resounded with hoots and yells; both levels, upper and lower, rippled with waving hands. The fans who'd had a little too much to drink did their best to support the players on the pitch. Dynamo were losing, but not hopelessly: the score was 0:1. In the second half the score didn't change. While the Locomotive supporters rejoiced, the Dynamo fans roared furiously and cursed the ref. The latter not only failed to try to get the Dynamo fans on his side, he made matters worse by imposing an extremely questionable penalty against their team. This provoked an explosion of rage from the fans. Nothing unusual about that: people go to matches to shout, take offence, and turn the air blue with curses. But on this occasion, something unexpected ensued.

By ill luck, a drum and a very inspiring drummer were stationed at the top of the Dynamo fans' stands. This drummer started a rhythmic chant immediately repeated by a thousand stamping feet: "The ref's shit! The ref's shit!" The fans on the upper levels, in a single charge, stormed the barriers around their enclosure, brandishing their fists and continuing to stamp in rhythm with the chant. The effect of resonance has been well described in junior high school physics textbooks. Every child has been told by their teacher why soldiers must never march over bridges in step: the substructure won't hold. Quite possibly each of the rioting fans on the upper level was individually aware of this law, but being swept away by the crowd and by their own ecstatic sense of injustice, they forgot this unfortunate fact. The upper tier splintered and, with a roar, collapsed onto the one below. Everything started crashing down. Panic broke out. The fans higher up leapt off the toppling stands, while those on the lower levels tried to burst onto the pitch, pushing against the metal netting that protected the grass. The pressure of the crowd forced those in front into the firmly cast chain-link, crushing them into the fence like soft fruit through a sieve. The crush was so horrifying that the next day the television didn't even feature any images from the scene. The worst of the accident was described in soberly restrained words: the law against showing violence was already in effect.

Lena's son was one of those who perished. And Lena, who had felt no particular emotion in regard to football, let alone towards Dynamo, conceived a fanatical hatred for everyone in football shorts and boots. Her fanaticism remained unknown, as she didn't see a psychotherapist about her passion for revenge, and she brought her despair whole to Novogorsk, without spilling a drop.

In principle, Nina understood the vendetta which Lena had waged against the unfortunate footballers. Although Nina didn't consider her action acceptable, she could understand the emotional motivation. She even allowed that, in the other woman's place and after a shock like that, she might have done exactly the same thing. But, as before, she failed to understand why she, Nina, had to pay with 25 years of her life for the satisfaction of Lena's revenge? Why couldn't Lena take the punishment for her own crime, which was meaningful only to her, and instead why did she, with help from her policeman husband, incriminate Nina, who had nothing to do with this mess? Thus even an understanding of the motives didn't free the former Novogorsk waitress from resentment. She couldn't excuse Lena.

The second fact that Nina dug up was that the attack on the footballers was not Lena's first murderous venture. Somehow, she succeeded in finding out exactly why Dr Moiseyenko had been forced to abandon her profession. And she sympathized with her whole soul with Dr Rozhdestvensky, whom Lena had robbed of the ability to have children. Unfortunately, Nina couldn't find out why she had punished him like that (in fact, she had nothing to do with the case, but Nina wasn't to know that!). Until the last moment, Nina never lost hope of penetrating the mystery behind this bizarre act. This was precisely why she, knowing that Lena would follow her like a thread after a needle, chose The Mounds (where Tatiana, Dr Rozhdestvensky's wife, had established herself after her husband's death) as her place of residence. She wanted Lena, who was undoubtedly trailing her, to be daily reminded of both her crimes; to see both Nina and Tatiana everywhere she went. She hoped that sooner or later this moral torment would lead to some purifying catharsis, perhaps even to genuine regret, tears and pleas for forgiveness... to something!

Days, months, and even years went by. At least three times a day – at breakfast, lunch, and dinner – Lena watched Tatiana and Nina, but nothing ever happened! She never broke down... She never burst into sudden tears, or clenched her fists, or lapsed into depression... To hell with her! She never even lost her appetite! Nina was shocked by this iron restraint; she was highly intrigued to know how much longer Lena could hold out. With every day, her mystification grew.

Poor Nina! She never knew the most insulting thing: that she, Nina, was the only person Lena regarded as a living reproach. Whenever she saw Tatiana, she felt justified and reassured that she, Lena, was also a victim. Nina couldn't have suspected this twist in the plot. Finally, I told her the truth about the relationship between Lena and Tatiana and thus solved the riddle. Nina was impressed by the news that Lena had herself been a victim in the Dr Rozhdestvensky affair and that she'd been crudely framed for it. She hurled her empty cocktail glass into the darkness with such force that it splashed into the lake, which lay at least fifty metres from the building. Undoubtedly, if war broke out tomorrow, I'd trust Nina to throw grenades from our trench. She was infuriated that Lena had somehow been exculpated and that it was Nata Sokolova who'd turned Lena into a victim, all those years ago.

"You understand that if only Sokolova hadn't taken it into her head that she could let herself…" Nina had suddenly begun slurring. She was searching unsuccessfully for the right words. "How the fuck did she decide that she could be the reason? That her desire was an inevitable and satisfactory condition for changing someone else's life? You see that if she hadn't fucked up Lena, she would never have decided to attack the footballers? And even if she had, she wouldn't have framed me!"

"Honestly, I don't follow you. Where's the logic? How does one relate to the other?" I really wasn't keeping up.

"You know I've been through the same temptation myself. When you're set up and named as the guilty party in a crime you haven't committed, you start believing that life owes you something. That you've got the right to commit a crime without being punished, as if they've stood you in the corner in advance by mistake, and now you can go and gobble all the sweets out of Mommy's secret drawer in the wardrobe, or break a vase, or hit your sister. Nothing more can happen to you because the punishment you've been given by mistake will be counted in your favour. That's the kind of philosophy you acquire. I think Lena came to the same conclusions I have. Honestly, I still consider myself entitled to commit something very unpleasant… cruel… possibly even vicious. It's just that until recently I couldn't settle what I should spend my last opportunity on. After all it would have to be something really worthwhile. I've been saving up this once-off indulgence for a long time. It would be simplest and most logical to blow my 'joker' on revenging myself against Lena. I've had this thought over and over again. I'd probably have decided on it sooner or later. But she got lucky…"

"Weell!" I shuddered anxiously. "What do you mean, she got lucky? They just drove her off in an ambulance!"

"Oh don't get worked up about Lena, she'll live," Nina said carelessly. "It's just regular food poisoning. They'll pump her stomach and clean her out. It's hardly a stab with a poisoned umbrella, it's just a goodbye scare, for old times' sake. After all she's probably been waiting all these years for me to attack her somehow. And now I've given her a few thrills as a leaving present. She'll panic for a few hours, then realize that life goes on; that I've let her go and there's nothing else between us. She can stop seeking me out and following me around. I won't try to be revenged on her again."

"So if Lena's been lucky, if she's going to live, is someone else in for it?" I scrunched myself up even tighter, feeling my knees go cold. Nina didn't give me a chance to get thoroughly horrified. I wanted to laugh when I heard how she planned to spend her "gift of impunity". The crime she'd conceived didn't require, in my opinion, either forgiveness or justification; it wasn't even a crime. I didn't try to talk Nina out of it. It was still better than if she made somebody else suffer.

Nina had decided to kill somebody who was already long dead. She'd decided to revenge herself on Misha, the man who had buried her in his book. She considered this wound crueller than her 25 lost years. She had simply decided to write a story in which she would kill him, equally indirectly. For some reason she seriously considered this symbolic gesture to be dreadfully real.

The snowball of tension that had been growing inside me all along finally melted. I started laughing hysterically, although there wasn't anything funny. But just then it struck me as ridiculously amusing that all of us, five passionate, personable women: me, Nina, Lena, Nata and Alla had all gathered in The Mounds because of this quiet, inconspicuous Tatiana. That we'd performed a round-dance around this emotionless, frozen statue of a woman.

It cracked me up that because of Tatiana (although she didn't know it) Nina had come here, bringing Lena on her tail. I was here because my son and my husband's daughter had decided it was a good idea to put me in the same home as my husband's mistress. The children were taking care of their own convenience: they felt it would be easier to keep an eye on us old ladies if we lived close together. Nata, too, had picked The Mounds because of Tatiana, the woman who had managed to marry Zhenya who had refused to acknowledge Nata's child. She'd also had an interest in keeping an eye on her. And she had coaxed Alla into this strange place, wanting to gather around her the wives of all the men whose children she'd borne.

And so we all circled around her, while Tatiana didn't even seem to realize how much was going on. Just as if she were living in a churning aquarium without even suspecting that she was at the centre of all this bubbling. Without meaning to affect anyone's life, she changed each of ours.

Yuri and Nina left The Mounds that same night. I pretty much stopped communicating with Yuri, but with Nina I carried on an animated creative correspondence; we would call each other to discuss the difficulties of working with words, the nuances of creating fictional characters.

Lena returned to the home the next day, extremely pale but looking all the better for it. Evidently, she got the meaning of her poisoning: she decoded Nina's message.

Alla stayed in the home. And although she still looked

gloomy, she seemed to flourish. A strange change had come over her: despite all her outward sorrow, her eyes sparkled with inner happiness. Clearly Yuri had found the right words for refusing her offer of love. He must have done a better job than Eugene Onegin. Since he hadn't put her off love itself, she retained a joyful awareness of how special other people are. Well done. Nina was a lucky girl: Yuri was one of the good guys. It was a shame I hadn't paid much attention to him when I had my chance; if I had, I mightn't have let him go.

Soon after Nina and Yuri left, sometime in the middle of August, Nata decided to gather all her children together and tell them the truth about their fathers. She prepared with great care, rehearsing in front of me what she would say and the order in which she'd say it. I listened with interest every time. At last she told me the secret of the birth of her second child. It turned out that her second son's father was a footballer from that very Dynamo team. He'd been very promising but he died young in Novogorsk, leaving behind (and inconsolable) not just Nata but also a widow with two kids. Had Nata ever suspected, when she allowed herself to alter that one word on her former lover's medical file, permitting herself to meddle with the chain of events, that she herself was putting in train things she could neither predict nor control?

When the momentous day arrived and Nata seated her children around the table, about to raise the curtain concealing one half of their genealogical trees, it turned out that they had already discovered their roots on their own. They had simply been waiting for her to reach a stage where she could speak openly with her children on a subject about which she'd always preferred to keep silent. Nata was hugely surprised when, at the close of her long, entertaining tale, Vagan laid before her a tidily bound, bulging folder.

"Mama, please take a look at this screenplay," her son said. "It's been on my desk for a week; I commissioned it as soon as I found out that I was going to become head of a cinema company. It might have lain on my desk for another year, or three years, or a decade, just as much time as you felt it necessary to keep quiet about yourself and about your relationships with our fathers. But I think it's a unique story. I want it to be told, and to be filmed beautifully. I think you are the right person to edit this screenplay, but without editing the truth behind it. What do you think?"

Nata was speechless. This document was that same final story, which she'd mentioned to me at the very beginning of my stay at The Mounds. She had wanted to use her own life as the subject, before closing the lid on her keyboard for ever. And yet while she had sat tight and waited, cunningly covering up her traces, the plot had grown all by itself: in a different place, on different soil and without her consent. A story which wants to be told will be told. And if the person whom the plot has chosen as its creatrix chooses to block the flow of information, then the energy spills over in a different place, through a different intermediary. Nata now had no choice but to edit and correct, swearing, someone else's screenplay: to look at her own life through a stranger's eyes. She was so completely absorbed in this process she didn't have time even to speak with me.

However, I didn't need her company. I had leaped head-first into word-juggling. My text was emerging thick and rich, like Irish stew. When Peter arrived on the next "children's day" and heard that my story had taken control of me, that I could no longer escape it, all he said was, "Well, finally! Granny was right. She said you were incredibly talented and creative, and she was sorry she wouldn't get to read the book you'd write after she was gone."

"Granny said that?" My eyes widened. "She believed I'd start writing books? That I had talent? Then why the hell did she insult me all my life, screeching that I'd let her down, that she'd wasted her life on me, given up everything for me, only to have me turn out a disappointment and never justify any of her sacrifices?"

"Well, that was just her way of looking at things," Peter shrugged. "She thought you needed to have obstacles and problems, illusions about not being loved or liked, that that was the only way you'd turn out the way she wanted you. She felt your environment had to provide resistance, to be strict and even cruel. That if your home was soft, cosy, and easygoing, then you would never try to get away, that you'd always depend on her. She just loved you very much."

"Fuck that kind of love! The old fool!" I yelled.

"Mama, but you love me just the way Granny loved you." I had nothing to say to that. I saw Peter off as soon as possible and returned to my laptop. On the table I found a review he'd left for me about his girlfriend Dasha's latest album. I'd already heard a few of her songs on the radio.

My novel, for the sake of which I'd agreed to leave my Moscow apartment and live in this dump, was taking shape all by itself. Now I really had a story to tell. I felt that I'd lived my story. It was time to write the afterword for this book, which is almost at an end.

Afterword

I've realized why, during my long years of dreaming about being a writer, all I did was sketch ideas, yet never managed to coax any of these seeds into a novel. I'd simply never really lived before. And therefore I had no living material. I'd spent my life waiting for some kind of outside force to force my fingers onto the keyboard. I'd craved a compelling desire. I'd wanted exterior motives. I had to live to the age of sixty to realize that my intention and my own self were sufficient reasons to write.

It comforts me that I'm not the only one like this. I can say that because, as I've unearthed the life stories of Alla, Nina, Lena, Tatiana, Misha, Zhenya and the others, I've seen for myself that I wasn't the only one to waste years so pointlessly. There are many of us like that in this residence.

Our problem is that we gave too much control over our lives to others; we were scared too often and for the wrong reasons; we faked indifference at the wrong time.

Our writers wrote their stories in other people's voices or didn't write at all, preferring to kill themselves in a daze of alcohol and drugs, if only not to speak out.

Our mothers surrendered their children to be brought up by others, if only to avoid taking responsibility for the next generation.

Our criminals weren't imprisoned for their crimes.

Innocent people punished unfairly never dared to protest their innocence, fearing still greater suffering.

Our lovers preferred to silence themselves, rather than look foolish and pitiful in their love, if only to avoid being true to themselves.

We didn't vote, we didn't write declamations, we didn't invent utopias, we made no demands, we didn't build barricades, we invented nothing, we boycotted no-one, we had no heroes. We didn't take responsibility for the fate of our country, or our children, or even for our own feelings and thoughts (we were brave in our kitchens, while beyond their boundaries life was a farce), for those close to us (oh! how we were terrified of starting relationships, let alone having kids), or even for ourselves.

We were much too afraid. Although no one frightened us. Ha... the irony of fate... Of course, to some extent we were justified by the historical memory from previous generations, when our great-grandfathers, grandfathers and parents fell into the great meat-grinders of their time. They sent us a message of terror: "Be careful! Be careful! Fear the worst!" But that was our challenge. Those words laid out our fate, not to fear, since others had already lived our worst fears for us, so that we could live our own lives. In this was the opportunity for growth and evolution: not to be afraid even when things are frightening. Where previous generations had written: "They're scaring us, but we're not afraid," we wrote, "They're not scaring us, but we're terrified." Each of us wanted to write a different story in the Book of Judgement.

We didn't have the strength of character to live our own lives; we didn't have the powers of concentration to invent our lives. We are constantly awaiting some kind of midwife to draw the new day out of us, compel us, induce our labour pangs, anaesthetize us, so that we easily and painlessly bring something new and genuine into the world, give birth to ourselves. We wait for circumstances to prod and pull us towards the future; so that all we need to do is relax, let the current carry us through life. But the truth, and the spice of life lie in the fact that life is only genuine when you live every single second independently. By refusing a minor test of strength, you fail the big ones. When you don't want to cook yourself lunch, or bake bread, or clean the house, or write your own story, draw a picture, file a complaint, change your child's nappy, you let go of your own life. When you aren't strong enough to reckon with even such tiny challenges, how can you hope to overcome something which demands greater effort?

You have to simply begin. Right away. Do something by yourself. Don't order pizza over the phone, but go into your own kitchen and mix a salad. Ring your mother and tell her how much you love her. In your own words. And don't send her a Hallmark card with a sentimental slogan written by someone else, and your signature at the bottom. Go to the gym and work up an honest sweat on the treadmill. Hug your child. Stroke your cat. Take out your crayons. Read the newspaper all the way through, so you know who to vote for when elections come round. Call the people you want to talk to instead of waiting until they miss you more than you miss them. Just do all these things. It's worth doing them while you still can. You don't have much life left, so live it now.

Over the last four months our residence has really become my second home. I no longer want to leave. Here they made me

GLAS TITLES ALSO AVAILABLE AS EBOOKS

VLAS DOROSHEVICH, *WHAT THE EMPEROR CANNOT DO.*
Tales and Legends of the Orient. ISBN 9785717201209

ANATOLY MARIENGOF, *NOVEL WITHOUT LIES & CYNICS.*
ISBN 9785717201148

MIKHAIL LEVITIN, *A JEWISH GOD IN PARIS.* Three novellas
by a world-famous stage director. ISBN 9785717201087

CONTEMPORARY RUSSIAN FICTION: A SHORT LIST.
Russian authors interviewed by Kristina Rotkirch.
ISBN 9785717201124

A.J.PERRY, *TWELVE STORIES OF RUSSIA: A NOVEL, I GUESS.*
ISBN 9785717201179

ARSLAN KHASAVOV, *SENSE,* a novel. Political youth movements
in Russia today. ISBN 9785717201018

MENDELEEV ROCK, two short novels. Striking and accurate
portrait of modern-day Russian youth. ISBN 9785717201056

OFF THE BEATEN TRACK, STORIES BY RUSSIAN HITCHHIKERS,
three novellas. ISBN 9785717201049

SQUARING THE CIRCLE, an anthology of Debut winners.
ISBN 9785717201063

ALEXANDER SNEGIREV, *PETROLEUM VENUS,* a novel.
A tragicomic story of the reluctant single father of an
adolescent son with Down syndrome. ISBN 9785717201025

STILL WATERS RUN DEEP, an anthology of young women's
writing from Russia. ISBN 9785717201032

DMITRY VACHEDIN, *SNOW GERMANS,* a novel.
Displaced persons and their cultural and psychological
problems in an alien society. ISBN 9785717201001

FIND THESE ON AMAZON & ALL THE MAIN PLATFORMS

give up all my baggage and helped me to hatch into reality. When I finished this book, everything was buzzing inside me: the tiny nuclear reactor that had been switched on inside me couldn't be turned off; it sent electricity surging through my whole body. I was overtaken by extraordinary attacks of tenderness towards everything. My throat seemed to squeeze shut with the pressure of unsaid words, and my heart was squeezed by the impossibility of finding the language to say the unsayable.

My throat closed up more and more often. Sometimes it was difficult to breathe, and even to swallow. They soon discovered that, besides tenderness, there was another reason for this: throat cancer.

When the news got out about my illness, Nina wrote a special chain letter for me. She says that if it's reproduced fifty thousand times, changing just one word in each copy, I will be reborn; in fact, I may not even die. I believed her. I write the letter every day; every day it reads like new. Now it's a completely different letter, and yet it still says the same thing. I will keep on writing it.